LOVE, SEX AND TESCO'S

By

Steve Carter

For Julie, Mum and Nicola

Chapter 1

The End of the Affair

I'm about to tell Rebecca something and Rebecca's one of those women who doesn't like to be told anything. It's why I've waited for her to drink half a bottle of Tesco's Finest Cava. It could be argued she's now finishing off my half, but I'm not about to raise that point with her as she is, for once, in a good mood. Still the thought of what's to come causes me to do a little shuffle at the doorway; a sort of in-out thing.

She sees me.

"Rob? What are you doing? The hokey cokey?"

"Eh? Me? Nothing ..."

"Well, for someone who's doing 'nothing', that was a pretty good impression of Hoffman in *Rain Man*." Her voice is composed but the creased lines across her forehead convey irritation. Still, I smile at the Hoffman reference. Rebecca's love of film is one of the things that really attracted me to her.

"You liked Hoffman in *Rain Man*," I counter.

"Yeah, but I don't particularly want to live with him," she says, stifling a yawn with the back of her hand. "Anyway, talking of strange men, you're acting weird. And, let's face it Rob, over the years you've set incredibly high standards for weirdness."

"A man must have standards," I retort, walking past the sofa where she's lounging like an exotic cat. I swig a mouthful of cold San Miguel and sink into a chair across from her. Taking a measured sip from her glass of cava, which it could be argued is rightfully mine, she fixes a stern gaze on me and waits for me to get to the point. "What are you watching?" I ask, feigning interest and taking a sidestep in the conversation.

"*CSI*."

"Is it any good?"

"Well, as you've watched four series of them on DVD you tell me," she says, pulling a small band from her long, brown hair and shaking it loose. Then she turns indifferently away from me and gazes at the TV.

"Who did it?" I ask.

"That bloke there; shooting at the police," she replies in a tired voice.

"That's always a bit of a giveaway."

I take another mouthful. I'm aware that the drink is providing the same stress comfort to me as a dummy would to a small child – though obviously, the small child doesn't enjoy the added benefit of getting pleasantly pissed. She refuses to get drawn into the mechanical conversation and continues to stare at the TV. I begin to wonder if I'm

1

ever going to tell her. Rebecca went to a counsellor last year who told her that we were 'emotionally detached'. She wanted me to go with her, but as I think it's all a load of rubbish I thought it might be better if I didn't. Anyway, I don't need a counsellor to tell me we're 'emotionally detached' when it's been a year since we even had a shag. Rather than say what I've come to say I elect to fill the void. "You all organised for tomorrow?"

"Yeah, all sorted."

"Got your tickets?"

"In my Gucci."

"Check it; the handbag queen." Another silence. Maybe a playful dig at her handbags was not what the moment needed. I absently peel off the label from my bottle of San Miguel. Fortunately, she feels an urge to get to the point.

"Come on Rob, spit it out." She's firm and says this in a no nonsense matter-of-fact voice whilst pausing *CSI*.

"Spit what out?" I edge, feeling a surge of panic swell up and somersault inside my stomach. Rather than look at her I turn my head away to find somewhere to put the bits of label I've torn off, stalling for a few more seconds of time.

"Just whatever it is you've come to say," she pronounces. "You're hanging around like a bad smell. It's obvious something's up."

I grip the bottle again, this time tighter, look directly into her big brown eyes and blurt it out. "I'm leaving you."

For a second her eyes widen and then, incredibly, she turns back to the television. It's as if there's something so intriguing going on in *CSI* that she can't bear to miss it and whatever it is, it's more important than the breakup of our ten-year marriage. When she turns back to me her face is expressionless. I don't know what to make of this reaction.

"So it's a good job I went to the estate agents yesterday then, isn't it?" For a moment, I'm unable to reply; then I realise she's only gone and put the house on the market!

"Without asking me?" I splutter.

"You're leaving me," she says evenly.

"But you didn't know I was leaving!"

"But I knew I was," she replies softly. It takes a minute to sink in. This sounds far too much like she's leaving me when I'm the one supposed to be leaving her.

"Bollocks. I need another beer."

"Get me another glass of wine while you're up will you?"

I slump back into the chair. "Get lost. The rest of that cava's mine anyway. You've already had more than half a bottle." She smiles sweetly and hands me her glass. I take it because that's what I do. That's what I've always done.

2

I walk back into the kitchen, get myself a beer and pour her another glass of cava, whilst my head takes a trip down memory lane. She was only 19 when we met. I was older – 27– and nobody thought it would work. It occurs to me that perhaps they were right. In part, it's because she's outgrown me; she's all *Sex and the City*, while I'm all sex and the footy. This is divorce number two for me and that means I have now become a 'common denominating factor'.

I wander back into the room with the drinks while the theme tune from *CSI* blares out. Rebecca is now ensconced in *Elle* magazine, obviously distraught at the idea I'm leaving her. She looks up as I hand her the glass. "Look Rob, for what it's worth, I am sorry."

Her attempt to look sorry could quite easily pass for wind. "No, you're not," I reply testily, sitting down.

"Rob. It is what it is. We don't love each other anymore, but I am really sorry."

"Why tell me about the house then? Why not let me think I was leaving you?"

"Who leaves who isn't important. We're just wasting time. We need to get on with our lives and I'm frustrated."

"No surprises there."

"Let's not do this," she sighs, closing the magazine. "So what are you going to do now?"

"Oh, I don't know." It's the truth. I don't have a clue. I haven't thought that far ahead.

"You could always go to your mother's," she says, running her index finger around the rim of the glass and making that irritating noise.

"I could also gnaw my right arm off."

"Rob!" she laughs.

"I'll probably go to Steve's, if he'll have me."

"God, the thought of you two living together," she says in commiseration.

"Anyway, are you gonna take care of selling the house? Do one of your organisational lists?"

"Count on it."

"Fifty-fifty split on the proceeds?"

"Of course, Rob. What do you take me for?"

"Just checking," I reply, glancing down at another empty bottle. "Anyway, what are you gonna do? Do you want any help to find somewhere?"

"Me? Err … well … I've got a flat in Didsbury lined up."

I stare at her incredulously.

"Fucking brilliant!"

Chapter 2

28 Days Later

I'm standing in the bay window of the lounge, looking out at the park across the road. It's a cold, breezy, winter evening and the last remnants of the rapidly fading light linger across the bare treetops. Rebecca's upstairs packing her final case. I can hear her banging around like a baby elephant. I smile and sit down to watch the TV hoping to find some solace in the screen. Instead I'm drawn to the photo of us on top of it, arms wrapped around each other, happiness etched on our faces. It was taken on our honeymoon in Antigua. It's funny, how when you live through those special moments, you can never imagine a miserable, future break-up point.

A minute later, Rebecca's popping her head through the door and she's all business.

"I'm off then Rob."

"Do you want this photo?" I ask, holding it out to her. "If I remember you paid that plonker with the monkey for it."

"No, you keep it," she says, not even looking at the photo.

I step towards her as she edges back into the porch. She has a small travelling case by her side and her hairdryer. The hairdryer; you know it's all over when the hairdryer goes. My eyes start to well up. Not because I don't want her to go but in the realisation that I do. It's the thought of ten years of my life disappearing out of the door. Rebecca doesn't cry though. She doesn't really do 'sad', just 'practical'. "Look, Rebecca I want you to know it's been -"

"Don't Rob. I know it has," she says, leaning forward and in one simple movement kissing me on the cheek, before bending down to pick up her bag. "Take care." With that she turns and strides down the drive to her VW Golf.

Not wanting to watch her drive off I close the door and stare at the walls around me, all the time thinking: why was it possible to reduce ten years of my life so easily down to a simple 'take care'?

When I finally pull myself together I realise I'm going to have to make a couple of phone calls, neither of which are likely to be much fun. I contemplate in which order to make them. No contest really.

I pick up the phone and dial my daughter Charlotte's mobile. She's in her first year at Lancaster University, studying for a fairly worthless – but great-excuse-for-a-student-piss-up degree in Media. I'm hoping to get her before she goes to the union bar. It rings a number of times before she picks up.

4

"Hiya, Dad. You okay?"

"Yeah. No. Look, I thought I'd better phone you. I wanted to tell you before you hear it someplace else. I've split up with Rebecca. It's all very amicable though." The line goes silent for a brief second. I can hear the sound of a jukebox throbbing in the background.

"Oh Dad, I'm really sorry," she eventually replies, "but I can't say I'm surprised. I've seen this coming for a little while. We all have, actually."

The way she says 'we all have' makes me feel like I've been starring in *The Truman Show*. Still, it's one of the many reasons why I love my daughter: she says it as it is. "So, you're not disappointed in me or anything?' I ask.

"Don't be silly! These things happen. Anyway, why would I be disappointed in you?"

"Dunno. I'm not the best dad in the world and now, it appears, I'm not the best husband either."

"You're a great dad. Just a bit … a bit different, that's all." I decide not pursue what that means.

"I'll take that as a compliment then."

"Are you okay? I mean, do you want me to come over this weekend?"

"No, I'm just a bit down, but I'll be okay. I don't need anyone on suicide watch if that's what you're getting at."

"You're terrible Muriel," she laughs, doing the voice from the film.

"Ignore me. I'm twisted."

"I know. That's why I love you. By the way, what's Rebecca doing?"

"She's gone off to some flat in Didsbury she had lined up."

"Oh." I can tell by the way she says 'oh' that she thinks Rebecca has left me.

"She hasn't left me. I left her."

"Right. So where are you now then?"

"Err … at the house." This isn't going too well.

"Anyway, it's not important is it? Who leaves who and all that blame nonsense?" The way she says it makes me feel like it really, really is important. "Listen, I gotta go," she continues, a little distractedly. "It's my round and there are a lot of impatient faces staring at me. For what it's worth, I'm really sorry Dad. Give my love to Rebecca the next time you speak to her."

"Yeah, I will. Love you. I'll catch you the following weekend. There's a Spanish season on at the FACT."

"Deffo. Sounds great. Gotta go. Love you too." I hang up and feel, for the first time in a while, a little bit better.

That leaves me with one more call to make. For the moment I avoid making it and look back out of the window. In front of the park gates a young couple walking their dog stop briefly to kiss. I don't know why, but

5

there are happy couples everywhere I look these days and all they do is depress me.

I realise it's time to make my second call. I pick up the phone and tap in my best mate Steve's number. He'll pick up. It's a Tuesday night so I know there's more chance that my 90-year-old, wheelchair-bound, agoraphobic aunt is out. He picks up on the first ring. "It's me," I say, trying to sound upbeat.

"Oh," he replies, making no effort at all to hide his disappointment.

"Sorry – were you expecting a call from the Olsen twins?"

"Nah, that's Mondays," he mutters sardonically. "You okay for Sunday's big game?"

He's referring to our upcoming match in the Halton and District Over-35's Indoor Five-a-Side League. We've been trying to win the league for two years and the new season is about to start. To me it's really nothing more than a kick about; something to do on a Sunday night, but to Steve it's life or death, or something much more important. "Yeah, I'm okay. I'll be there."

"'Cos this year it really is -"

"Our league for the taking."

"Exactly," he says, my sarcasm completely lost on him. "Anyway, what do you want?"

"Listen, I need a favour. I don't suppose there's any chance I could stay at yours for a few weeks?" It takes a moment for the penny to drop.

"God, you haven't blown another relationship have you? Can't you work it out with her?"

I note Steve's use of the word 'her'. He holds Rebecca in the same high regard that a Greenpeace activist holds a Japanese whaling captain. "No, I can't work it out with *her*. It might be a tad difficult working it out with *her* given the fact that she's currently living in a flat in Didsbury."

"All right, all right, calm down," he says. "I get the picture. Yeah, whatever. You can stay for as long as you like. It's not like you'll be intruding on my non-existent sex life."

"Cheers mate."

"How are you holding up?" he asks, in a suspicious tone.

"I'm a bit down, but I'll just have to get on with it, I suppose."

"Well, we don't want all this break-up nonsense affecting your performance on the pitch. You're useless when you've not got a woman."

He's harsh but fair: I thrive on female company. I don't know why, because women drive me demented. They make me clean up, they stop me from watching sport and they make me go shopping when it's the last thing in the world I want to do. But I am totally, absolutely and completely useless without one. "We need to get you dating again," he continues. "You know? Straight back on the bike after you fall."

6

"Err ... I'm not too sure about that. I -"

"I am. We can't win that league with you moping about the pitch and crying like a baby all the time."

"I'm hardly that bad. I just said I was a bit down."

"But you have to admit when you're happy with a woman you play better. Remember when you first started seeing Rebecca you were like Maradona for about a year."

"Hardly."

"Then, when she started to go to counselling, you were totally pants."

I knew I'd regret telling him about that.

"You're losing the plot. Anyway - and I'm not saying I agree with you – I wouldn't even know where to start dating."

"You should try the Internet. Everyone's doing it. I've even tried it myself. It's a sure thing."

"Any luck?"

"No, but that's just me."

"I don't fancy it; all chat room perves and nutters from what I've heard."

"It should suit you down to the ground then. Or try that, what's a name? The Soulmates thingy in the Guardian on a Saturday," he says, now making some kind of repulsive eating noise in the background; a sure sign of his waning interest.

"But that's just full of literary agents and antiques dealers who live in London."

"I would have thought some of those highbrow types would be right up your street. They'd probably love nipping off to see those boring Borgman films you're always banging on about." I ignore the 'Borgman' wind-up.

"I don't think lonely hearts is really my style," I tell him.

"The problem is, you don't have any style. I don't know. Try an escort agency. But whatever you do don't let this affect your game. Because this year it really is -"

"Our league for the taking."

"Exactly. Look, the door's just gone; it's probably the Olsens. I'm off."

With this the phone goes dead in my hand. I wander despondently into the living room, reach for the Guardian on the coffee table and find the Soulmates ads.

Five minutes later the paper is in the bin. This is about all the time it takes for me read three adverts.

The first advert sets the tone perfectly for all that follows: *Female, 33, likes going out/staying in.* I like a woman who knows her own mind!

The second ad is also less than enthralling: *Single mum, 34, voluptuous figure seeks partner any age.* We men have long since worked out what 'voluptuous' really means, but on the upside I'm 38 and it is any age, I guess.

Wearily, I read the next: *White witch, 32, seeks man to make magic with; must like cats.* I really, really, don't like cats and they really, really, hate me.

I glance down at my laptop and muse: the Internet?

Chat rooms, perves and nutters.

Has it really come to that?

Chapter 3

One Hour Photo

It's mid-December and the wind is kicking up a real racket outside. The next door neighbours' Christmas reindeer have blown over in the 40-mile-an-hour gusts and are glowing eerily under a wooden garden table. Pulsating fairy lights are draped over frosted windows and a large pine Christmas tree in the living room creates an almost picture perfect scene. I close the curtains and glance around at the lack of festive decorations in my own house, then sigh as I walk over to my laptop. I'm currently feeling at a bit of a loose end. It's clear to me that I'm showing all the signs of FEDEPS, or Female Deprivation Syndrome. There's no such thing, but try telling my mood that.

It's late on a Sunday evening and I stare at my laptop screen.

Internet dating.

It really has come to that.

I close down the porn site I've inadvertently opened, go to Google and type into the search bar *find a date UK*. I press the return key. A list of sites appear, all claiming that they can help me locate a perfect partner. At the top of the page an innocuous looking site catches my eye called *www.UR-date.com*. Not particularly clever or original, but it appears to offer a straightforward dating service.

After 15 minutes of clicking around its numerous features, I find myself more than a little interested. The first thing I have to do is create a username. After an inordinate amount of time, I come up with *Vinpetrol*. This is because one of Rebecca's mates said I looked a bit like 'a poor man's Vin Diesel', whatever that was supposed to mean. It's the best I can come up with and it gets me on to the site that will change my life.

Not that I have the slightest clue about all of this when faced with the initial challenges of being *UR-date's* newest member. Firstly, I have to fill out a profile page. The first question is a portent of things to come: *What is your hairstyle?*

Great, I'm being forced to confront one of my biggest personal hang-ups. It suddenly feels less like a dating website and more like a visit to the psychiatrist's couch. I click the drop-down menu. I'm forced to choose between *bald/ not much* and *shaved/ part shaved*. I go for the latter as it has the aroma of choice rather than the stench of resignation that pervades the former.

I read the next menu: *Please describe your looks*. There's a plethora of options ranging from *ugly* to *stunning*. I know in my heart of hearts that I

9

lie somewhere in between these two choices, but where? In the end I plump for *quite good looking.*

Ten minutes later and the task is complete. Grinning with smug self-satisfaction, I briefly imagine all the dates my amazing profile will get me. I log off and pay tribute to a good night's work by taking myself off to bed.

After work the following evening I log on excitedly and click a link to see how many emails I have. It turns out to be a rather disappointing *none.* I click another link and find out that my profile has only been viewed three times. So what? I think. Rather than wait for the ladies to contact me, I'll contact them.

The obvious place to start is with the *matching* facility. This is where my profile tick boxes are matched with any prospective partners' tick boxes. At that moment my computer dings and the email counter moves from nil to one.

Bingo! Let's go. Action stations. For a brief moment I imagine myself as Tom Hanks in *You've Got Mail.* I open up my email. I read it. The reality is that I'm more like Tom in *Forrest Gump.*

Dear Vinpetrol.

Welcome to UR-date! As you do not currently have a photo of yourself on the site, you might like to know that members with photos receive up to ten times more mail and are three times more likely to go on dates. You can upload a photo anytime by clicking on the enclosed link and following the instructions given.

Having shaken off the initial disappointment that the email isn't a prospective date with La Jolie I click the *matches* button and look at the profiles. The site gives priority to those matches that have photos.

So, despite all of the check boxes I've ticked in my profile, it's highly likely that I'll need to put a photo on to have any chance of a date. The catch-22 being that if I do put a photo on the site, it's highly unlikely that I'll actually get a date, because - and I'm not kidding here - the Elephant Man was more photogenic than me. I decide, for the moment at least, I'm not going to put a photo on *UR-date.* Instead, I'm going to put my faith in the belief that not all females are shallow bimbos searching for Brad Pitt lookalikes with gigantic wallets. After all, the email didn't say that members without photos don't get *any* dates; it only intimated that those with photos got more. No, I'll take *UR-date* by storm with my wit, repartee and intelligence.

If storming *UR-date* meant getting two replies to forty emails in seven days then I achieved my objective. Still, both replies came with photos, which seemed promising at the time. Ironically, both photos led to dates that turned out to be total disasters.

A local lady called Pam sent the first photo. It came as an attachment in an email asking if I wanted to meet for a drink. She'd read my profile and thought I sounded nice. I saw her photo and thought she looked nice. I arranged to meet her on Wednesday after work in The Lion for a drink.

It didn't go too well.

Steve agreed to drop me off on his way home. He stopped at the nearby garage to fill the car up with petrol. I got out and trotted off to the pub on the opposite side of the road. Before he'd even paid for his petrol I was back in the passenger seat of his car with my seatbelt securely fastened.

It had taken all of ten seconds for me to locate her in the corner and then make a hasty retreat before she noticed me. She was barely recognisable as she'd sent me a photo that must have been taken at least ten years, and three stone, ago.

On the way back home in the car I debate the rights and wrongs of what I'd just done. "I feel like a tosser, mate," I say.

"Well, you shouldn't," he tells me. "Everyone knows that the rules of dating etiquette no longer apply if you use old photos. So what you did was totally legit."

"Yeah, so why do I feel so bad? I should have sat down and had a drink with her, at least. Imagine how desperate she must be to use an old photo like that?"

"Mate, you're desperate. But did you send her a ten-year-old photo of you when you had all your own hair?"

"No, but I hardly think -"

"No, dead right you didn't. But if you had, you couldn't have complained if she'd run off to her mate's car like a frightened little girl, could you?"

"Err ... I suppose -"

"No. There's rules and there's rules. And some rules must be obeyed: no old photies."

And the debate was *finito*. Still, I kept off the site for a week after that.

If that was bad the second date was worse. A stunning, blonde Russian lady called Lydia replied to one of my attempts at repartee in an email. We corresponded for a few days and she seemed normal enough. She even assured me that the photo on her profile was a very recent one.

I agreed to meet her at Piccadilly. She was even more stunning in real life. All of which should have warned me that all was not well. I mean, as Steve succinctly pointed out when I showed him the photo, "Why would she be interested in you?"

It quickly became apparent a little while after we got into the bar. "Would you care for another drink?' I asked, standing up and thinking that everything was going smoothly.

"Yes soon, but, I would now like to talk about future," she replied, leaning forward to take hold of my hand.

I seriously thought she was about to do a bit of palm reading.

"Please sit down and relaxing," she urged. I sat down opposite, slid my hand free and looked at her whilst she went on. "I would like to marry you please."

"I'm sorry. I'm not following you." And I wasn't.

"Ah! Let me explaining. I have to go home soon, back to Moscow. My visa expire. I am wanting to marry quickly so I can bring little boy Sacha to England. You want see picture? He lovely boy. No trouble. I will make excellent wife. He will make excellent son." She started to open up her purse and take a photo out of it.

"No! I don't want to see that, really. I think there's been a misunderstanding. I thought this was going to be a date. You know? A date: where we get to know each other."

"Yes. Get to know first. That is good. Then we can later marry, yes?"

"Yes. No! I mean no chance. I've only just ... I don't -"

"This make me sad. No can't marry. I not understand. You want date woman, but you do not want marry?"

"Well, no, yeah, sort of, eventually I suppose. Look, I'm sorry but I'm not marrying anyone at the moment. Can't we just have a drink and a chat?"

"Vodka. Big. Thanks you." With that she gave me a shoulder that was colder than the Russian steppe in winter.

I stumbled towards the bar and made an attempt to get the barman's attention. As I turned back to look at her, there was a guy sat at the table, his hand enveloped in hers. I caught the word 'marry' before I buttoned my coat up and headed outside to catch an early train back.

I didn't even feel the need to debate this one with Steve, though as you can imagine, he found the whole thing hilarious.

So here I am, contemplating whether to jack it all in and go celibate. Come to think of it, I am celibate. I hadn't realised how difficult it would be to find someone to go to the cinema with. I can't remember dating ever being this hard. In the end I decide to give it one last shot. I'll bite the bullet and put a photo on *UR-date*.

As I must be one of the few people in Western civilisation who doesn't own a digital camera, I seek to rectify the situation. On my first available 'free' on a cold and crisp Thursday morning, I reluctantly make my way to the IT department. I focus on trying to appear confident as I stride in, but there's no doubt in my mind this won't be easy. You see, the IT department is controlled by a computer super-geek called Simon Drysdale.

Worse, Drysdale is a bit of nemesis. He plays for our arch rivals, and reigning Halton and District Over-35's Indoor Five-a-Side champions: *The IT Crowd*. Well, I say 'plays for' given his physical attributes it could be argued that he merely blocks up the goal. If all this wasn't bad enough, relations between the two of us are not exactly cordial. This is ever since Steve took a swing at him after our ignominious 4-2 defeat to Drysdale's mob in last season's big title decider. Steve accused Drysdale of moving before he took a penalty which Drysdale saved. To be honest, Steve was wrong: Drysdale wasn't so much 'moving' as 'wobbling'. Still, it didn't stop a heated after match discussion, a misplaced punch and Drysdale threatening to go to the police. So it's fair to say that he and I are not on each other's Christmas card lists.

Also, Drysdale is fiercely territorial about all school computer equipment. His job description is 'to facilitate the use of IT throughout the school'. The problem is he's interpreted this phrase to mean 'be as awkward and obstructive as possible'.

The Hoover Dam is probably less obstructive than Drysdale.

So, a minute after entering his office, I find myself quickly embroiled in an argument over whether lending me a digital camera is indeed 'facilitating the use of IT throughout in the school'.

"Look, I just want a camera, okay?" I say, throwing my hands up for effect.

"But I can't just give you a camera. Not unless I know what it's for." He turns his back on me to check the progress of a virus scanner on the monitor behind him. "You might want to use it for something that's not legitimate."

"Not legitimate? What do you mean?"

"You know? Something that could compromise the school's IT policy," he retorts, hitting the keyboard like he's playing Mozart's second piano concerto. "Or something that's got nothing to do with teaching and learning."

"Look, all I want to do is take a few pictures with it, and upload them on to a website." Well, it's the truth. I take a sharp intake of breath at this point and then play my ace card. "Do I have to go to the Head about this?"

Although I have no intention of going to the Big Guy I sense it's the only way to get Drysdale to co-operate without giving away my real purpose. It's working too. Like a virgin's promise, I feel him beginning to weaken under the threat of the Head. "Well, it's pretty irregular ..." A quick change of tack is all that is needed and the camera will be mine.

"Look, I understand. You're just doing your job. Let me do mine. I'll have it back by Monday I promise."

"You sure it's for a legitimate purpose?"

"Trust me – it is." He looks at me as if trusting Hannibal Lector with his Tesco's Finest Chianti would be a safer bet. I flash him an insipid smile. He then wanders over to a large metal cabinet. Taking a key from the chain attached to his jeans belt he carefully unlocks it as if the crown jewels themselves were inside. There, on the shelves directly facing me, still unopened in their boxes, are around 25 top-of-the-range Fuji digital cameras.

"Wanna demo?" he says, taking one out of its box and handing it to me.

"Nah. Cheers. I've used these before a few times," I say, holding out my hand. "I'm sure I'll be okay."

"Okely dokely," he chants, as he hands the camera over. He then swirls adroitly round on his New Balance trainers and sits back down. Picking up a copy of the *NME* he turns his back on me, runs his stubby fingers through his greasy, black hair and shouts over his shoulder, "see you Sunday."

This is a wind-up; a reference to the 'big game' between his lot and ours. He then starts to hum what sounds like a very bad version of *Stairway to Heaven*. It's clear that I'm dismissed. Not wanting to take the bait, and thinking about any possible dates that might come my way because of the camera, I put it inside a small carrier bag and hurry off down the corridor to the sanctuary of the Humanities stockroom.

Six hours later and I'm sitting in my kitchen, trying to work out the intricacies of a Fuji digital camera. I have another look at the instructions. The main problem is where to put the camera so that it takes a decent photo of me.

The moon springs to mind.

I scan the house desperately, only to find surfaces that are too high, or not high enough. Eventually I find the only place that I can put the camera where it can see me sitting down: on top of the telly. This means moving the honeymoon photo, which is good because it's totally putting me off. Anyway, I figure that to take a decent snap I'll have to set the camera on a delay, then run and sit down, whilst simultaneously attempting to appear as if I've been sitting down all night. I take a few practice shots at this and it turns out to be more manageable than I'd thought.

The next dilemma is what to wear. I settle for my black, Ted Baker crew neck and a pair of even blacker, Beckhamesque combats. To be honest, I haven't shaved for two days so the best I can hope for is that I will appeal to those women who claim to like 'a bit of rough'.

I now have to decide what the *mise en scène* of the photo will be. My first thought is minimalism. Then again, having only me in the photo seems like a bad idea. So, I will strategically place items in the photo that draw attention away from err ... me. Shit! This is getting complicated.

Ten minutes later, I'm carrying my electric guitar - which I can't play - and a dilapidated copy of *Private Eye* down the stairs. The magazine will say that I'm both intelligent and that I have that certain quality that women claim to place high on their agendas when looking for a man: a sense of humour. The guitar indicates something, but I'm not sure what.

Five minutes later the camera is on top of the TV and pointing in the general direction of the sofa, which has in its immediate vicinity an electric guitar, a coffee table with a very old copy of *Private Eye* and a fairly desperate looking bloke. The timer on the camera has been set to ten seconds and I try to look nonchalant.

The phone starts to ring.

I wonder whether I should answer it, but the ringing is spoiling the ambience. I go over to the camera, flick it off and reach for the phone.

"Hello?"

"Hi Dad. Are you okay?" Normally I love it when Charlotte rings, but her timing, like mine with the camera, is way off.

"Yeah, fine," I tell her. "Are you?"

"Yeah. I've got an essay to do on contemporary Spanish cinema and it's got to be in by Friday. What you up to?" Under normal circumstances I don't lie to Charlotte, but there is no way I want her to know what I'm doing. So I judge a little, white lie to be in order.

"Nothing, really. I'm sat here trying to figure out how to use a digital camera."

"Get you. Welcome to the 21st century."

"Very funny. I'm more *au fait* with technology than you might imagine."

"Whatever, Dad. Listen, I've phoned for some advice. What can you tell me about Almodóvar?"

"Err ... he's gay."

"Seriously."

We spend the next ten minutes discussing her essay. I put the phone down, take a deep breath, reset the timer and rush to the sofa. The camera sounds the five seconds to go with a beep and I pull a face that I'm convinced must look more nonchalant than a down-the-line Roger Federer backhand.

I end up doing it 37 times.

On the first photo, the nonchalant one, my face looks like I'm taking a very painful dump. The next 25 all capture what must be my hidden feminine side, although it doesn't look too hidden. The photos are so bad I convince myself that there are lighting issues at work.

I fiddle with the lighting menu, but the next ten make me look like a serial sex offender. Dressed all in black and not having shaved does nothing to discount this particular impression. The strategically placed guitar in the background enhances the effect and looks like it could be used as some kind of obscene weapon to torture my victims with.

15

Eventually, I manage to take two photos that suggest I'm not about to ask girls for their last boyfriend's mobile number, or tie them to a bed and plug in an electric guitar.

I run upstairs, insert the USB cable into the computer and begin the fairly simple task of uploading the photos onto the *UR-date* site.

I think my luck is about to change.

Chapter 4

Les Étrangers

If my luck changed in December there wasn't any noticeable evidence. Christmas came and went; the most depressing feature being the loss of the 'big game' to Drysdale's mob for the third straight time. It was another painful 4-2 defeat marred, yet again, by Steve publicly questioning Drysdale's parentage in the pub afterwards. Worse, he blamed the defeat on me: "if you had a woman we'd never have lost."

The defeat meant that we were going to need some help from other teams if we were going to win the league. On a personal level the game mirrored my own relationship failings with Rebecca: I started off well, scoring early on, only to fade away in the second half and become completely impotent by the end.

On a more positive note I did at least manage to talk Charlotte into going to watch a rerun of *Pan's Labyrinth*, though we were both painfully aware that she was acting as a sort of surrogate date for me.

So by January my mood is as dank and dark as the days that constitute the month. About now I'm beginning to form the opinion that *UR-date* is a complete waste of my time. This is very much my mindset on a cold, still, grey Sunday afternoon; the sort of day that possesses all the ingredients to push any rounded rational being into a deep depression. The house appears to be much bigger than it did before and my sense of isolation is never greater than when I pass the tiny box room on my visits to the bathroom. Rebecca used it as a sort of dressing-cum-make-up room. The sheer emptiness of it perfectly echoes my own solitary feelings.

It's almost dark outside even though it's only a quarter past four. I'm sitting on the sofa mindlessly watching a pointless premiership fixture on *Sky Sports*. As I sit staring at the TV screen the sudden realisation that I might never go on another date ever again hits me. I switch off the box and sprint upstairs. It's still with no great level of expectation that I boot up the laptop and log on.

As usual, there are no contact emails from *UR-date*. In fact, only five women have looked at my profile in the last seven days. I'm feeling more despondent than ever when I hit the *Matches* button. The computer scans the database and spits out my top 10 possible dates. Some of them I've seen before; some I've written to but received no reply, and some I really don't like the look of. The ones I don't like the look of seem to be using their police arrest photos to attract dates. Anyway, I'm pretty sure that they feel the same about my photo. I look at it for a while, then decide that there's not much point in trying to take a better one, as the fact is, where photos of me are concerned, this one is as good as it gets.

Finally, I check my personal statement. It's attached to the end of my profile and is an opportunity to give prospective matches details about me that aren't covered by tick boxes or drop-down menus. In short, it might be seen as a last chance saloon to win dates over despite the photo. On closer inspection I wonder if mine is perhaps a little too boring: *I like to think of myself as intelligent with a good sense of humour. I really enjoy female company and friends say I'm very easy going. Don't think that I'm here to sweep you off your feet, I'm not. I'm looking for someone to go to the cinema with initially, as this is a real passion of mine.*

I think about altering it, but in the end I decide not to as it's basically the truth. In my latter years I've developed a healthy respect for the truth, in very much the same way that a criminal who keeps getting caught develops a healthy respect for the law. I click around aimlessly for a while and I'm at the point of logging off when I notice that a chat box has opened at the top of the screen and a message has appeared. It's simple and straight to the point and, amazingly, directed at me: *Hi! How are you? I just read your personal statement, and I really like it as it's a bit different to the usual rubbish you get on here. Though I'm a bit disappointed you aren't going to sweep me off my feet, lol. Wanna chat?*

It's from someone with the username of *4thrite*. This is the first time I've chatted in real time, so I've not much idea what to do. It takes me a moment before I think of the obvious and check out her profile.

First of all she's got no photo. This is a bit unfair: she can see me, but I can't see her. Disappointing, but it still constitutes a measure of interest from the opposite sex. When I get to the end of her profile I read her personal statement, which explains why there isn't a photo: *I'm less interested in looks than personality, which is why you won't find a photo of me on the website. Of course, that might mean I look like Quasimodo's sister, but if you want to find out you're going to have to take that chance.*

The only thing that worries me about her profile is that the check box stipulating number of children says she has *three or four*. On the other hand, I've long ago ditched the idea of finding someone of my age who doesn't have kids. But *three or four*! I glance down to look at her age. She's 36; 36 is good. I don't imagine many 22-year-old girls are forming an orderly queue to get at me. I laugh at myself for suddenly becoming picky. She has enough qualities for me to enter into some kind of discussion with her, the most important one being she's the only woman on this site showing any interest in me whatsoever. Only at this point do I realise I've been arsing around for five minutes without replying and she's probably cleared off. I quickly type a reply: *Hi, that's me: definitely no sweeping off the feet going on here. Thanks for the comment on my personal statement.*

I immediately worry that she'll find my comment either too bland or too forced. I wait anxiously for a reply. There's always the chance that there won't even be one. After a couple of lines from me, women on here have a tendency to disappear. In fact, I've made so many women disappear I'm surprised the police haven't come looking for me. So I'm pleasantly surprised when a reply comes back: *Sorry I'm taking a while to reply; I went out to a club last night. I've got a bit of a hangover.*

Wow, that's a positive, she likes a drink. I hit the keyboard: *No worries. I've been known to enjoy the odd hangover myself. What part of Manchester are you from?*

The reply is quickly forthcoming: *I'm in Wythenshawe. I've lived here 20 years now.*

Wythenshawe! Alarm bells start to ring at this point. I can't say I know a lot about the area really, but it has the reputation of being as rough as the proverbial bear's arse. I begin to develop a possible mental image of the kind of woman I'm talking to. I picture a track-suited harridan in her mid-thirties, squatting over a knocked-off Amstrad computer, munching pasties, whilst simultaneously downing large glasses of Cherry Lambrini. All this is taking place in her fifth floor refurbished council flat, whilst her multi-ethnic brood cause havoc on the estate. That is when they aren't otherwise confined to quarters by ASBOs. Still, beggars can't be choosers: *That's not too far from here. Anyway, like my profile says, I'm really interested in films and love going to the cinema. What's your favourite film?*

Dunno. What's yours?

Balde Runner.

Before I notice I hit the return key. Talk about a Freudian slip of the keyboard. Why do I have to be such a pretentious idiot? I could easily have said *Ferris Bueller's Day Off*.

It's because I'm a bit nervous and desperately trying not to appear desperate. Also, my fertile imagination is running away with me. I'm now imagining this Wythenshawe lady as a bit of a closet intellectual, the *Educating Rita* type. A woman, who's missed out on the flower of educational opportunities, suffered a life blighted by teenage pregnancy and fiscal hardships, but who at this very moment is reaching out in the prime of her life to grasp at a few precarious petals. All she needs is a little highbrow conversation with me to help her escape the day-to-day drudgery of a humdrum, council house existence.

Her answer comes back fairly quickly: *I've not really heard of that one; who's in it?*

Oh well. Perhaps she's a great shag!

Okay. So it's clear we're not going to be doing a great deal of film chat. So I decide that maybe a change of topic is in order here: *Have you been on this site for long?*

19

This is something of a disingenuous question. When you view someone's profile it tells you how long they have been a member: *Not long, since early December, you?*

Just over a month. To be honest, I've had so little interest I'm thinking of jacking it in.

No sense in beating about the bush. She gets my drift though: *I have heard that there are ten times more men on here than women. If that's true, it's going to be tough for any bloke. I'm not having any problems :-)*

I like that comment. It's really confident and I love confident women. I find them very sexy. Also, ten times more men! To paraphrase a line from *Sleepless in Seattle*, 'it certainly feels true'. I type back: *Well, it's tough for me, I can tell you. What's your real name? Or do I just call you 4thrite? What's the name about anyway?*

It's Jenny. Everyone calls me Jen. I guess the username kind of sums me up. I like to get straight to the point. What about you? And what's your username about?'

My name's Rob and don't worry about the username. I always think that if you have to explain a joke it's not worth the effort.

LOL.

What follows after these exchanges is a really comfortable and interesting conversation. She's easy to chat to. I relax and begin to open up to her in a way that I wouldn't have believed. I ramble on about how much I love Charlotte, how I became estranged from her when she was young, and how I regret missing out on the later part of her childhood. I tell her that, even though Charlotte and I have a great relationship, it's not a normal father-daughter relationship. The truth is Charlotte tends to behave more like the parent than I do. I babble on about the fact that the house is sold.

In return, she tells me about her recent separation and how difficult it is as a working mum dealing with three teenage boys.

Eventually we get back to films (presumably her head's no longer cabbaged) and she extols the virtues of *Slumdog Millionaire* and *The Matrix*; pretty good choices really. I also learn that *The Matrix* is a religious film. Well, at least according to her it is.

During our whole time online I find her lack of pretension and honesty alluring, and when she finally tells me she has to go, I feel a little dismayed. I look at the clock. It tells me I've been talking to her for well over two hours. We end by promising to talk to each other whenever we are both online.

As she signs off, and disappears back into the real world, I'm left with the rather disconcerting feeling that although she was the only person on the site I was talking to, she was not reciprocating the exclusivity of the arrangement. Her replies sometimes took a few minutes to come through, whereas I replied almost instantaneously.

Chapter 5

Don't Answer the Phone!

Throughout the last week I've managed to encounter Jenny on UR-*date* almost every day. I've learnt that she's around most evenings after nine o'clock. So I make it my business to be online at the same time. This probably qualifies me as an e-stalker, but I don't care.

In the ten days we've been chatting and writing to each other, I've become acutely aware of what a seductive medium email is. To my surprise, it turns out to be a really positive way to start a new relationship. Yes, it does have its drawbacks: written conversation is much easier to misinterpret and subtle nuances can be lost. But there are many positive aspects to it, including the fact that we've avoided the shallowness of building our relationship on the muddy foundation of looks. In reality, this has nothing to do with me. I'm particularly shallow and I'd love to see a photo of Jenny, which just goes to show what a slow learner I am. No, it's more to do with the fact that she steadfastly refuses to send me one. This is in spite of my constant badgering.

It's another particularly cheerless and blustery evening, made all the more miserable by the fact that I've received the order to 'vacate the premises' from my solicitor. I have to be out by February the 14th. The irony isn't lost on me, I can tell you. At this moment, the prospect of Valentine's Day holds all the romantic allure of a dirty weekend with Mrs Thatcher in Chernobyl. My impending exit from the house has forced me to badger Steve into clearing out his spare room. And, even though he's going above the call of duty by letting me move in, I'm not really looking forward to it. I'm also in the process of buying a much smaller house, which isn't likely to complete for another couple of weeks. So, whilst I'm only going to have to stay at Steve's for a relatively short time, it's still going to feel like a long haul.

Anyway, I'm online chatting with Jenny again. This evening the conversation in cyberspace flows particularly easily. I have a feeling that, for once, she's giving me her complete, undivided attention. I'm prattling on about my form group and it must be whilst I'm jabbering on about this that Jenny realises my preoccupation with her looks hasn't been aired. So it's perhaps typical of a woman that this should be the precise moment she chooses to surprise me. A chat window opens up and reads: *Look, I'm going to send you a photo of me. I don't really have many photos, but I'll send you this one, which was taken on holiday last year. I have to say though; it doesn't really look like me.*

So the point of sending it would be ...?

Nevertheless, I guess it must look something like her, so I wait impatiently for the file to download and open the attachment.

I'm completely gobsmacked. What appears on the screen in front of me can only be described as some kind of weird, alien life form; a life form which obviously exists by gorging itself on bright, white light whenever it gets the chance. I type back: *Wow! Thanks. You appear to have a real 'energy' about you. You're obviously someone who lights up a room as soon as they walk in. LOL.*

I'm really hoping this will shame her into sending another one, but it doesn't. Instead she simply replies: *Glad you like it! I admit there is a touch too much light exposure. But it all adds to the mystery really! Look, got to go, you wouldn't believe the ironing I have. Hope you don't mind but I've passed your name on to a friend of mine, Gail. She'll probably contact you. Her username is Gail5873. Have a chat with her!*

I am not altogether happy about this last comment. It feels a bit like she's pimping me out to one of her friends. I sit, think about it for a moment, and decide to do what any man in my position would do: I bring up Gail's photo to see if she's fit.

In front of me is the photo of an attractive, extremely well-endowed redhead in her late thirties. I'm sure she has no shortage of UR-*date* takers but she isn't really my type. Then I realise that even if it was a photo of Nicole Kidman, she still wouldn't be my type. You see, I'm, ever so slightly, falling for Jenny – at least, virtual Jenny. Though weirdly, it still hasn't occurred to me that we could ever move to a stage where we'll eventually meet.

As I contemplate this another chat box pops up. I'm suddenly getting more action than the marines in Helmand province: *Hi, I'm Gail. Jenny suggested I write to you. She says you're really funny online and you've been making her laugh. She really likes you.*

I'm suddenly rushed back to my schooldays. I feel like a 14-year-old kid in the playground again. Jenny 'likes me'! So I type: *That's nice. I really like her too. But I'm a little perplexed as to why she wanted me to talk to you. No offence.*

The reply is quick and to the point: *None taken. She tells me that you're interesting and thought we'd get on. We swap contacts all the time so it's not as sinister as it seems and we have an unwritten rule where we don't step on each other's dating toes.*

That certainly alleviates some of my anxieties. I start to ask a few questions and in no time at all the conversation is going well. It quickly becomes apparent that she's very much like Jenny – smart, fun and very easy to chat with. She's so easy that I become a little too confident. Now, it's my experience in life that whenever I become a little too confident with a woman, I'm sure to be heading for a spectacular fall. It all goes horribly wrong shortly after Gail tells me about her plans for a date the next evening. She's going out for a meal with someone she's met on *UR-date* and they're going to share a cab home afterwards. For some stupid reason I think it would be funny to type: *And then is it back to yours for coffee?*

I'm smiling at my brilliant attempt at humour as I type it. I'm not smiling when the reply comes back: *I beg your pardon! What the hell are you inferring? Am I giving off some kind of signal that suggests I am an easy lay or something?*

What? Where did that come from? The abrupt termination of my brief dalliance with virtual Jenny flashes before my eyes. I imagine Gail rushing off to email her with the news that I'm a pervert. This is going to necessitate very careful handling if I'm to emerge from this disaster unscathed. I pound frantically back: *Sorry. I really wasn't inferring anything. You're not giving off any signals. I was merely cracking a little joke; one that appears to have backfired.*

I sit chewing my nails while cyber nutter Gail mulls my reply over. It feels like an eternity before the box opens up: *Well, that's ok. It's just that I worry about the signals I give off sometimes.*

What? Like the ones that indicate you're an absolute nutter?

After that I smooth things over for ten minutes, soothing what appears to be a very fragile ego, log off and go to bed.

To tell you the truth, she's exhausted me.

It's a Saturday morning, a couple of days after my little run-in with Gail. I'm standing in the kitchen with a cup of tea in my right hand, waiting for the toaster to pop up two Warburton's potato cakes. I haven't spoken to Jenny since the Gail debacle. I've kept out of her way because I'm worried Gail's told Jenny I'm to be avoided at all cost. I'm also worried that I'll cop Jenny's virtual wrath the next time we chat.

The toaster spits out its contents and I snatch the piping-hot potato cakes, pop in another and rush upstairs. I reckon I've avoided Jenny for long enough now, so I search frantically for her online.

When you search for a member via their *UR-date* username, the search will tell you if they're currently online, or give you the time when they were last online. After logging on I receive the cruel message: *Not currently online. Last online 10 minutes ago.*

I curse my luck. I can't believe I've missed her. I start to write an email which will explain my side of the Gail story, but when I write it the whole thing sounds even worse than it was. I close the computer without saving the email and speed downstairs to investigate the burning smell coming from the kitchen.

When Sunday arrives I try to find her again. At the point when I begin to think that it's really not meant to be, I strike gold. It's around 10.30 p.m. when I see her profile, showing *currently online.*

I brace myself. I need to type something that's very circumspect. How should I play it? Do I refer to the conversation I had with Gail, or do I pretend it never happened? Before I've made up my mind the chat box in the top left hand corner pops up: *Hey you! I thought you were avoiding me. What have you been up to?*

I waste no time in replying: *I thought you were avoiding me! I was looking for you yesterday and today but I couldn't find you. I was wondering if I'd said something that might have upset you.*

You can take this reply exactly for what it was: an elbow dipped in possibly scalding bathwater.

Well, you have upset me a little.

I knew it. I can never get away with anything. That nutter Gail probably couldn't wait to tell her. However, I decide to play dumb for a little while longer in order to give myself some thinking space: *'Err ... how's that?'*

When the reply comes back I'm more than a little surprised. It could be that I've misjudged Gail: *Well, we've been chatting online for two weeks and you haven't even offered to swap phone numbers with me!*

Swap phone numbers? This is a bolt out of the blue. Okay, time to think. So, it couldn't hurt to swap phone numbers could it? I mean, it was only swapping phone numbers wasn't it? It didn't mean going out on a date, or meeting, or anything. Eventually we might talk to each other on the phone. I couldn't see it happening anytime soon, but it would happen. It had to. Then, sometime way down the line, we might even think about going on a date; go to the cinema maybe. Yeah, sounds good. But for the moment, we're just swapping phone numbers. It can't hurt at all.

Well, if you really want my number, here's my mobile number ...

As I type in the last digit, my mobile starts to vibrate. I can't move; I'm rooted to my chair with fear. Surely, that can't possibly be Jenny? I stare at it, but it continues to buzz and, no matter how much I stare at it, it doesn't stop.

Then it dawns on me: it's a coincidence. When you think about it logically, it can't be Jenny because the mobile began to vibrate almost immediately after I'd finished typing the last digit. It's just that my phone doesn't recognise the number on the screen. So, I'd better pick up as it might be important.

"Hello?"

"Hiya! It's me, Jenny!"

She says 'it's me, Jenny', in such an explanatory way that she must have known I wouldn't know it was her. I'm on the back foot already and it's something I'll get quickly accustomed to. The first thing that goes through my mind is, how did she do that? That trick could impress even the most sceptical magic circle member. Next I think: wow! She sounds like Noel

24

Gallagher's big sister. She actually (or ac-tew-al-eh, as she would say it) pronounces her name as 'Jen-eh'.

"Hi! Nice to finally speak to you, although it's a bit sooner than I might have imagined," I say, pulling myself together. I can't really think of anything else to say as I'm still in shock. I'm also wondering how she could possibly have made the phone ring so quickly. I can't help thinking there's a night school somewhere in Wythenshawe teaching a GNVQ in stalking where she's picked up a few tricks.

"Well, no point in waiting around. I got the feeling that if I waited for you to ring I'd probably (prob-ab-leh) be waiting for some time."

"No, I would def-e-nit-leh ..." I'll have to watch myself; that accent is catching. "No, I mean, I definitely would have called you within a few years."

She laughs at my weak joke. Well, I think it's a laugh. It sounds more like a hyena in pain. "Eh cheeky, (cheek-eh) you're not skittin' my accent are you?"

"Course not."

"Good job!"

I laugh at this. She certainly has no pretensions and I doubt her airs and graces are on show very often either.

From that moment on, I decide that not only do I like virtual Jenny (Jen-eh), I like the real one too; accent or no accent, raucous laugh or no raucous laugh. Of course, on realising that I like her, the nerves hit me and I start to talk bollocks. I don't stop for at least ten minutes. The only time she interjects is to ask a question or make the odd affirmative comment. Finally, she puts me out of my obvious agony by telling me she has to go. "Look, it's been really nice, but it's late and I have work in the morning. The world of facility (facil-et-eh) management waits for no one. I also have three teenage boys that should be in bed but are still on their computers. Listen, do you fancy coming out with me? We could meet a week next Friday. It would be nice to get off the computer and talk to you face to face."

"What do you mean? Like a date?" I say, not really getting it.

"No. Not a date. More like two people meeting for a drink to see if they have anything in common."

"Isn't that what a date is?" I think briefly about my track record on here *vis à vis* dates.

"That depends on your definition of a date. Mine is that it's not a date. It's just two people meeting for a drink to see if they have anything in common."

"Well, that's okay then. I didn't go on *UR-date* to go on a date. I wanted to see if I could meet someone to see if I have anything in common with them," I reply.

25

We both laugh; she carries on. "Do you know the Castle Hotel on the business park in Warrington?"

"I think so. What time were you thinking?"

"Well, I can get out of work by four? It's up to you. I'm easy."

"Okay. I'm off on half-term, so it doesn't really matter to me what time."

"Let's say four o'clock then?"

"Err ... okay."

"Right, see you then. And don't worry; I can tell we're really going to get on."

With this she hangs up and, at the end of the call, I find myself staring at the phone in a very similar fashion to the way I stared at it when it first rang. I don't know how that happened. I thought we were only exchanging phone numbers.

Ten minutes later, lying wide awake and staring at the bedroom ceiling, I'm trying to work out how I managed to get myself invited on my first ever totally blind date, aged 38.

Chapter 6

Blind Date

It's the day of the blind date and Steve is in the kitchen enjoying his third half-day's flexi-leave since I've been here, and I've only been here a week. He's studying the Guardian crossword on the table in front of him and I'm pacing around, cup of tea in hand, like Pavlov's dog waiting for a bell. "Do you know what? I really don't want to go," I pronounce.

"Whatever," he says, not even bothering to look up. "You know you're going; you've already told her you will."

"No," I insist, placing my cup of tea on the table. "I've decided I'm not going."

"Look mate, it's just big match nerves," he assures me. "You're probably just worried about how badly it's all going to go and how ugly you are. By the way, has she seen how ugly you are?"

"Yeah, I put a photo on the website where I'm in serial killer mode."

"Good move. The serial killer look gets the desperate ones interested. Do you think this one's desperate? What am I saying? 'Course she is; she asked you out."

"She reckons she has no shortage of takers." I sit down in an effort to stop myself from pacing around the kitchen, but then immediately stand up again.

"Look on the positive side," he says, placing his pen behind his ear and rocking back on his chair. "You haven't run off on her yet, so that has to be some kind of first. Anyway, I don't see what you have to lose?"

"Err … my dignity? I can't believe I'm going on a totally blind date," I groan, sitting back down. "What if she's a bit of a moose?"

"Then, my amigo, it would be a match made in Heaven," he says, leaning forward and pencilling in five down. "As a matter of no interest whatsoever, didn't you tell me she sent you a photo that doesn't look anything like her?"

"Yeah, I think she could be well … you know, a bit mad."

"All the better; you love mad women."

It's true, I do. I've always been partial to mad women, perhaps because my mum's one. They say we all end up dating our mothers. I shudder at this thought and, not wishing to dwell on it, shift my argument.

"She's got this really strong Manchester accent. It makes the Gallagher brothers sound like they've been to Eton."

"What? Do me a favour. In the area of dodgy accents you are on decidedly boggy ground my friend. Your accent makes you sound like a gay John Lennon! Are you trying to tell me she's NTB?" (None Too Bright)

"No, no! She's smart and funny, or fun-eh as she would say. But ..."

"Go on."

"She's got kids," I say, shifting again. "And I don't want that kind of pressure. You know, the kids? I hate kids."

"Course you do. You're a teacher. All teachers hate kids."

"Well, I'm not looking to be a daddy to any new ones. The idea of having to parent someone else's kids isn't my idea of fun. I mean, I didn't win any parent of the year awards for my efforts with Charlotte."

I stand up again and Steve slides my cup of tea back across the table to me. "I think we are getting a little bit ahead of ourselves here. It's a blind date. It's not like you're ever going to get to meet them. I mean, you've usually run off well before they even start talking about their kids," he says laughing. "You've got to admit this is all doomed to fail right from the very start. Internet dating? As if ..."

That's typical Steve for you. Where any dating's concerned he's about as optimistic as a short-sighted hedgehog that needs to cross a motorway during rush hour. "If I remember rightly it was you that put me on to Internet dating in the first place."

"Did I? Well, you still can't stand her up – it's not right Rob and you know it."

"You never said that in the car when I stood the other one up."

"That's because she'd broken the dating rules about old photos. This one hasn't done that."

"No, she's sent one where I can't tell what she looks like."

"It's not the same thing. She's not broken the rules so you gotta turn up."

I look over at him as he gulps the last remnants of his tea. He looks so smug going on about dating rules as if they really exist outside of his tiny little head. Worse, the smug look is also because he knows he's won and the resignation must be etched across every line on my craggy face.

I consider my options.

I mentally run the gamut of them from a-z: I don't have any options.

I have to go. "All right, but just remember that I didn't want to go!" I moan, in such a way as to indicate that any ensuing disaster will be his fault.

"They can put that on your tombstone," he chuckles. "Here lies Rob – he didn't want to go." Delighted at the brilliance of his little quip he stands up, turns towards the door and heads outside, rather smugly, for a ciggy.

That I 'didn't want to go' was only half the truth. Part of me really did want to, but that part was swamped by my recent dating experiences. I walk over to the hall mirror and look at myself. Even if I fancy her she's not going to fancy me. I look up at my thinning hair and have a sudden brainstorm.

I sprint up to my bedroom and pull out a tattered, old holdall from under the bed. I rummage through its contents, all the while looking out of the window to make sure Steve is still outside smoking – which he is. Then I go to the bathroom and quietly lock the door. A short time later, after an unfortunate incident with a spray can that I pulled from the bag and the new, white bath towel that Steve's mum bought him for Christmas I creep, rather sheepishly, out of the bathroom to embark on a frantic search in my wardrobe. I'm desperately looking for my black beanie hat, which I eventually locate in my sports bag along with last week's unwashed football kit.

I can't think how I can avoid being seen by Steve on the way out and the inevitable sarcasm the hat will attract if he spots it. I wait quietly at the top of the stairs, listening for his movements. Just as I've given up all hope that he's ever going to move, I hear the sound of the kettle being filled and rush down the stairs at top speed. "See ya later!" I yell, banging the front door firmly shut behind me.

Before he has time to realise what is happening and, more importantly, spot the beanie, I haul my reluctant backside into the Audi A4 and drive to the pub.

When I arrive ten minutes later, I get out of the car and make my way across the car park. I notice in a wing mirror that my demeanour has all the enthusiasm of a stretcher-bearer who's been ordered on to no-man's-land on the first day of the Somme.

So I'm sitting here, waiting for Jenny, while my hand taps the table in front of me. I peer through the cracked face of my watch: it's five to four.

Five minutes to go.

I'm dressed from head to toe in black, which seemed like a good idea before I put the beanie hat on. Now I worry that I look like I'm about to rob a bank. Still, there's no way José I'm taking the beanie off. You see earlier, in the bathroom, I sprayed my head with a can of Years Younger and now my scalp resembles a full-blown, satellite photo of the lunar surface. The jargon on the tin of Years Younger tells you all about its amazing, hair thickening properties. What it doesn't tell you is that if you have less hair on your head than you do on your arse, you're unlikely to see any tangible benefits.

However, I can now tell you a couple of things for certain: firstly, if you spray Years Younger on to a bald head, it develops the colour and consistency of diarrhoea. Secondly, if you use Steve's new, white bath towel to try and wipe said diarrhoea off it makes an incredible mess of both your head and the towel. So the beanie hat is a cover for the large, brown spots that have developed on my scalp. At best, these spots resemble some kind of hideous bacterial infection. At worst, they look as if someone has, quite literally, shit on my head.

And you wouldn't believe how much it itches.

I take another glance at my cracked watch face. It looks like the one I ran over in the car and the one that Steve broke trying to prove I couldn't have broken that one by running a car over it (don't ask). I guess I'm the sort of bloke who's always breaking things: watches, glasses ... marriages. It still keeps good time though – good enough to tell me that Jenny is ten minutes late. I get the distinct feeling that I'm being stood up. I look around the pub. Apart from me, there are four other people here, which isn't surprising at ten past four on a February Friday.

When Jenny finally enters I very nearly miss it, but I'll never forget it. It's 4.25 and there's not a hint of sheepishness about her.

She *saunters* in.

I know it's Jenny instantly, although I don't know *how* I know. It might be because I've seen the photo she sent that doesn't look like her. She doesn't notice me at first, so all I can do is watch her looking around the pub trying to locate me. When her gaze finally rests on me, I feel a surge of panic.

Then she waves at me. I repeat: she waves at me. She doesn't know me, has never even seen me, so what is she waving at me for? She can't know I'm me ... but she does. Just as I know it's Jenny, she knows it's me. She approaches me quickly. Her walk is purposeful and elegant; her face is lit with an expression that borders on the mischievous.

It's very clear to me that the date is going to be even more traumatic than I'd imagined, because I now realise this is definitely not Jenny's first ever blind date.

Jenny has now reached the table and is politely holding out her hand and, from where I'm sitting, it's holding all the aces. I rise halfway to my feet and reach out to shake it limply. This isn't surprising. Everyone says I have the limpest handshake they've ever come across. "Hi, we meet at last!" she says. My limp-wristedness clearly hasn't daunted her and she beams a smile at me that almost knocks my head off. "Who would have thought it? Would you like a drink?"

Shuffling about in my seat, I quickly realise that my protocol radar is off: I should be offering to buy her a drink. Before I can make the offer my hand goes involuntarily to my head and starts clawing at the incessant itch beneath the hat. She glances up and stares as, like *Dr Strangelove*, I use my other hand to drag it down to my side with no small difficulty. She drops her gaze back and looks at me, while tilting her head to one side. Her facial expression indicates that she thinks I'm a nutter. "Hi! No! Please let me get you one," I blurt out.

30

"No, it's fine," she replies, taking off her scarf and wrapping it over the chair. "I'll get it. What do you want?"

"Best stick with diet coke," I reply, wondering if this is her ploy to get to the bar and do a runner. "You know? Driving ..."

While Jenny's at the bar ordering the drinks, I get some breathing space. I look over at her. She has a great figure. She's slim but shapely, and she's pretty – not that intimidating sort of pretty which can be hard to look at sometimes – she's pretty in that easy-going, Renée Zellweger way. She has pale, steely-blue eyes, short blonde hair and looks at least five years younger than the 36 she admits to on the website. She also looks taller than the 5'4" box she ticked, which gives her a certain stature and she's most definitely not in any danger of being sued under the Trades Descriptions Act for the *very good looking* box she also ticked. She's wearing cut-off jeans and a white, crew-necked top that could have looked ridiculous on someone of her age, but doesn't. She also has an unzipped Adidas leather jacket that wouldn't have looked out of place at a *Motorhead* gig, which also looks pretty darn good on her.

To my surprise, and huge relief, a minute or two later she's back from the bar and plonking two drinks on the table. "Cheers," I say.

"Cheers!" she repeats, taking a large gulp out of what looks like a small rum and coke. "God, do I need this."

She's now sitting directly opposite me with her legs confidently crossed. She puts the drink down and stares into my eyes. I feel a little disconcerted to say the least. I need to do something so I begin to talk, although talk isn't really an accurate description. I begin to ramble, to gush, to spew forth a load of old crap. "Did you find it okay? Of course you did; you're here aren't you?" I say, clawing once again at my head. "I mean, did you have any difficulties finding it?"

"You mean, with me being late?" she replies, eyes glinting.

"Are you late? I hadn't noticed," I say, face flushing. "Thanks for the drink."

"It's not a problem," she tells me, her eyes now locked on to mine. "I am a little late though (a little late!) due to someone dumping a shitty (shi-teh) job on my desk at the last minute."

"Well, you look really nice," I tell her, wondering how the hell I made that quantum leap in the conversation. She isn't taken aback though.

"Oh, this old thing," she says, grabbing playfully at her leather jacket. "It's an Adidas original, only three prototypes ever made."

"Why, are you rich?" Oh no, quantum leap number two.

"Hardly. Why, are you? I could do with a rich man," she laughs.

I laugh though it's a little forced and then realise something I wish I hadn't:

I have a hard-on.

31

I'm not sure exactly when this happened, but as far as I've been able to ascertain, a hard-on isn't a good thing to have on a first date. Neither is it likely to make the sort of favourable impression that gets you a second one. The scale of the problem is this: I estimate the lump in my combat pants to be around a hard eight. That is to say, Steve and I have a system by which we measure our hard-ons, using a scale of one to ten. A full-on ten is often described in soft porn novels as 'raging'. As I haven't had sex for a year, I couldn't tell you what a 'raging' feels like these days. So I'm reduced to crossing my legs, shuffling around on my seat and bemoaning the fact that I'm wearing my thin, black combats rather than my thick, black jeans.

My predicament is partly Jenny's fault. She's pulled her chair around from her side of the table so that she's facing me head on. Then placing her foot on the lower bar of my chair, she's put herself right into my personal space. I now have a head on view of her incredibly toned stomach and gorgeous little belly button. "Is everything okay?" she asks, noticing my squirming on the chair.

"Yeah, yeah, 'course it is. I'm having a great time."

"Glad to hear it," she replies, her eyes glancing up to my head. "Is your head itchy?"

"Err ... no. Why?"

"You keep scratching it."

"Do I?"

She doesn't answer but breaks out into a smile and leans back in her chair away from me. "Listen, do you fancy something to eat?" she asks, looking at me and smiling like a veritable angel. It's clear that I would be totally stupid to turn down this invitation.

"No thanks. Err ... I'm not really hungry," I reply.

This, I judge, will totally throw her. It's a brilliant move on my part. She will now have to go home and eat, which will draw proceedings to a halt. I can then exit stage left, taking my itchy head, number eight hard-on and any chance of a repeat date with me. Not that I believe she's hungry anyway, as she must be eight stone soaking wet.

As usual I'm wrong on all counts.

"Okay, suit yourself," she tells me, and waltzes off to order what turns out to be a very large chicken tikka.

When she returns, I've recovered a little from the trauma of it all and we talk about the safe subject of our respective jobs. "I work for a software company in Warrington," she informs me. "I'm a facilities manager. The money's okay, but the main reason I stick with it is because the people I work with are really nice. It's not too taxing if you're organised and, having three boys at home, I've learnt to be organised."

Ah, the kids!

32

Now that I've actually seen how attractive she is I'm more than willing to reconsider my previous position. I suspect she's making a point with this last comment. I can't blame her. I always think it's important to know the rules of the game before you start to play. That way you can't complain if it goes belly up. So I let her know I understand the rules. "Teaching's not great money, but it pays the bills," I tell her. "It can be really stressful with the kid's behaviour, but at least I don't have three kids to look after at home while I'm trying to do it."

There: I've acknowledged that the three kids don't put me off. Game on.

"No, you have more than 30," she jokes.

"Yeah, but I don't have to take them home with me every day."

"That's a good point."

"How old are they?" I enquire, trying to further establish the rules.

"The youngest one's 11. The oldest one 15."

"All boys, you said."

"All boys." She holds my gaze as she says this, and it's a firm hold. One that says: 'you know the rules now. Do you still wanna play?'

I flash back my best 'yes, I still wanna play' smile and we change the subject.

We continue to chat as the food arrives. She breaks off to thank the young waitress, and after indicating that she doesn't require any sauces proceeds to eat, totally unfazed by the look on my face. The expression I'm wearing is probably comparable to the one on the faces of the Titanic's band when the icy water first hit their knackers.

The reason for this is that she absolutely demolishes – and I mean *demolishes* – her meal. Not that this halts the conversation at any time. It doesn't. She multitasks by talking and eating right the way through it, without ever looking undignified. I'm now looking down at an empty plate and I wouldn't be surprised if she had taken some of the enamel off the top of that too. She puts her cutlery down and smiles again. She has a very pretty smile. "Well, that wasn't up to much, but I was really hungry."

"I can't wait to see you eat something you do like!" I say, and she giggles. I realise that, like her online persona, she's very easy to be around.

"I'll have to be going soon," she says, leaning forward with her elbows on the table. "I'm still living with my ex until he finds his own place. He's going out tonight and I need to get back for the kids. But it's been really nice to meet you at last."

I glance down at my watch. It's nearly six. I don't know where the time's gone. "You too," I reply. "If you have to go, let me walk you to your car."

We get up and I'm more than relieved to find that my knob is back to normal. I follow her out of the pub and into the badly lit car park. The

33

key moment has arrived. Do I have the courage to ask her for another date? If I do will she reject me? Despite the head scratching and hard-on problems, I think it's gone well.

We've stopped by her car now. She's zipping her jacket and hanging around in that uncomfortable way that you do at the end of a first date. I look briefly into her eyes, desperately trying to steal any clues that might be written in them, but nothing's there. Words fall out of my mouth.

"Anyway, it's been really nice," I manage to say.

"Yeah, it has," she says, taking her car keys from her pocket. "It really has been nice to meet you."

Somehow I get the idea that the whole thing has been really nice. But she's now getting ready to go and I need to do something quickly. Eventually, from somewhere, I get some strength. "I don't suppose you would like to -?"

"How about Sunday? If Harry's not booked the night already, I might be free. We could meet then. Should I text you?"

I panic at this. We have a match Sunday evening and there's no way I can dump my mates, the same mates who have stood by me during my break-ups, on the off-chance of a date with her. So I'll just have to tell her no. "Yeah, Sunday would be great! I'll look forward to it. Let me know."

God knows how I'm going to explain this to Steve. To make matters worse I add, "It was really nice."

I can't believe I've said it again.

She doesn't seem to notice. She turns quickly, beeps the door open and slides elegantly into her Peugeot. I walk over to my car and watch as she reverses with expertise, waves at me then drives off like she's just missed the flag in the British Grand Prix. As soon as she's out of sight I fling my hat off and start to claw at my head with all the fury of Michael Jackson filming a Pepsi ad.

Driving back to Steve's house I keep looking at myself in the rear-view mirror. I'm smiling like Andy Dufresne listening to Mozart in *The Shawshank Redemption*. I crank up the CD player to the max and start to sing along to the *Arctic Monkeys*. When I arrive at Steve's there's a text message on my phone. It reads: *'I told you we would get on – I love it when I'm right!!! xxx.'*

When I get out of the car, Steve is standing in the doorway. He's holding the new, white bath towel his mum bought him for Christmas out in front of him in a very accusatory manner and it looks like someone has, quite literally, shit all over it.

Chapter 7

The Second Time Around

I'm lying on the sofa holding my stomach with both hands. It's cramping so badly that, if I didn't have at least a rudimentary grasp of biology, I could swear I was about to have my first period. It's now Saturday afternoon; roughly 24 hours after my blind date and I haven't eaten a morsel since yesterday. This is unusual as I normally have the kind of appetite that gets you forcibly ejected from all-you-can-eat buffets. I groan as another spasm painfully grips my stomach. It could be a particularly bad flare-up of my irritable bowel syndrome. However, the fact that I went to the toilet three hours earlier, and smack on my regular time, makes me worry that this feeling might be something much worse.

And I'm not the only one suffering from an irritable condition. Steve's annoyed when I tell him I might not be available for the game due to a possible date with Jenny. "What do you mean you might not be available for selection?" he says, switching the TV off with the remote.

"It's just that I might be going out with Jenny again," I say.

"But you can't do that! We have a big game tomorrow night. The team we're playing are only two points behind us and we are only-"

"Two points off the top."

"Exactly!"

"It's not definite," I add. "It might not happen. It depends on whether her ex has booked the night or not."

"Well, I wouldn't worry about it. You've got a bad record on the repeat date front." Before I can answer back, he takes himself outside for a smoke.

Mulling over the conversation, my thoughts are interrupted by my vibrating mobile. It's a text from Jenny and one that I've been dreading. It says: *'Harry is out 2morro. He booked it on the calendar b4 me so I can't make it. Sorry!'*

Now, I don't know Harry, but I do know that I don't particularly like him at this moment. Why has he booked it before her? How come he put his name down on the calendar before she did? Okay, so he might have been following the previously agreed procedures of a separating couple still living together in difficult circumstances, but really, who does he think he is?

But in my heart of hearts, I've been half expecting it. I always fear the worst when I'm on the brink of getting something I really want. At times like these in my life a kind of self-defence mechanism kicks in and I begin to rationalise as a way of coping with disappointment.

Okay, what's positive about this development? For one thing, I'll no longer be walking around with a 'stupid grin' on my face, which was Steve's accusation when I returned yesterday. According to him I looked like Jack Nicholson did after smashing the door in *The Shining*. So the removal of this grin will please my housemate no end. To be totally truthful, my telling him about not being able to play was a bit of payback for the fact that he's made himself three cups of tea so far today, and hasn't made me one. He never, ever, makes a cup of tea without asking if I want one too. So the grin must have really annoyed him. On the rare occasions when he's not pleased with me he puts sugar in 'by accident', but that's about as vicious as he gets. Anyway, it will cheer him up when he knows that a) I can now play and b) he thinks I've been dumped in the process.

At least the knotting feeling in my stomach has subsided. Now I know that this should be a positive development but, get this, I actually feel worse! I can't for the life of me explain this weird state of medical affairs. There's a kind of emptiness where the knotting once was. Perhaps her text has caused it. I feel like, well ... like I might have been dumped.

I have to work this out. The Big E or not the Big E? That is the question. The more I think about it the more confused I become. She can't make tomorrow when she said she could, yet she did appear to be keen as we left the pub on Friday. Perhaps the text is some kind of test? A way of finding out if I'm as keen as she is. God! Real, seen dating is even harder than blind dating. Thankfully, after a little while, I start to trust my instincts and common sense prevails. I reach for my mobile and thoughtfully type: *'Don't worry I couldn't make it tomorrow anyway as I have car problems. See you around x'*

As I'm about to hit the send button the temporary insanity departs. *"See you around?"* What's that about? No. I realise she can't make it, end of story. The person I wrote to on *UR-date* didn't play games. She wasn't ambiguous, she was honest and painfully so at times. So the text said what it meant: she simply couldn't make it. I recall how frequently she talks about how we have a 'real connection' whenever we correspond. All I need to do is not lose the plot; easier said than done in my case. Also, I must show her that I'm still keen, but that I also have integrity and I can't be messed around. But I mustn't make her feel vulnerable. I search my mind for a satisfactory text reply that will encapsulate those values and ideas.

At this point I would settle for any reply that feels like it wants to enter my head, but my head is blanker than Paris Hilton's on being asked to calculate Pi to two places. Suddenly the phone vibrates in my hand. I look down at the screen: *'We can meet on Tuesday. But I'll have 2 b back fairly early. Call me & I'll give u directions 2 a pub I know.'*

36

Shit, I'll have to have an actual conversation with her now and all because I couldn't think of a satisfactory text reply. Not to mention the fact that we're going to meet in a pub that she knows and I probably don't. Also, not to mention the fact that I'll never find it in a million years, because she's a woman and women have all the directional sense of a helium balloon with a knitting needle inserted in it.

Furthermore, I'm not going to be able to meet her until Tuesday. Tuesday is a long time away. But that knotting feeling is back and now it doesn't feel so much like IBS. Strangely enough, it feels good to have it back. It's made me realise how much I want to meet her, how much I want to spend time with her; to look at her flat stomach ... to have her provocatively place her long legs on it ... Careful! My trousers are stirring here. I dial her number.

It goes straight to voicemail.

Now this really frustrates me about women. They send you a text asking you to phone them, and when you do – immediately I might add – it goes straight to voicemail. You're then left with the option to either hang up or leave a message. My phone messages always sound like I have a day release pass from the Care in the Community programme.

As I'm wondering whether to leave a message or not, her name appears on the screen – *Jenny*. I press the green accept button. I am, even by my low standards, amazingly calm. "Hiya. I called you, but it went to straight to voicemail," I answer.

"Sorry, I was on the phone to my mum. She's not been very well and I wanted to see how she was."

"I hope she's okay? It's just that I don't really like leaving messages as I don't always sound like myself." What a stupid thing to say. She doesn't sound worried though and her voice shows no indication that she thinks I'm the idiot I am.

"That's fine," she tells me. "I take it you can make Tuesday for a drink and maybe something to eat? Say around eight?"

"I'll check my diary – just give me a minute."

I haven't got a diary. The truth is that I'm free any night of the week that she wants me to be. But I don't want to seem too keen. I stand with the phone in my hand and Steve passes by. He must have caught the back end of the conversation as he's looking at me in an odd way. He knows it's more likely that scientists will find dark matter before my diary's found.

I flash a sarcastic looking smile in his direction and he returns it with gusto before disappearing back down the hall. I start to talk again, having left enough time for her to imagine that I am, indeed, checking my diary. "Yeah, that's fine. Might have to re-arrange a few things, but it should be okay."

"Well look, don't cancel anything on my behalf as we can always rearrange."

"No! No! It's fine." A hint of panic is not so much noticeable in my voice as the only thing actually in my voice. Unpleasant thoughts of her rearranging my date on Tuesday with one of her many *UR-date* contacts leap into my mind. "No, I really can make it. It's not a problem," I insist.

"Okay," she replies. "Have you got a pen? I'll give you directions to a pub I know near the airport."

I can't help thinking I'll be lucky if I don't end up at Heathrow Airport by the time she's finished. She gives me the name of the pub and the exit junction off the M56. She then gives me a set of directions that I may even be able to follow. "Okay then, see you Tuesday," she says, as she finishes.

"Okay. Tuesday at eight, and don't be late!" I say this last bit in the style of the Big Bopper singing *Chantilly Lace*. She laughs at the joke, but she doesn't say she won't be.

I put the receiver down and catch my reflection in the hall mirror. I look like I'm auditioning for a part in *The Shining* again. I walk, with more than a slight spring in my step, into the living room. Steve takes one look at my smile, gets up from the sofa and goes off to make himself a cup of tea.

I now have 72 hours, more or less, to kill before the big date. I need to try and take my mind off it. I consult the calendar to see it only has one entry for the weekend: tomorrow night's 'big match'. Kick-off is six o'clock, which will help to pass some time. The lads will be going for a pint afterwards so I'll tag along with Steve. Although uneasy thoughts are beginning to surface as I remember last week's game; in particular the part where I'd called John, the club manager and captain 'a right wanker', at which point the referee kindly suggested that I leave the pitch. Consequently, we drew a game we should have won and dropped two points behind Drysdale's mob.

I sprint down the hall to the kitchen to where Steve is sat aimlessly scanning the Guardian's sport section like he has all day, which, when you think about it, he has. "Steve. The date's off. I can play."

"The date's off being another way of saying: I've been dumped."

I ignore the barb.

"John hasn't said anything about last week's game has he?"

"You mean, about how you called him a wanker," he replies, looking up from the paper and fixing me with a knowing smile. "And how you got sent off, and how we drew a game we should have won?"

"That's all water under the bridge now and at least you're not bitter. No, I meant about the team for tomorrow. Did he say anything about the team? I am playing aren't I?"

"You mean, you can't remember what he said about whether you were playing or not, because you weren't there, due to the fact that you'd been sent off and then stormed off in a huff?"

"You're really enjoying this aren't you?"

"I always enjoy myself when you act like a complete knob."

It's obvious he's still sulking and I can see I'm going to get nowhere with him in his current mood. Another approach to the problem is required.

Ordinarily John's an easy going bloke who doesn't hold grudges. However, given the fact that this is the third game in a row in which we've had a small contretemps, he could very well be suffering from compassion fatigue.

I get an idea. I can squirm out of this and maintain some dignity after all. In Thursday night's game, John almost came to blows with his best mate Mark. I switch on my computer and begin to write an email:

Dear John,

I have to say... I am a little hurt. When I saw you fighting with Mark the other night I was reminded about how you and I used to fight... I know this is coming across as a little needy, but I still think that maybe... you know? We could fight again... sometime.

I know we decided that we would fight with other people; it's just that...it's all come a bit soon for me.

Look, don't say no straight away... think about it... I am sure we could fight again... even if it is just once more.

Yours in anticipation

I hit send and head downstairs to check the Everton score on the television text. They're losing again. Why my dad ever took me to Everton matches as a lad I'll never know. They've less chance of getting into Europe this season than a radical Muslim cleric with rabies. I leave the screen on the usual '*Everton nil*', go back up to the computer, open Outlook Express and click send/receive. John has already replied. I open his email and laugh out loud at his reply:

Look Rob,

I enjoyed our fighting while it lasted, but I have moved on now and you clearly haven't.

It's not you, it's me ... I think it is only right that you know that I have been fighting with other people every Thursday for a while now and, well, to be honest, I'm enjoying playing the field a bit. I have tried to stop myself because I know I might be getting a bit of a name for it, but finding new people to fight with every week has made me realise that I'm not ready to commit myself to fighting with just one person.

Our fights were great fights and I'll never forget them, but for now, at least, I'll be making an arsehole of myself elsewhere.

I'm sorry.

John

ps Don't worry you wanker, we only have six tomorrow so you're in!

At least that will help to take my mind off Tuesday.

Sunday's game consists of a victory, in which I score two goals and keep hold of my temper. The even better news is that Drysdale's mob, surprisingly, only draw and so we move level with them on points. This is, in part, due to the fact that Steve livens up their match by throwing Hula Hoops at Drysdale from the balcony and getting their game temporarily stopped. This is perhaps the very first (and only) recorded case of 'small emulsified potato snacks stop play' in a football match. 'Hulahoopgate', as we later christen it in the pub, breaks Big D's concentration and he lets in a soft goal right at the end.

After the game, a few pints are consumed in The Bear's Paw and a pleasant night is had by all, provided your surname isn't Drysdale, that is.

Monday and Tuesday daytimes go pretty quickly. I'm back in the house of pain after the half-term with my nose firmly pressed to the grindstone. Meetings after work on both nights ensure that the time ticks along pretty quickly.

And so, once again, I find myself in Steve's bathroom about to head out on a date. This time, though, there isn't a can of Years Younger held threateningly above my head. Instead, I splash on some of the Armani aftershave Charlotte bought me for Christmas. Back in my bedroom I check that the can is still under the bed safely hidden away from Steve. I won't be using it again; my scalp was itching like a bitch all Friday night. Not only that, if Steve knew I was prone to spraying my non-existent hair with hair thickener, life wouldn't be worth living.

It's 7.30 p.m. when I set off for the airport with Jenny's directions on the dashboard. I follow them to the letter and have to admit to feeling quite staggered by the fact that they are both clear and correct. Even more amazingly, I arrive at the pub with absolutely no detours necessary.

Walking across the pub car park I can see the freezing weather isn't putting any of the hardy smokers off as they huddle together for warmth under the patio heaters. I brush past them and step up to the entrance. A heavy, wooden door leads into an olde worlde bar where an enormous log fire is crackling and hissing in the middle of the room. It's very quiet inside.

There's a middle-aged couple sat close to the fire speaking in soft voices and an old bloke with his head buried in a newspaper that's spread out in front of him. The remnants of his Guinness slosh about in the bottom of his glass as he gives it a final swirl before polishing it off. He looks up and nods at me. I say hello then order a diet coke which I take to an empty table by the window. There's a chalked *specials* board on the wall which I read to pass the time. I've dressed in black again, but I'm not

40

wearing my beanie hat. I'm also reasonably calm though there are still one or two butterflies fluttering around in my stomach.

As I move my eyes down from the board I see her walk past the group of smokers outside. She displays the same air of confidence as last time, but somehow it feels less intimidating. A few heads turn as she walks past – I like that. She's wearing a long, black coat and jeans. She's understated, yet elegant and bristling with an alluring self-assurance that I'm very attracted to. She enters through the door. I get up and kiss her lightly on the cheek. This time I insist that she sits down while I buy her a drink and when I return from the bar, I sit directly opposite her. I've made sure there is no room for her to move her chair around and close in on me, but I'm wearing my thickest jeans just in case. "You look really nice," I say, because she does.

"Thanks. You don't look so bad yourself," she grins. I blush a little but manage to quip.

"Oh, this old thing? She laughs but she's looking at me intently. I deflected her looks when she talked to me on our first date, but I'm holding them a little longer tonight. I feel like we're beginning to tentatively explore the start of something very new and exciting.

The main topic of conversation is our respective exes. Hardly surprising when she has 18 years invested in hers and three children to boot. I have two exes, Charlotte, and a combined total of nineteen years to talk about. We're on safe, fertile ground and we babble on. "I never really got on with Charlotte's mother," I tell her. "We were young and on the verge of splitting up when we found out she was pregnant. So we got married. I guess these days you wouldn't do it but back then I felt I had to."

"What about your recent split?" she asks. "What went wrong there?"

"Rebecca? Oh, I don't know. We got on. We still get on. In the end it wasn't enough though; for both of us really. What about you and Harry?"

"It's not easy to say. There were lots of reasons, but it finally came down to the fact that I couldn't cope with his controlling behaviour and he couldn't cope with my insecurities. I'd asked him to change but he couldn't. He asked me to change and I couldn't. *Voilà*: grounds for divorce."

"I can't imagine you having insecurities," I say, because I can't.

"It's hard to explain where they come from really. They only seem to emerge at certain points ..." She tails off, and I'm on the ball enough to know that I don't really want to probe any further.

"I just wanted someone to go the cinema with and I don't control. I have enough trouble controlling myself never mind anyone else."

She laughs openly and without reservation at this. I should point out at this juncture that the noise emerging from her mouth is loosely associated with the noun *laugh*. To be honest, it's more akin to the noises you might hear from the monkey pound in Chester Zoo at two in the morning, after an escaped lion wanders in. However, she's completely unperturbed by the looks of alarm displayed on everyone's face in the pub.

After that I'm a little more comfortable. Like the earlier settling of my irritable bowel the crap gushing out of my mouth has slowed to a trickle. I even manage to make a few more witty quips and decent one-liners.

We both order food this time and having already watched her eat I have no worries about my lack of table etiquette. We talk and talk and the time goes by very, very, quickly. All too soon, she's looking at her watch in a regretful way. It looks as though proceedings are coming to an abrupt halt. "I'm sorry, but I really have to go," she says, finishing her third diet coke. "I need to sort the boys out for school tomorrow and do some ironing. If you want to we could meet up this weekend? I'm free on Friday night. We could go clubbing it."

CLUBBING IT! If this means going after a few baby seals down on Southport beach I'd be more interested. But no, to my horror, she is actually suggesting going to a nightclub. These are not words I want to hear; a trip to the cinema maybe, but definitely not clubbing it. So my reply surprises even me. "Clubbing it? Yeah, I could be up for that," I say casually. Could, if I were 20 years younger!

"Great, I'll call you tomorrow when I've sorted a few things out."

"Okay. I'll walk you to your car."

We walk outside. She closes her black, leather coat and wraps her arms around herself. I stand in front of her shivering. It's absolutely freezing. Though she's loitering a little, her body language suggests that she really needs to go and as she reaches the bonnet of her car, she stands awkwardly. It's the first awkward moment of the evening. Then suddenly, it occurs to me: her awkwardness is on my behalf. I should kiss her. I step forward and place a small kiss on her cheek, then stand back pleased by my efforts. Her face lights up and breaks into a smile, the first shoots of which indicate bemusement. Bemusement at the fact that it was such a formal kiss, I suppose, but then her smile blooms fully and I see patience and understanding there. She walks to her car, zaps the door open and turns her head towards me. "Drive safely," (safe-leh) she says softly.

"I will."

On the way home my phone beeps. It's in my pocket and I know instinctively it will be a text from her. I break the law and almost total the car trying to read it. It says: *Thanks for a wonderful evening. Don't forget this Friday :-) X'*

As it turned out, it was not a Friday I was likely to forget in a hurry.

Chapter 8

Motel

Today is Wednesday. As luck would have it, I have a couple of non-contact periods this morning and, as any teacher worth their salt will tell you, the less contact you have with the kids the better the job. It's probably not understating the case to say that the kids ruin teaching.

Historically, non-contact periods used to be known as 'free' periods. The name was changed in the 1980s, presumably because it suited neither teaching unions nor government to imply that teachers were merely sitting around the staff room reading the Guardian jobs page.

At this moment I should be catching up on my backlog of marking. However, the backlog has grown to such huge proportions that if it was pulped into toilet paper it could probably wipe the arses of a large part of South-East Asia.

Instead of tackling this backlog I'm sat at one of the computers sipping hot coffee in the staff room. The staff room is on the second floor of the oldest building in the school. This room was originally the library and it still has that musty smell and intimidating please-be-quiet air that libraries often have. It's a place where thousands of books have been mulled over and you can feel it all around you. Not that I'm mulling anything as substantial. No, I'm currently mulling the possible ramifications of going clubbing with Jenny on Friday night. For me, the crux of the matter lies in the fact that she lives in Manchester and I live in Runcorn. The thing I'm really interested in can be boiled down to the frothy consistency of one sticky question: what are the sleeping arrangements going to be?

I have to confess that until now, I haven't even considered the possibility that I might be on the point of breaking my 12 month duck. When you've been on a losing run that stretches this far back into the distant past, as any football manager will tell you, you take it one game at a time. No, I'm more concerned about the distinct possibility that a Friday night from hell is hanging over my head like the sword of Damocles.

You can see why I might not be overly keen on the idea of 'clubbing it'. One of the reasons for joining the Internet dating site in the first place was that I didn't fancy the club scene. Still, I'm about to learn another salutary lesson: with Jenny, nothing pans out the way you think.

As I walk back to my room, I see Drysdale approaching me in the corridor. It's too late to avoid him because he's already seen me and is waving like I'm a plane that's been sitting on Manchester Airport's runway for three hours. I know exactly why he's after me; it's why I've been avoiding him for the last few weeks. Well, that's not entirely true. It's only one of the many reasons I've been avoiding him.

"A quick word in your shell-like if I may," he shouts. I stop and brace myself for his onslaught. "The camera. You said you were bringing it in?" he complains.

"Yeah. And I will," I tell him, trying to sound like he's pissing me off, which he is.

"When? You said that two weeks ago. I would like you to return it please; it's IT property."

"Look, I said I'll bring it in and I will. Tomorrow." I'm lying through my arse at this point. The truth is that I lent it to Steve, who wanted to take some pictures at his sister's wedding. Unfortunately, I let slip, while he was in a very inebriated state, that the camera was Drysdale's. The camera was last seen heading towards the River Mersey at a great velocity.

"Well I need it tomorrow and, if I don't get it, I'm going to have to take this further," he says in his most threatening, computer-geek voice, which is not very threatening at all. I feel at this point that the best form of defence might be attack.

"What's the rush anyway?" I say, raising my voice. "You've got more cameras in that cupboard than a coach full of Japanese tourists."

"I would hardly call it a rush," he replies, his face contorting in frustration. "Anyway, I don't have to explain IT policy to you."

"No. But you should explain it to somebody, as no one in this school has a clue what it is." I turn away and walk off leaving him clenching his keys in anger. To his credit though, he doesn't allow me the last word.

"Yeah, well, if I did explain it you wouldn't get it!" he bellows down the corridor. I briefly contemplate shouting back 'just like you're not getting the camera', but think better of it.

It turns out that the Drysdale conversation is just about the high point of my day. After breaking up two fights at dinner time, being told to "piss off you baldy bastard" by one of our more challenging year 11 boys and getting a bollocking from the Deputy Head for not doing some shitty, pointless paperwork, I'm now driving home in torrential rain.

When I get in, I thank God for small mercies: Steve's not home yet. It takes me ten minutes to open the door. He's told me the lock can be tricky, but I think it would be easier to get in a nun's knickers than into his house. Eventually, I head down the hall and plonk a large pile of marking, which I have absolutely no intention of doing, on to the kitchen table. Why I insist on bringing it home I do not know.

One of my History colleagues once asked me why I always took marking home if I never actually did it. "I have every intention of doing it until I get home," was my reply, and it proves to be true once again as the mere thought of it makes me sick.

I glance at the kitchen clock to see that it's only half-past three. I make a calculated decision not to tell Steve the real time I arrived home. With a bit of luck I can avoid one of those 'teachers, you only work half days and you still get 12 weeks holiday a year' conversations he enjoys so much. Shit, he takes half a day's flexi-leave whenever he wants and goes out for a pint every Friday lunch time.

I turn to stare at the pile of marking and find my left hand making its way to my inside jacket pocket. To my utter dismay, I find a red pen. Before I know what I've done, my right hand extracts an exercise book from the pile and opens a page. My head begins to swirl. With a gargantuan effort, I close the book and hurl it back on to the pile. A second later, a red biro follows and I find myself striding down the hall to my bedroom.

This is the room that Steve said was "a little bit cold at times." I get the feeling he's involved in a scientific experiment to recreate the surface temperature of Pluto in here – it's more like a flask than a room. I jump into bed wondering how it could possibly be colder inside the room than outside. Leaving my clothes and a big, woollen coat on, I pull up the duvet and three extra blankets. In ten minutes I'm fast asleep. I don't stir until there's a knock at the door; it's Steve with a cup of tea.

I squint at the clock. It's 5.30pm. "What time did you get in?" he asks, in far too friendly a tone for my liking. Shit! I'll have to play it safe.

"Around 4.30," I lie.

"Yeah, right! I got in before that," he retorts, placing the tea down on the bedside cabinet and turning back towards the door.

"Well, it must have been a little earlier then."

"Yeah, try about 3.30 – teachers! You only work half days, and you get 12 ..." Fortunately, he passes out of earshot as he goes down the hall. I sip at the cuppa and wonder what time Jenny might ring.

One of the worse things about a new relationship is waiting for a call that you've been told is coming. The power lies with the one who says they'll make the call; the other party can only wait and wonder if it will even come. If you have any self-respect you don't pre-empt it, as this gives the appearance of being needy. I'm trying desperately to hang on to my self-respect by not phoning her.

In the end, I don't have to fight my better instincts for long. The call comes at six. "Hi, it's me," she says, in a jolly-hockey-sticks voice.

"Hiya, you okay?"

"Yeah. Just got in from work. Long day."

"Yeah, me too," I say.

I hope she doesn't have thermal sensors on her mobile phone. If she does, she will detect a very red face at my end. "Look, I thought I'd ring about Friday night and the arrangements. You still okay to come?"

45

Ah! The Arrangements. Here's my chance. I should broach the subject carefully and with no little discretion. "Yeah, about that. I was wondering what -"

"I thought we could stay in a motel. I've already checked and they've got a room available at the one near my work. It'll be handy for me and it's also quite close to you, isn't it? But I'll have to book it soon, as they're holding it for me as a favour. I didn't want to be presumptuous and book it. So what do you think?"

To be honest, I didn't hear a word of what she said after the utterance of the word 'motel'. After a year, I'm so desperate to have sex that even the word motel gets me going. A motel has much seedier connotations than a hotel. It conjures up all kinds of ideas in my warped mind and none of them particularly gentlemanly. I don't know how long it is before I reply, but it feels like an eternity. Eventually I bluster, "Yeah! All right then. Okay. I don't mind. Means I can have a drink. Not that I'm an alcoholic or anything." I cringe as I say this, because I sound as if I'm pretty certain I am an alcoholic. "It's just ... where are you thinking of?" I venture to ask.

She gives me the details of the motel. I know it, vaguely. She then proceeds to give me some less important details. "It's fairly cheap,' she tells me. "It means I can go straight there after work and get ready. And it must be only ten minutes from you, which is good. We can meet in the room."

This is good news indeed. Trying desperately to keep the word motel from my thoughts, I proclaim, "Sounds fantastic."

Perhaps, at that moment, I appear a little too enthusiastic for comfort. As my hopes rise, she pops them fairly quickly and sends them plummeting back down to ground zero. "I don't want you to think I'm forward, or for you to get the wrong idea. It just makes it easier for us to go out and have a drink. And it's a twin room. I wouldn't share a hotel room with just anyone, but I feel safe with you."

I don't know whether to be pleased by that remark or insulted. After a year without sex, I probably give off a reek of safety that's so powerful that I might as well come with a kite mark from The Royal Society for the Prevention of Accidents. "Of course, err ... what wrong idea could I possibly get?" I ask, giving out a little laugh at my own fake joke.

"Okay, well, just to be clear. Should we say about seven?' she asks, ignoring my laugh. "We can eat at a Chinese place I know nearby and then hit the town." I can't help wondering if hitting the town means 'clubbing it'.

I sincerely hope it doesn't.

"Okay, seven it is. I'll see you there. I'm really looking forward to it."

"Me too."

And, despite the fact that it's been made perfectly clear that my least favourite Chinese meal '12 month duck' is still on the menu, I really am looking forward to it.

When Steve comes back with a second cuppa ten minutes later, I tell him about the Drysdale incident earlier on in the day. "The fat bastard" is his studied reply.

"That might be," I say. "But I'm down a digital camera and he's up my metaphorical backside."

"Did he mention the footy?" he asks, ignoring my comment about the camera.

"No. I've told you before. He rarely mentions the footy."

"That's because he has absolutely no talent, except for being fat."

"Yes. That aside though, what about the camera?"

"Do you think he was trying to psyche you out?"

Sensing that this is going nowhere, fast, I switch tack and tell him about Jenny and the motel – not because I want to brag, but because I want his read on things. I don't know why any sane person would want his read on anything, but his read seems to be fairly clear. "Wow! You're totally game on there mate!" he cries. I think about this perspective, but can't quite see things in the same positive vein.

"No, I'm not so sure. She was pretty clear about it. It's just a drink and I don't want to go there and get the old hopes up. Besides, she was eager to explain it was a twin room."

"No, no, mate. Game on! Think about it. She checks you into a hotel room, sorry, a 'motel' room, without even asking you. Why? She knows you'll say yes. She doesn't even have to ask you; she knows there is no way you won't say yes."

I feel I need to stop him here. If I'm not careful, his unwarranted enthusiasm could easily sweep me away like I'm an empty crisp packet on a windy, Blackpool beach. "Whoa, hold on. She didn't 'check me in'," I insist. "She had the room held, while she 'checked with me'. See the difference? 'Checked with me'. 'Check me in'. Shall I walk you through it? Anyway, she sounded like she doesn't do this sort of thing all the time."

He's distinctly unimpressed by my last comment. "Nah! That's the secret, see. You try to sound like you don't do it all the time, when, really, you do. I bet she does it all the time. She's obviously one of those predatory women; the black widow type, patrolling the Internet, searching for vulnerable men. Let's face facts: there are very few men more vulnerable than you at the moment. I'll bet you're probably just another in her long line of victims, well, if victim is the right word. Anyway, let's not lose sight of the main fact: this is still a serious opportunity for a shag. So, beggars can't be choosers. By the way, just so we're clear on this, you didn't say no, did you?"

His voice could not be more imploring if he was eight years old and asking his mum if he could stay out for an extra half hour to play football with the big boys. "I might have, but I didn't. But I don't want her to think I'm easy either."

"Yeah, right. You, easy. Anyway, she can probably smell your desperation all the way from Manchester. Your smell must be similar to that aftershave called *'Eau de Desperacion'*." With this last insult, he sails towards the important point. "Just think! The possibility of a real shag," he states jealously. "Who would have thought you still had it in you?"

With this, he stands up and leaves the room, shaking his head as he goes. I give in because I realise I'm on dodgy ground. The motel does make her sound a bit predatory – at least, when taken out of context. But I heard the rest of the conversation and he didn't. It's only the thought that it's probably been even longer since he had sex that makes me leave it there. Honestly, he is such a tosser at times and couldn't be more wrong on this one.

Except, a 'motel'!

Even as I think about it a hard eight hits my trouser leg.

Chapter 9

On The Town

It's Friday night, the last day of February, and I'm driving towards Warrington. Warrington masquerades as an upcoming, hip new town, but really it's nothing more than a gigantic service station sitting between three major motorways. Still, it'll do for my purposes this evening.

I'm on my way to meet Jenny. It's a cold, dark evening and the rain's smashing against my windscreen. The wipers on my Audi are currently working overtime, but I still can't see where I'm going. I can only drive a maximum speed of 20 mph and I'm worried that I'm going to be late. My destination is a small motel.

No, this isn't a scene from *Psycho*, but it's almost as scary.

Eventually I find the turn-off that leads me to the business park and I spot the motel on the right. Thankfully, when I arrive, the rain is beginning to recede a little. Scanning the car park, I'm instantly relieved to see that her silver Peugeot is already here. I get my overnight bag out of the boot and head for the reception desk.

When I get there I ask the receptionist for the room number that should be booked under the name of 'Jenny'. She looks on the computer and tells me that there isn't anyone booked in by that name. Shit! I'm forced to make a decision. Either I ask the receptionist to go through a list of the names of people staying here, which would give her the – correct – idea that I don't know the surname of the person I'm spending the night with, or walk off like a complete idiot in search of a room I have no hope of finding. I immediately do the latter.

I never think logically in situations like this so I don't even consider phoning Jenny and asking 'what room are you in?' "I think she's on this corridor," I mutter incomprehensively in the direction of the receptionist. I then wander around the motel like a complete nutter for ten minutes.

Eventually the penny drops and I phone Jenny on the mobile. She tells me she's in room 105. I tell her I'll be there in a minute.

Sometime later, after coming to the conclusion that the motel must double as some kind of novelty maze, I phone her again. She answers and, hearing the background noise, it sounds like she's already in a nightclub. "Where are you?" I ask, feeling more than slightly stressed.

"In room 105," she answers, as if her whereabouts is blindingly obvious.

"I know that! The problem I have at this moment, is not actually knowing where room 105 is."

"Where are you now?"

49

"If I knew that I wouldn't be asking you where the room is," I reply, putting my bag down. "I don't know! I've been wandering around the motel for about three hours." She laughs loudly. I tell her I'm by the stairs.

"Go back to reception and take the door on the left. Head through to the fire escape, I'm the third door on the right."

"Okay, see you in two hours," I groan. She hangs up and goes back to her nightclub.

I eventually find the room. Actually, it wasn't too difficult; all I had to do was follow the sound of the blaring music and the hideous screeching noise that accompanied it.

When I get to the door the screeching turns out to be a hairdryer; it's so loud I imagine its core temperature must be similar to that of the sun. The silky, blonde hair I'd so admired when I first saw her was either painted aluminium strips or a wig. I pause at the door and press my ear up against it. What's going on in there?

The noise emanating from inside the room causes all kinds of things to start racing through my mind. Is it some kind of wild sex party, into which I've been innocently recruited? Are middle-aged businessmen having their gonads roasted with Jenny's hairdryer while she's dressed as a kinky dominatrix? What will happen when I go in? Will she grab me while I kick and scream, force me on to the bed and have her wicked way with me? It's the hope of the latter that pushes me on.

I knock loudly. She opens the door, hairdryer in hand and attired in the most unflattering grey bath robe. "Hi! Is the music a bit loud?" she shouts, over the music.

"A tiny bit!" I yell back.

"What?"

"I say, it's a tiny bit loud!" Shouting for all I'm worth. She ignores me, takes the bag from my hand and walks inside. I follow apprehensively, looking into the bathroom to check there isn't anyone tied-up in there.

Once inside the room, I can see it's one of those cheapo, £65 a night, no-frills jobs. I don't even notice the décor; all I'm interested in is the bed. Like the alcoholic who makes it to the bar in time for last orders, my mind set is fixed to 'make mine a double please'.

It's a double. Yes!

This is just what the sex doctor ordered. Well, it would have been, except that in all my excitement I've missed what's going on at the other side of the room. Next to the window there's another bed. A small cot bed, on which Jenny is placing the bag she's taken out of my hands. "You can sleep on here if that's all right?" she tells me, with a hint of mischief in her voice. I try not to look too disappointed.

"Yeah, course it is. No problems. It looks quite … quite cosy."

50

She reaches across to a cheap looking CD player and turns the music down. "Sorry, (sor-eh) didn't catch that," she says loudly.

"I said it's okay. I'll be fine on there. Very comfortable." She looks at me and I catch her steely, blue eyes. A faint smile breaks at the corners of her mouth and I wonder if I am reading too much into it. It seems to say: 'a faint smile has broken at the corners of my mouth and you haven't got a clue what it means'. She turns the music back up slightly and looks over her shoulder. "Why don't you sit down? I'll be ready in about five minutes."

I notice that, like most women I've met, she's extremely comfortable when giving out orders. I don't mind because it means I don't have to work out what the protocol is in situations like these.

She then switches the hairdryer back on and continues to set fire to her hair. After she's finished drying it she gives me another smile, wanders into the bathroom and shuts the door. She's gone for what seems an eternity, but in reality, is only ten minutes. Still, it's long enough to sit on the end of a bed, twiddling your thumbs in a strange motel and wondering if you're finally going to break your duck.

When she emerges from the bathroom I can only say that it was well worth the wait. She's dressed in a tight, black top, short, black skirt and a pair of stunning black, leather kinky boots. She wanders past, totally unaware of the effect she's having on me, takes a final look into the mirror and touches up her lipstick. "Right, let's go," she says, in her finest Wythenshawe accent. "You won't be surprised to know I'm absolutely (absa-lute-leh) starving."

I can't move right away and she graciously gives me a few moments whilst I wipe the slobber from my chin and use my opposable thumb to push my tongue back into my mouth. We head out into the dark, dank Warrington night in search of food, drink and the promise of unforeseen pleasures.

The first thing I do is watch her demolish another humongous meal in the nearby Chinese restaurant. I now realise why the UN have their doubts about our ability to sustain food supplies into the next century. Anyway, we talk non-stop during the meal and I'm once again conscious of the looks she elicits from males within her vicinity.

As we leave the Chinese I make an attempt to find out what we're doing next without putting the idea of clubbing into her head. "So, what now?"

"There are a few good bars I know. Let's have a couple of drinks."

"Great," I say, trying not to sound too relieved.

"Then we can find a club and have a dance." Fuck.

As we hit the second bar of the evening and consume our third drink I realise, delightedly, that the date is going really well. I feel completely relaxed with her for the first time. She radiates self-confidence, which somehow rubs off on me – albeit aided by the fact that I'm consuming alcohol. I begin to wonder if the warm glow that's pulsating around my body could be the early throes of love, but decide it's more likely to be the three bottles of San Miguel I've knocked back so far. Anyway, I'm relaxed enough to be talking in general terms about women, sex, and my failings in these areas, to this gorgeous creature seated very close to me. As we talk, I open up on one of my favourite sexual subjects.

"I can never spot the signs. I reckon I've lost out on loads of possible shags just because I can't read them. I mean, a woman has to literally throw her knickers at me for me to get that she's interested."

"If a woman wants you to get the signs," she replies, "she'll do it in a way that you just can't miss. The women you weren't sure about must have been messing you around or they weren't really interested."

"No, I don't think so. In my experience they thought they were making it clear that they wanted me. It's just that I didn't pick up on their signals. Several women have told me that I was so oblivious to their advances that they just gave up! They couldn't be bothered making it even more obvious."

"Well, you needn't worry about me. If I'm interested, you won't be in any doubt." She winks her eye and makes the noise of a camera shutter. The gesture seems the perfect invitation to raise something else that's been on my mind. "How do you get to be so confident? I'd love to be as confident as you."

"Confidence is a state of mind," she muses. "It isn't something you're born with. You should have seen me before I went to counselling."

COUNSELLING!

"Seriously?"

"Yeah, seriously. Deep down I'm not as confident as I look, believe me. I have issues, Rob. When you get to our age everyone has baggage."

"Well, you certainly know how to carry yours around with you."

"Oh, I do!" she laughs, and nods at my empty bottle. "Drink?"

The invitation signals the end of the discussion for now and I can't say I'm unhappy about that. Issues? Baggage? Counselling! It all seems a bit heavy so I'm glad we've left it. Thinking about it, it's probably some kind of test. Women are like that; always setting little tests. Like some sexy, gorgeous exam board for men.

I nod as she points to the San Miguel and she takes off in the direction of the bar in her micro skirt and kinky boots. It's a little hard to believe that she's out with me and even harder to think of her on some shrink's couch, but it's still a great feeling to be out with her.

Talking of great feelings, the San Miguel is hitting the spot. I'm not sure, but I feel, more and more, like this could be the night. As she walks across what passes for a dance floor, out of the darkness there suddenly lumbers a gigantic, ape-like figure. Worse still, it appears somehow to have learnt my name and is shouting it at the top of its voice. "Smith! Mr Smith!"

I recognise the owner, and his distinctive voice, almost immediately. It's an ex-pupil of mine, Vinnie Johnson. This is potentially disastrous. Vinnie Johnson holds the dubious distinction of being the only pupil from our school ever to receive a professional rugby league contract and a two-year prison sentence (suspended) in the same school year. This not only qualifies him as a hard bastard (prison sentence), but it also means he is none too bright (professional rugby player). Vinnie left the school about four years ago and I'd heard through the grapevine that he hadn't made it to the big league. I'd always got on with him and in some ways would have been pleased to see him except, like his rugby tackling, his timing is somewhat out on this occasion. He reaches the table after pushing right past Jenny. "Bleedin' 'ell Mr Smith mate! Ow ya doin?" he says smiling, in a not dissimilar way to a large Silverback Gorilla.

"Fine, Vinnie. It's nice to see you. What are you up to?" I reply, glancing anxiously over at Jenny who is now, thankfully, at the bar.

"Ah! You know? Out for a drink with the lads. Try and get a shag later in Mr Smith's. The usual crack."

"How's your dad?" I had met Vinnie's dad a number of times on parent's evenings and, despite his fearsome reputation, he always seemed to me like a decent bloke and father.

"Still inside, but out for Christmas," Vinnie tells me. "He never did it you know. Well, not this time, anyway. Mr Smith, mate, it's great to see you." He extends his hand and I place mine inside it. I almost black out with the pain. "Hey, Mr Smith, you shake hands like a big girl!"

Spending 11 years inside the British education system meant that Vinnie, a man who could probably crush me with one of his farts, is still conditioned to calling me Mr Smith. Still, the fact that he's even learnt my name, and can even remember it, is an educational achievement of no small note.

One of the more touching things about my job is that even the most difficult ex-pupils apparently bear no grudges and are always, seemingly, pleased to see you when they bump into you socially.

Yet, a drunken Vinnie at this point represents a small threat to the smooth progress of my date. A date which, I am hoping, will end in a satisfactory climax. In fact I'm finding it difficult, looking at my date, to think of anything other than a satisfactory climax. Meanwhile, said date is back from the bar and is standing angelically behind Vinnie, clutching two more freshly purchased bottles of San Miguel. How could any man not appreciate this woman's qualities?

53

I pull my hand out from Vinnie's, gesture for Jenny to pass me my drink and turn to Vinnie saying, "Vinnie, this is Jenny." Vinnie turns 360 degrees and, not being particularly blessed with social graces, looks Jenny up and down for a moment, then turns back to me.

"Tell you wot Mr Smith, you're a dark horse," he says excitedly. "She's pretty fit. Ow've you managed that? No offence, like."

"None taken Vinnie. Let's just say I have hidden depths," I laugh.

Thankfully, at this very moment, something across the room catches Vinnie's eye and he demonstrates the ADHD he was diagnosed with in school. He quickly loses interest in us, grunts something along the lines of "Gotta go. Nice to meet you both, innit?" and strides purposefully across to the other side of the room. Ten seconds later, what can only be described as a 'mêlée' is well underway. 'Mêlées have a tendency to follow Vincent Robert Johnson wherever he strays in life.

Jenny and I down our drinks and use the disturbance as the perfect excuse to venture out into the cold, February air. Outside, we fasten our coats and brace ourselves against the biting wind. "So what do you wanna do now?" she asks. Oh no. It looks like clubbing hour has arrived.

"I'm not bothered really," I lie. "Whatever you want."

"To tell you the truth, I'm a bit tired. Would you mind if we left the clubbing for another night?"

YES!

But wait, there's bad news as well: she's tired. Or is she just saying that? I never have a clue what women are up to. "No, that's fine," I reply, trying not to sound desperately relieved.

We head back to the motel. Jenny links arms with me and snuggles close in an attempt to beat the cold. I don't resist. It feels really good to have any level of physical affection after being without it for so long. As we walk down the side of the canal towards the bridge, it's deathly quiet. Our eyes adjust to the dark and we catch sight of something that stops us in our tracks. This is too much. Under the dark arch, a large, young male and a slightly overweight, young lady are rumbling bovine-like on the ground. They are taking full advantage of each other and, for once, I really am stuck for words. Thankfully, Jenny isn't. "That looks like fun," she says, squeezing my arm and playfully pulling me in the direction of the motel.

Ten minutes later, we're sitting on the double bed facing each other. The motel room, in stark contrast to the chill outside, is really warm. I can't help smiling as the heat is probably the lasting residue of that hairdryer.

I suddenly realise that we've reached the moment we both knew would arrive from the start of our date. The moment when we would be forced to confront our emotions, look deep into our souls and ask ourselves the timeless question that men and women have asked throughout the ages: 'are we shagging, or what?'

I, for one, have taken about a nanosecond to reach an affirmative to this difficult question. However, I know females tend to give the question, and its answer, a teeny bit more consideration than us men. I scan her face for signs, but she is impassive. So, I try to avoid looking like I've already made my mind up. This is in the vague hope that I might not have desperation written all over my face. During my year of female imposed abstinence, I've learned not to get my hopes up, because, more often than not, that's all I find I'm getting up.

Jenny has, by now, slipped her boots off and is looking at me in a way I cannot fathom. I look uncertainly at the cot over my shoulder and she notices my apprehensive glance. Still, she says nothing, so I make a decision. It's time to sink or swim and so I take the plunge. 'So?' I say, staring at her in the most non-threatening way I can, whilst also trying to look coolly detached.

"So what?" she replies playfully.

"So, what are the signs? Are they good, or are they bad?"

"What do you think?" As she says this her eyes open slightly and they almost dance across the bed to me. A year without any hint of sexual action evaporates in an instant and I pounce. Seconds later, we're kissing passionately and immersed in the process of taking off each other's clothes, item by item. A Mills and Boon variation might describe us as being 'in the wild throes of passion'.

I've always loved the removing-the-clothes ritual ever since I first discovered 'spin-the-bottle' at the ripe old age of 12. After suffering some early setbacks I developed a 'spin-the-bottle' technique that was the terror of all the 12-year-old girls on my estate and the envy of most of the boys.

But this is better than 'spin-the-bottle', much, much better. I gently slip down her skirt and she expertly manoeuvres me out of my jeans. Now, my first 'raging' in a year is exposed to an un-expectant bedroom. I remove her last item, well, not counting the bra. I have never mastered the technique of bra removal. Bras were clearly invented by a woman, with the sole purpose of proving that women are, indeed, the more intelligent sex. So instead, Jenny takes it off. As she does so she turns unexpectedly away, pulls at something in the cups and throws them across the room. Curious, I glance over and spot what looks like two chicken fillets staring back at me from the floor. Jenny grabs my head and turns me back toward her. "Women's secrets," she whispers, into my ear.

Then, I omit a tiny sound which I can only describe as a gasp of pure delight. Forgetting quickly about the chicken fillets I can now see every square inch of her body below me.

It's absolutely stunning.

At this moment, my face resembles not so much 'the cat that's got the cream', but more the cat that 'accidentally got locked in the Associated Dairies main storage fridge'. I raise myself above her with my 'raging' in my favoured right hand and try to press home my 'advantage' – and she breaks away from my kiss. "Have you got a condom?" she asks, like an air-stewardess asking for my boarding pass.

Now, I know all about safe sex and I can tell you that, for me, a condom is about the safest form of sex that there is. You see, I've never managed to actually maintain an erection whilst putting one on. It's a mental problem linked to all the paraphernalia of pulling it over. It sort of, gets to me: the pressure and everything. Still, I'm not about to mention this right now. "Sorry, no I haven't," I reply meekly. "I didn't really want to be so presumptuous as to bring one." This was sort of a lie. I just hadn't thought things through. Of course she would want safe sex, of course she would want to use a condom, and, of course, I hadn't thought about any of this.

"That's fine. I have one. I'll go and get it."

Before I can tell her that for the purposes of my libido at this point, she might as well go and get a huge, hairy-arsed, fat man and sit him on my face, she heads off to the bathroom. Meanwhile, I'm reduced to sitting on the edge of the bed and attempting to look cool about the whole thing.

In a microsecond, she's back and handing me a small packet, which I glance at. It's a Durex Extra-Safe. I almost laugh at the irony; she doesn't know how 'Extra-Safe' she is. Still, looking down, I have something approximating a blustery 'seven'. This is a massive testament to seeing her, kit off, striding over to her bag in the half-light and looking like Aphrodite on heat.

She lies back on the bed, rolls over to turn on the lamp and I'm in the presence of her almost perfect bottom for the first time. I move up the scale to a hard gusting 'eight' and hope briefly floods through me. She's so sexy I might even get through this without humiliation. I rip open the Durex with my teeth in a feeble attempt to convince myself that I'm a sexual animal ready to mate. I pull it out.

It looks like one of those burst balloons you clean up after children's birthday parties. Like all condoms it also smells, to me anyway, like it's been previously used. (Something I often ask myself: 'do condom makers take recycling that seriously?') I take it between my thumb and forefinger, and pull it over my, by this time, slightly breezy 'five'.

What follows is amazing. I fail miserably.

No, that isn't what's so amazing. What's so amazing is that she totally understands. No judgement, no false sympathy, no patronising, no complaining and no jokes. Only real tenderness and complete understanding are displayed. I fail miserably and she understands.

56

I can't believe it. I hadn't realised that a woman like Jenny could be interested in me. Not only that, but she doesn't even seem to care that much. Instead she pushes me down on the bed, looks hard into my sheepish eyes and kisses me softly on the lips. "Don't worry about it," she whispers softly in my ear. "It happens. Anyway, we don't need that to have a good time."

An hour later, I can categorically, and without fear of contradiction, say that she was right.

Chapter 10

Just My Luck

I awake the next morning with the feeling of a warm woman wrapped around my neck. A tingle runs down my spine as I realise I'm wearing Jenny like some kind of favourite, winter scarf. It feels so good to have someone lying next to me in bed. I turn over to look at her but as I do so, she too turns and I'm left looking at her back – which I don't mind at all, as it's the nicest back I've ever seen. Without thinking about any etiquette that might be appropriate, I begin to plant small kisses on its smooth, slightly freckled surface. This action elicits small moaning noises from somewhere beneath the duvet. "Mmmm, that's nice! I see you're awake. Did you sleep well?"

"Yeah, what time is it?" I say, feeling an unprecedented urge to lightly bite her back.

"Mmmm. About nine, I think. Why, you in a hurry?"

"Well, I have footy, but it's not until 12 pm and it's not too far from here. It's just that I have to nip to Steve's first to get my kit."

"Do you have time for breakfast?" she asks, breaking away from my bites and turning towards me. "I'm starving and, anyway, it's included in the price of the room. So, as I'm half Scottish, and hate wasting money, you'd better say yes."

I rarely eat breakfast, but I don't want her to think I'm one of those Dracula type shags: the ones who disappear as soon as first light comes along. I want to make a good impression, because I definitely want to see her again. In fact, I'm hoping to take her out again later this evening. "No, breakfast would be great," I reply. "I could eat a horse."

"That's settled then. Breakfast it is. Let's say in about an hour. In the meantime it seems to me that I'm in your debt for the moment and I'd like to pay you back."

"Surely, I'm in your debt as I haven't given you any money for the motel room," I say, a little naïvely.

"I'm talking about last night," she says, stifling a giggle. "It seems to me that I'm the one who had all the … fun."

I can see where this is going and I quickly make a decision that I do not want to face a repeat of last night's condom foibles. "No, not at all. I had loads of fun. Just because I didn't … well … doesn't mean I didn't enjoy myself. I don't have to … to … err …"

"Come? Do you mean to say the word come?"

Up until this point in my life I have never heard the word said in a way that so approximates the pleasure of the action. The way she enunciated "come" is making me think about how nice it would be to do it. She's nestling down in the bed and is looking deeply into my eyes. Coming to my senses sooner rather than later, I realise I need to extricate myself from this situation. So I go for a tried and tested male out-card. "I'd rather not if you don't mind. I've got footy later and, well, it can affect the performance."

The way I say this you would think I have a Champions League semi-final against AC Milan later today, rather than a five-a-side kick-about with a bunch of middle-aged blokes at Frodsham Leisure Centre. Still, it seems to have the desired effect. "Oh! Err ... oooohkaaay. Have to say though, I haven't had too many men turn me down for a game of football. But if you're sure ..."

"Yes! I am. I am. No offence."

"But I am offended," she laughs. "And we've still got an hour before breakfast to kill. Why don't you turn over? I'd at least like to touch you."

Now this seems like an unusual request to me. Contemplating the thought of where she might want to touch me, I turn, ever so gingerly, on to my side, facing away from her. I needn't have worried.

Seconds later I'm purring like a cat as she begins to run her fingernails over my body. The next 30 or 40 minutes are absolute ecstasy. More than anything, it feels really good to be on the receiving end of her touch. I'm struck by how much I've missed physical affection over the last few years. I have a feeling that I'm at the point of huge sea changes in my life. It's clear that her touching me this way means she feels something similar. As her nails dig deeper into me I realise how much I love her touching me like this. I need her to touch me, more than this though, I need her.

Then, and at what seems like the very high point of my ecstasy, she suddenly and without warning says, "Do you know what's mad? If I ever touch men like this they often get the wrong idea and think it's something more serious than it is. I hate it when that happens. I mean, why can't a woman touch a man without it meaning some kind of commitment? You understand that don't you? You're just enjoying this for what it is, aren't you? Me touching you."

At this point she is sending out the most confusing messages since David Beckham was first introduced to predictive text. As I'm trying to come to terms with the possible ramifications of her statement she continues to place her hands on nerve endings I had no idea I possessed. For me, the whole thing feels a bit like your girlfriend informing you that she's ditching you for your best mate, whilst simultaneously wanking you off. "Absolutely," I agree. "Why should it mean anything when you do thaaaaat! Mmmm."

"I know," she continues. "Do you know what I can't stand? Needy men. The thing I liked about you so much from your emails, and meeting you, is that you're soooo not needy. You come across as really ... really independent. I like that in a man."

"Err ... mmmm! Yeah, right, totally independent me. You know, could you just stop that for a minute? I -"

"It's like, I'm going out on this date tonight with a guy from Wrexham that I met on *UR-date* and I feel totally comfortable telling you about it. Because I know you're an adult and that you're mature enough to deal with it."

She is now looking at me with a genuinely pleased expression on her face. It's a look that says: 'do you know? You really are such a mature guy and not at all needy, and an adult, and I'm so pleased I can tell you this'. She looks so extraordinarily pleased that, somehow, I begin to feel really pleased with myself. Hey, I'm a great guy! Not needy at all! An adult! Mature! She's pleased she can tell me this! I flash a smile back at her that wouldn't have been out of place at a double glazing sales conference. "No worries. I'm off out tonight with my mates anyway," I say.

As I say it, I can't get away from the feeling that I've just been mugged.

Half an hour later we're in the pub attached to the motel and eating the included-in-the-price-of-your-room breakfast. Jenny is thoroughly engaged in the process of devouring her 'full English', whereas I'm too preoccupied to eat. Firstly, I keep looking at her boobs, which seem to have increased in size again. Also, I'm absent-mindedly nibbling on a piece of brown toast and obsessing about this girlfriend-stealing tosspot from *UR-date*. As I do, I wonder just where I've got the ridiculous idea that Jenny is my 'girlfriend'. It sounds way too needy. So needy, in fact, that there's no chance of me verbalising it within a 100 miles of her.

We have briefly touched on this subject in our email conversations and she made it perfectly clear that she would more readily admit, at this point in her life, to being the secretary of the Simon Cowell fan club than she would admit to being someone's 'girlfriend'.

So, as Jenny continues to eat her way through Travelodge's profit margins, I'm working out my options for the evening. Instead of another great night on the town with her, followed by another attempt at real life sex, it's looking increasingly like a night in front of the telly is looming. The evening ahead doesn't seem like a particularly exciting prospect.

Meanwhile, it's clear to me that she's booked another hotel somewhere with this guy from Wrexham. I wonder if I should pry a little or take the more difficult course of action and back off. In the end I decide to take the latter route. This, I deem, will come across as decidedly less 'needy'.

Across the fake mahogany pub table, Jenny is still not in a particularly talkative mood as she tucks into her food. So it's not with any great expectation that I strike up conversation. "I have to say that I really had a good time last night," I say, as an opening salvo. "We should do it again sometime."

"We'd better, or I'll be really upset!"

"When's good for you? Not tonight, I know." I can't really help making this little dig, but she brushes it off with the same ease you would dandruff from a funeral suit. "Well, I can fit you in Tuesday; if you can fit me in?"

"Great!" I curse myself at that. It was said a little too enthusiastically. I realise I'm now becoming paranoid and that I don't know where the state of Enthusiasm borders the country of Needy. And that last comment probably means I've whipped my passport out and crossed the border. If I have, she hasn't let on and seems enthusiastic herself. "Why don't we go back to the Romper?' she says. "I can't go far as the likelihood is, after this weekend I'll have to confine myself to quarters a little. You know? Get in early."

"Suits me as I have work the next day anyway," I tell her.

"It's a date then."

With this, she begins to attack the last sausage on her plate. I watch her intently for the rest of our time together. She chats pleasantly with the waitresses and she puts them totally at ease. Even though the meal has been paid for, and there's no bill, she leaves a tip that is certainly more than generous. It's very difficult not to like her. In fact, so far, I haven't found one single thing I don't like. I've even found myself adjusting quickly to the accent and waiting eagerly for the next raucous laugh.

When we leave the pub and walk back to the hotel car park it begins to rain. As neither of us is in possession of an umbrella, Jenny suggests we run. We reach the cars. "See you Tuesday," she says, kissing me hurriedly on the cheek. "I'll text you later."

"Yeah, see you Tuesday."

I climb into my car and turn the key. The CD player bursts loudly into action. As I drive past her we wave at each other. Through the rear-view mirror, I watch her climb into her Peugeot. I put my foot down and head back for my ever-so-important match.

I can't concentrate on the way home. I'm completely gutted about her upcoming date. Why did she have to tell me? Of course, I know the answer to this already, she's told me so many times on email about how important honesty is to her. So I guess she's just practicing what she preaches.

Ten minutes later, Steve is waiting for me to take him to five-a-side. He's sitting in the front room with body language approximating your mother when, as a teen, you've stayed out all night for the first time without permission. "Well?" he says, tapping his foot on the floor.

"Well what?" I reply, somewhat disingenuously.

61

"Come on. Did you?"

"Did I what?"

"Look, you know the closest I get to sex these days is vicarious sex. If other people aren't telling me about the sex they're having then I'm not having any at all."

"Looks like you aren't having any sex at all then. I really like her so I'm saying nada."

"You did, didn't you?' he shouts, jumping up excitedly. "You jammy bastard; it's all over your face. Go on, tell me something, anything, one little thing to keep me going." I hesitate for a moment. Probably best not to tell him about the fact that I totally failed to get it up at the appropriate moment, but no harm in throwing the little doggie a bone.

"She was wearing a really short skirt and has the best legs I've ever seen." With this, he grabs the cushion next to him and begins to suffocate himself. From under the cushion I hear a muffled noise that sounds like a grown man weeping. I can just make out: "You bastard! You *know* I'm a leg man."

Half an hour later we're in the car and on the way to the leisure centre. Steve is prattling on about the game tomorrow night. "If we win tomorrow that means we can win the league next Sunday if we beat Drysdale's lot."

"You know, you're obsessed with Drysdale. I think you fancy him."

"Be serious for a moment."

"I am being *serious*. I think you really do fancy him." He lets out a sigh of biblical proportions, crosses his arms and turns his head to look out of the passenger window. The rest of the journey is made in a highly enjoyable, uncomfortable silence.

The following evening is a *tour de force* for our team. We beat *DFS Furniture over 40s* 5-1 and Steve scores a great hat-trick, which he talks everyone through a number of times in the pub afterwards. Even better, *The IT Crowd* only win 1-0 and we now have a better goal difference than them. It's all set up for a decider next Sunday and we only need a draw, but as Steve says, keeping all things in proportion, "we don't want a draw, we want to murder them."

Though I do hardly anything constructive for the rest of the weekend, the time passes quickly and Tuesday evening arrives soon enough. I know the way to the Romper, so the short journey down the M56 will be a little less stressful. Steve isn't around to wave me goodbye when I leave, partly because he's still sulking about my refusal to divulge any goings-on in the motel. "That's what mates do," seems to be the main tenet of his argument.

So he's taken himself off to the local pub with the tacit agreement from myself that I'll turn up for a quick one if I get back early enough.

I reach the pub on time and go inside – and it's no great surprise to find that she isn't here yet. We've agreed to meet around eight. In future, I'll stick well clear of words like *about, around, sometime after,* for very obvious reasons.

Jenny walks in at *about* quarter past, which I take for being a result. She strides purposefully towards me and kisses me on the cheek. She's much more conservatively dressed this time; she's in smart black, tailored pants and a white, button-up blouse. She confessed to me on email, a little while back, that this is deliberate; she wants to know that her dates are interested in her for more than sex appeal. I don't care; she looks great to me.

We order a couple of drinks from the bar and look for a table together. The pub is quite busy for a Tuesday night, mostly with small groups of office types probably trying to save themselves the hassle of cooking a late meal for one. Eventually we find a small table by the window and look at the menu. I order our food at the bar. When I return, I notice she's watching me intently. I break the silence. "So, how's it been the last few days?" I enquire.

"Good. Busy at work, but that's how I like it." That's a real female perspective on work; I love it when there's nothing to do.

"God, I hate it when I'm busy. Basically I'm just lazy," I say truthfully.

She throws her head back and laughs. "I don't think so. I don't think you can be lazy and be a teacher these days."

"The government might not agree with you," I counter.

"Well, they're a bunch of tossers anyway."

"I have to concede you might have a point there. How was Saturday by the way?" I slip this into the conversation ever so matter-of-factly. I also try to say it in the least needy way that I can, like I'm asking about her ironing load.

"Oh! That. It was okay. He was nice and everything, but not really my type." Result!

I suddenly want to ask, for no possible reason I can comprehend, 'and did you shag him?' But, fortunately, a little voice in my head suggests that asking that question might not be the 'adult' thing to do at this particular juncture of the relationship. Instead I muster a superb, "Ah well. Not to worry. That's life."

She looks at me puzzlingly, as if trying to work out if my voice holds any trace of sarcasm. On guessing that it doesn't, she says, "I won't be seeing him again anyway. Actually, I've been thinking – I'd really like it if we could see a bit more of each other. What do you think?" As she says this, her hand reaches over the table and grasps hold of mine. I have to say this is a bit more like it. Forget not being needy!

"I would really like that. Are you doing anything this Thursday?"

"Sorry, I can't do Thursday; Harry's staying out that night."

"Okay. Then what about this weekend? I can do Friday or Saturday."

Now considering she wants to see a bit more of me, the look on her face gives the distinct impression that if she does, it isn't likely that it's going to be this weekend, or anytime soon. Instead, she squeezes my hand. "I can be a bit disorganised at times Rob," she says, tracing her forefinger up and down mine. Carefully choosing her words she goes on. "I'm really sorry. I meant to tell you on Friday, but forgot. I'm going skiing in Austria on Saturday so I won't be able to see you for a week or so."

On hearing this, my head doesn't so much start 'swimming', as starts to plough its way across the English Channel, doing the butterfly for all 23 miles. I can't really say anything for a moment. Then I say the very first thing that pops into my head. "Right. Well, I'll miss you."

She sits back at this and searches my face for any clue that might indicate insincerity. "That's so sweet Rob. I'm going to miss you too. But it's only for a week and we can see each other as soon as I get back. I booked it ages ago with Gail, but now she's not going."

I've recovered enough at this point to start asking a few pertinent questions. "So who's going? I suppose it's one of those girly, ski holiday thingies, eh?"

"Not really. It's a bit mixed. There are about 30 of us. Mostly guys I think and I don't actually know any of them."

From what I've heard these mixed skiing holidays resemble Roman orgies at times. It's a wonder the snow doesn't melt with all the shagging that goes on. "Should be fun then," I reply, staring up at the roof.

"Yeah, there's supposed to be some right characters going. I get the impression it will be a laugh." Yeah, a hoot. I can't stop laughing already.

I really don't want to think about all the 'right characters' that are going. She's now grabbing my hand and squeezing it so tightly that, unbelievably, and despite everything that she is telling me to the contrary, I feel secure. "So will you text me? Keep in touch?" I ask.

"Yeah, course I will. But don't worry; it's only for a week."

And it is only a week, but what a week.

Chapter 11

Seven Days

They say that a week is a long time in politics. Well, let me tell you something: a week's much longer when your newly-found, prospective girlfriend is about to go off skiing for a week in Austria, believe me.

I haven't seen Jenny since we left the pub on Tuesday when she dropped the skiing bombshell on me. It's Thursday evening. I dial her number and hope her phone isn't engaged. It rings for a short time before she picks up. Our conversation begins a little awkwardly. I'm as guilty as she is as I focus on asking carefully worded, neutral questions. This is an attempt to disguise any emotions she may interpret as 'needy'.

"So, what time are you leaving Saturday?" I ask, feigning cheerfulness.

"Well, the flight's at quarter past seven. So I'll leave about six as I live so close to the airport."

"Isn't that cutting it a bit short?"

"Rob, my life is all about cutting things short." I don't know what that means, but I hope it is nothing to do with John Wayne Bobbitt.

"Got everything packed?"

"I can tell you don't know me very well yet!" she says, banging the phone around. "I'll probably pack Saturday morning the way I'm going."

"Who's having the kids?"

"My brother's coming down from Scotland to have them. It's really good of him. He's a bit of a star for doing it. Especially as my mother's found out and, let's just say, she doesn't fully approve."

"I can't say I thoroughly approve myself." I say this in a tone that's very clear I'm attempting light-heartedness. I really don't want to piss all over my new romantic bonfire and it's definitely not going to work to my advantage by playing the hard-done-to boyfriend. Hopefully, there will be every chance to play that starring role in the future, but for now, I stay on the sure-footed ground of good-natured humour. "So, it's definitely a week then? You haven't misread the tickets or anything?"

"It'll go really quickly," she assures me. "I'm looking forward to seeing you again, really I am."

"Me too. More than you know." I leave this comment hanging in the air. I wait to see if she is willing to pluck it out and throw something back to me.

She isn't.

"Rob, I'm really sorry, I have to get off. There's so much to do," she says, now distracted by large amounts of teenage shouting in the background.

'Well, I'll let you go then."

"What have you got planned for the week?" she asks, seemingly as an afterthought.

"Oh, you know? This and that. The usual stuff: moving house and shit."

"Oh, of course! I forgot. I'm so wrapped up with myself sometimes. Sorry. Is everything set?"

"Yeah, looks like it's all going ahead on Wednesday. I signed the papers this morning. I'll keep busy anyway, while you're away." The line goes quiet for a few seconds. It's as if I have transgressed some previously agreed protocol not to say anything vaguely awkward. When she finally speaks there is no trace of rancour in her voice, or indeed any emotion that might lead me to understand how she's feeling.

"Well, I hope it goes well for you and I'll see you as soon as I get back. Maybe I could pop by for a reconnoitre of the new house?"

"You could if I had any idea what a reconnoitre is," I laugh. She laughs too, and for the first time it feels as if we're not trying too hard.

"So can I come for a reconnoitre, or not?'

"I'll be offended if you don't. Look forward to it."

"Me too. Gotta go Rob. I'll text you when I get there."

"You'd better, or you can forget reconnoitring."

She giggles and merely says, "Bye."

"Bye," I reply, and flip my phone shut.

Jenny flew out to Austria this morning. For some reason, my life feels like a film that a DVD player has placed on pause. I know the play button won't be pressed again until next Saturday, when the film will resume and an intricate plotline will enfold that I cannot second-guess. I'm in a state of limbo and I don't expect this will change until she gets back.

Not that I'll be able to see her straight away anyway. Her ex is moving out of the house while she's on holiday, so there's no way she'll be able to see me when she returns. No, I'm going to have to wait. I'm also going to have to deal with the anxiety I'm feeling. My unease has been brought on by the fact that there are 20 horny British men in the group she's out on the slopes with – and she's an extremely attractive and sexual woman.

And here's another thing. I really don't want to think of all those handsome shag-a-holic ski instructors that might be waiting to prey. The best way to get through this is to realise that, as yet, we haven't made any commitments to each other. She is, for the moment, free to do what she pleases with whom she pleases; I'm going to have to lump it. I could take the view that the same rules apply to me too. I'm free to do what I like. It's just that I don't feel like doing anything.

At least today is Saturday and I have five-a-side football to get me out of the house. Better still, I'm going to the cinema this evening with

Charlotte to see *Nine Queens*, an Argentinian film. The thought of this makes me feel slightly exotic, intellectual and very superior. It has to be said, Jenny should be glad to have someone so exotic and intellectual. She should put a stop to any shagging around with those ski instructors. So, whilst I am bound to miss Jenny, my confidence has risen due to my exotic intellectuality.

Getting out of the house is doubly pleasing as, not only will it take my mind off any shenanigans that might be taking place in Kitzbühel this evening, it also means I won't be sleeping in that fridge of a bedroom that Steve has kindly provided for me.

Charlotte's housemates have all cleared off to Dublin for the weekend, which means I can sleep on the sofa at hers. I take a sadistic comfort from the fact that the State no longer pays for the good old student piss-up and all monies spent on Guinness will be clawed back retrospectively via student loans. I only have three nights left at Steve's house anyway. One night less in that fridge of a room is a verified Brucie bonus.

As it happens, the football turns out to be highly enjoyable. I score a hatful of goals as we take the spoils. Steve backs three winners in the afternoon so he, too, is in a good mood for once. So good, he says that he might even get the radiator in my room fixed.

If the day was a good one, the film later on is even better. The evening is enhanced by the thought of sleeping in a warm room for the first time in a few weeks, but the icing on the cake is a late night text from Jenny. It comes through at around midnight as I'm enjoying a discussion about the film and a glass of cava with Charlotte.

"Dad, you're so wrong about the direction," she informs me in the way that second year university students do when they think they know absolutely everything. "You must admit it was stilted."

That's typical of a university education in Media Studies. All it does is ruin your enjoyment of everything. "I thought it had a great twist at the end," I tell her, downing the last of my cava.

"You must have seen that coming! I saw it coming from the opening titles," she giggles. Just then my phones buzzes and I reach for it with perhaps a touch too much enthusiasm. Charlotte certainly thinks so. "Something or someone important?" she asks, with a cheeky grin.

"Could be," I say, attempting to appear nonchalant.

I look down at the screen. The text is nice, especially the last bit: *'Hi, am having a really nice time. Everyone is gr8. But I have to say I'm missing u! xxx'*

Trying to ignore Charlotte who has, by now, got up from the sofa and started to hover behind me, I type a quick reply. I hope it doesn't make me sound too needy: *'I'm missing u 2. I see your staying up having a late one! I'm off to sleep in a real live warm room! Gonna do some house packing for the big move tomorrow. xxx '*

Charlotte wanders back to the sofa and sits twirling her long hair between her fingers. Eventually she lets curiosity get the better of her. "Come on Dad, tell me, who are you texting? Is it your new girlfriend? Are you in love?"

"If you must know it's someone I met on the Internet. And if she thought I thought she was my girlfriend it'd likely be the last time I ever saw her. Her name's Jenny."

"Oh my God! The Internet! I wouldn't have put you down for the Internet."

"Well, I was getting desperate."

"That's too much information," she screeches in mock horror. "So, what's she like?"

"She's really nice; very attractive. She works for a software company. Three kids."

"Three kids?"

"Yeah, well, when you get to my age women have kids. Well, a lot of the normal ones do anyway."

"So is it serious?"

"Not yet. I've only seen her a couple of times, but I really like her."

"Oh Dad. That's so sweet."

"Don't go buying any wedding presents just yet," I say. With that my phone buzzes again. Charlotte diplomatically gets up and wanders off to the kitchen to get a refill.

"I'll leave you two love birds to it then," she says, and winks.

I smile back at her and, flipping open my phone, read the text: *'I'm off to bed now. I will text you 2morrow. Nite xxx.'* I hope and pray that she's off to bed by herself.

Sunday, and the day of the 'big game' arrives. The morning and afternoon pass without too much excitement. I get a few texts from Jenny saying that she's having a good time and enjoying the skiing. I try not to think about some handsome Austrian instructor telling her she is not holding her poles stiffly enough.

Apparently, according to her text this morning, the group that she's with is 'totally bonkers'. I'm not sure if I wouldn't prefer it to be totally boring and miserable. I seem to be developing all the traits of a jealous boyfriend – and I don't much care for jealousy as an emotion. With increasing difficulty, I resolve not to be jealous if at all possible.

Meanwhile, Steve paces up and down the kitchen stopping occasionally to flick through the Observer sports section. When he isn't muttering something derogatory under his breath about Drysdale, he's outside smoking.

At six o'clock we make the ten minute drive, in silence, to the leisure centre. Our match is scheduled for seven. At five to seven our team have assembled on the balcony. John is talking tactics but I'm not really listening. My head is somewhere in the Austrian Tyrol. Steve notices and elbows me in the side. The other game finishes and we walk down the stairs past a bunch of sweaty, panting, middle-aged men.

When we get on court *The IT Crowd* are already at the other end, having entered by the far stairs. We start to warm up and the ref blows his whistle to signal the teams to get ready. As I'm doing my final stretch I immediately become aware of Drysdale walking slowly towards me. My senses sharpen. The whole scene suddenly becomes reminiscent of Clint Eastwood approaching Lee Van Cleef for the final showdown in *The Good, the Bad and the Ugly*. My head starts to hear, "OOOWE-OOOWE-OOH, DERN-DERN-DERN." What on earth is the fat bastard doing?

The whole place, which includes the five spectators on the balcony, descends into a hush. Drysdale is now standing three feet in front of me. "Smith. I want that camera" he says, placing both hands on his hips. "You'd better bring it in tomorrow."

The hairs on my neck spring up and I can feel the eyes of my team mates boring into the back of my head. I look over to my left and see Steve with his mouth trailing on the floor. Time seems to stand still for a moment before I turn back to face my own personal Lee Van Cleef. "Do you know what? I'll bring that camera in Drysdale, and when I do I'll be sure to shove it right up your arse!" At that moment his shoulders involuntarily slump.

"That's threatening behaviour. I'm going to see the Head about this tomorrow," he lamely retorts, before scuttling back off to his goal. I turn round to find ecstatic beams on my team mates' faces.

Ten minutes later, we are three nil up and strolling to our first ever Halton and District Over-35's Indoor Five-a-Side Champions' title.

It's 11.45 later that night. I'm lying in bed, half drunk, clutching a crappy, platinum shield medal whilst texting Jenny. I'm buried beneath a duvet, an extra blanket and two coats. I'm also wearing a large woolly jumper and a pair of tracksuit bottoms. Although I'm not a bit tired, I have the light off. This is because I like the way my phone lights up when she replies.

We've been texting back and forth for a bit and the tone of her texts suggests that she's missing me as much as I'm missing her. I wonder – how is it possible to miss someone so much when you barely even know them?

At about a quarter past midnight we say goodnight for the evening. I turn my phone off and close my eyes. I'm quickly asleep and dreaming about Jenny in a very intimate way. At least, I am until a loud knock on the door wakes me and Steve pops his head in. "Sorry. Did I wake you?"

"Your timing could be better."

"We are the champions, my friend," he sings, rather tunelessly. I notice he's still carrying the silver championship cup around in his hand.

"You sad act. Are you ever going to put that down?" I ask.

"Yeah, eventually. Anyway, just popped in to tell you that we are having a little problem with the heating again," he says, clearly revelling in the fact he's woken me.

"I never would have guessed." He gives me a strange look, buried as I am beneath the last three months textile exports from mainland China.

"Are you wanking underneath all that?"

"You're projecting again. Remember – the doctor's told you that's what you do because you don't have a girlfriend like me."

"I especially don't have one that I just met and that's just gone off to Switzerland."

"Austria."

"Eh?"

"She's gone off to Austria. Kitzbühel, if you must know."

"I mustn't."

"Anyway, we've been texting," I inform him. "So fuck you."

"Must be true love then. By the way, I was thinking, aren't there loads of handsome ski instructors in Switzerland?"

"I'll take your word for it; being gay, you'd know. And it's Austria."

"I've heard that some of those skiing weeks are just one gigantic shag-fest."

"You can't have done, or you'd have already been on one. You know? With you not having had a shag for years." At this, he takes a small step and is almost into the room – it's as if my insults are some kind of invitation. "Look, do you actually want something?" I say, flicking my table lamp on and sitting up. "I'm trying to freeze to death in here and you're just interrupting me."

"Well, I was just wondering ..."

"What?"

"Well I was interested in asking ... err -"

"I have work in the morning," I point out. "You know? Work! Where I have to get up. Not some piss-easy civil service job where you can stroll in on flexi-time at ten o'clock. So what do you want?" He steps backwards slightly and looks down at his feet.

"Just tell me whether she was wearing stockings when you -" He bolts for the door, but not before a large parka coat hits him at something approaching light-speed.

"Oh yeah ... and the shower's bust!" Two more nights to go.

The next morning I get to briefing a little late. As I slip through the door the Head's waffling on about 'standards and consistency'. All the faces gathered are either yawning or aimlessly looking away. I catch a glimpse of Drysdale out of the corner of my eye. He's glaring over at me, so I smile back. He looks away and I realise he's not going to the Head.

The rest of the day is a walk in the park.

It's Monday night. Steve and I have a developed a bit of a tradition over the last three Mondays. I go down to the local Bargain Booze, bring back a box of San Miguel and we then proceed to drink them far too quickly. We do this sitting in his kitchen, whilst talking bollocks. Okay, so it lacks the historical and cultural tradition of the Running of the Bulls in Pamplona, but we like it.

This evening, by San Miguel number three, the subject has moved to women and sex. It's a subject where I usually have more to say than he does, my supremacy in this matter being rooted more in historical tradition than current practice. He likes to ask the questions.

"So, if you had to estimate, how many?" he asks.

"Well, it's not a case of estimating. I have the exact number indelibly inked into my brain. It's 12."

"You're telling me that you've only ever had sex with 12 women?" he asks incredulously. "We all used to think you were shagging anything that moved when you worked in the offices."

"Well, I regret to inform you that I wasn't. Anyway, I don't just sleep with anyone. I have to really like them."

"God, you're such a girl," he says, clearly pleased with the fact I've not run up hundreds. "You sure it's only 12?"

"There's more chance that I'd lose my knob after a visit to the toilet than forget how many women I've slept with. It's not like I haven't mentally listed them, hundreds of times I might add, and thought, 'oh no! There must have been more than that'."

"What do you reckon an average number is?" he asks, letting out a rather large belch.

"What? For blokes our age?"

"Yeah."

"No idea. Maybe 20 to 30." I can see his face drop at the realisation that he's distinctly below average. So, being the good friend that I am, and bearing in mind he's given me somewhere to crash these last couple of weeks, I pounce. "So, what about you?"

"Hard to say, really," he tells me, shifting around uncomfortably.

"Hard to say, but not hard to touch if Mary from accounts is to be believed."

"I was pissed, everyone knows that."

"So, how many?" I repeat.

"Six. But there wasn't one that wasn't really fit," he says, with a passion that belies the statement.

"Six!"

"Six is impressive for me as everyone knows I couldn't pull a pint, never mind a woman."

"So who was the best then? Of your six?"

"You remember that little Tabatha one? The girl who worked in the overpayments office?"

"The little, dark haired one?"

"Yeah, well, she used to give me one in the car park every time we went to the pub after work."

"How come she did it every time?"

"Well, it was every time, if I agreed to pay for the drinks. It was a kinda deal."

"Sort of like the one between a hooker and a client? That kinda deal?"

"My lawyer has told me not to comment as it's all *sub judice*," he says, breaking into a grin. "What about you? Who was your best?"

"Well, not counting Jenny because you should never discuss current beaus."

"Whatever."

"I'd have to say I don't know."

"You can't make your mind up," he says, starting to roll up a ciggy.

"No, I don't know *who* it was!" At this, he takes a large gulp from his San Miguel bottle and leans forward in his chair. It's fair to say I have his full attention.

"What do you mean you don't know? How can you not know?"

"Do you remember that office Christmas party when the lights fused …?" He raises his hand and I stop there; it's just as well.

We sit in comfortable silence. As I crack open number seven, he stands up, stretches, picks up his tobacco and leaves the kitchen. I smile inwardly because I can't help thinking that a man who bans himself from smoking in his own house might be a tad difficult to live with.

In bed later I notice a missed call from Jenny. I don't return it because I'm pissed and it's one o'clock over there. I switch off my phone and put it on the bedside cabinet next to me. I then try to fall asleep, whilst attempting, with absolutely no success at all, to imagine Jenny naked.

Tuesday passes off without any incident. Despite some nice texts from Jenny, I spend the evening in a solemn mood, packing and thinking about the move the next day.

The removal firm turns up at eight o'clock sharp on the Wednesday morning with all my furniture. I have to say that the bastards are far too efficient for my liking. I was hoping that the move would take all day and occupy my mind, but the selfish gits are done and dusted by 9.30am. They've unpacked everything and I'm left alone in an empty house, surrounded by the relics of my previous life. This leaves me with far too much time to think.

At ten o'clock I actually consider going back into work, but thankfully the madness subsides and I read the paper for a bit.

One thing that's become evident is that I really don't like my new house. I should never have bought it. There was an element of panic when I put in my offer. I was convinced that I wouldn't be able to afford a better one. There should be a new law, I think – a law that prevents anyone going through a separation or divorce from buying a house for at least six months. This would protect them from estate agents, but more importantly, from themselves. Then they wouldn't get stuck with a shit house that they don't like. What makes it worse is that the people I bought the house off left it a complete tip, yet I can't be arsed cleaning it up.

I wonder what to do with the day. I don't, as yet, have access to the Internet or Sky TV, so staying in the house isn't an option. Steve's at work, so going to his and dragging him out to the pub is also not an option. This leaves a visit to my mother's. I think again about going to work and teaching the afternoon lessons. No, I'll go to my mother's, but I'll have to shower first, because she has a thing about people who smell, and for the last couple of days I've been getting only cold showers at Steve's. In her previous existence, my mother was probably Sherlock Holmes's bloodhound as she can smell a workman with BO from ten miles.

As I make my way upstairs I can't help noticing that the heating hasn't yet kicked in. It's a particularly cold start to the month and there's little sign that the house is heating up. When I get to the bathroom I start to run the shower. It isn't working.

It must be easier to get a hot shower in the Gobi desert than in North West England!

Chapter 12

The Mummy Returns

It's my 'ex' wedding anniversary today, which seems almost prophetic in a weird sort of way. This is because Jenny sent me a text last night out of the blue, and in an ironic twist of fate, my life feels like it is about to take another tumultuous turn: '*Have talked my bro into having the kids 4 1 more night! I can meet u in the pub at 8 and then u can show me ur new place. I hv missed u so much xxx*'

It's nine o'clock on Saturday morning and I've enthusiastically confirmed my meeting with Jenny for eight this evening. I don't have anything planned until five-a-side football at midday. This gives me nearly three hours to kill. I suppose I'd better think about cleaning the house. It will, at least, give me something to do. So I spend the first part of the morning cleaning the kitchen – as best a man can – whilst having the sense to resolve that Jenny won't get within a mile of it when she comes over this evening.

Next, I figure the bathroom will need to be absolutely spotless. I know, from previous experience, that women can be funny about bathrooms; their standards of hygiene are usually slightly higher than ours.

Ten minutes later, and well pleased with my labours, I sit down to watch my newly installed satellite system. Whilst flicking through the channels, my thoughts turn to the hospitality needed to make the evening a resounding success. A nicely cooked meal and a bottle of wine will be a fitting romantic gesture and set the correct tone. The tone will, initially, be one of bridled passion. We'll smoulder away, eating our meal, only to later flare into unbridled passion as we watch a Meg Ryan DVD on the couch. I need to think very carefully about what to serve, so I wander upstairs to track down the takeaway menus.

I eventually find them in a shoebox, in the room I've taken as my main bedroom. As I tip them on to the bed, it occurs to me that maybe sex will be on tonight's menu. This thought makes me feel more than a little apprehensive. Yes, sex would be very tasty, but on the other hand, I didn't exactly move mountains in the bedroom department last time. In fact, it would be more accurate to say that I barely kicked over a small molehill last time.

Condoms! I wonder how many Durex sell every day. The number of used ones we found in bus shelters when we were kids would suggest that most blokes aren't cursed with my particular problem. All over the planet tonight blokes will be getting it up with a condom. Why do I have to be such a wimp?

Then, I notice the bed. I haven't changed the sheets. Well, that's not totally true. I haven't actually put any sheets on the bed, yet. I meant to get round to it, but three days in a house isn't much time to be thinking about unimportant stuff like sheets on a bed. Anyway, some women are happy enough to do it on the couch. Jenny could be one of them.

Somehow, though, I doubt it.

I stumble over to the airing cupboard and pull out a set of plain white ones, checking carefully for stains as I do so. A year without real sex has left its various scars on me. The fact that I'm a man and I know far too much about all manner of stain-removing, cleaning products is just one of them. Thankfully the sheets are reasonably fresh, so I return to the bed to attack the duvet.

Half an hour later I head back downstairs, but not before I've resolved to perpetrate all manner of sadistic tortures on the sick bastard who invented the double duvet cover. A man and a double duvet cover were definitely not meant to ever cross paths.

Once downstairs, I meticulously plan tonight's meal. I do it to the point of military precision. A number 21, a 33 and a portion of egg fried rice; all washed down with a couple of bottles of cava. Such a feast should be enough to charm any prospective date in the direction of an almost freshly washed, double duvet cover. I circle the numbers on the menu.

Half an hour later and I'm at five-a-side, lazing around the pitch. My lack of interest, much to the frustration of my team mates, is obvious. My mind is clearly elsewhere and, what's more, I don't care. I'm thinking about the old football chestnut of 'no sex before the game'. I appear to have reversed it. I'm operating a 'no game before the sex' policy. I'm probably being a little over cautious – as it's only my second shag in a year, I should have plenty of energy left. Come to think of it, there's a good argument to say it will be my first shag in a year. Anyway, I take loads of stick for being a 'lazy, fat bastard' in the showers after the game, but like the leisure centre's shower water, it all runs off my back.

After football I meet my father at his favourite Frodsham watering hole. This is a weekly habit of ours and things go well for a while, but soon his proto-fascistic jabbering kicks in and my head begins to spin with gibberish. "They're ruining it."

"What?" I must have tuned out for a second.

"The immigrants. They're ruining it."

"Ruining what?"

"This country." Oh no – not this again. Not wanting to go there and having agreed not to talk politics with him on many occasions, I make the mistake of asking a rhetorical question.

"How are they ruining the country?" I say, slamming my drink on the table.

He mistakenly believes this is an invitation to debate. "Go on. Let's hear it then, know-all. Explain just what it is the rest of us are missing," he says.

"We have a low birth rate. Someone has to work to support future generations. QED we need immigrants," I say, rather smugly.

"Yeah, but the immigrants are taking all our jobs," he replies, with his time-tested argument.

"How are they taking your jobs? You're 66 and you haven't worked for 13 years!" I look over at him and his face is thunderous.

"I can't work. I have a bad back," he argues.

"You were on invalidity for your bad back for years and yet you have a golf handicap of seven. That's the problem with you and your golf club cronies. Nothing better to do than sit in the clubhouse all day drinking gin and tonics, reading the Daily Mail and spouting National Front dogma about immigration."

"Yeah, but the point you're missing is that they're all on benefits these immigrants and they're costing this country a fortune."

"You're on benefits."

"I'm entitled to my benefits. I paid in and I'm only getting back what's mine."

"Or what's the taxpayer's?"

"Do you know?' he says, taking a deep breath. "Have you ever considered for a second you might be wrong about anything?" That hurts because I haven't really. It might explain why my relationships don't last. Anyway, with this, he looks at me in a way that tells me we've reached our usual impasse.

"Want another drink?" I ask, looking down at my shoes. He nods and I wander off to the bar. At times like these I wonder how my mum managed to live with him for as long as she did.

He starts talking to an old guy sitting at the next table, who has obviously been listening in. Very quickly, the two of them are nodding in agreement like a couple of toy dogs in the back window of an old Cortina. I look over at my Dad. He has all his own hair, perfect vision and he's a fascist. It would seem that the only genetic propensity I took from him was the one to put on weight easily.

A short while later, I return to the table with his drink and a glass of Belgian wheat beer for myself. I should have known better, because he spots the latter. For the next five minutes, I'm forced to listen to his views on the common currency and how he will chain himself to Frodsham police station railings if they ever attempt to change the pound in his pocket for the euro. I take a big swig of my beer, breathe deeply and look at the clock.

It's nearly three; five more hours to go.

I get home at half-four and as soon as I'm through the door, my mobile buzzes. It's a text from Jenny: '*Hi just got off the plane. Gonna get my head down when I get in. Am knackered. Can't wait to see u later xxx!*'

I quickly text back: '*Gr8. See you at eight in the pub xxx.*'

After my lunchtime drinking session, the 'getting of the head down' idea seems like a good one. Afternoon drinking always makes me tired. I decide not to mess up the impeccably made bed so I get my 40 winks on the couch in the living room and, before too long, I'm having some very bizarre dreams. There are gigantic, flaccid penises wearing see-through raincoats chasing me around a campsite.

Perhaps it's the beer.

At 6.30 I shower, get changed, then phone the Chinese and place an order for collection under an assumed name, which Steve will collect for me. The favour has cost me a special fried rice with a portion of Kung Po ribs, and all because I'm barred from the only decent Chinese restaurant for miles due to 'racist behaviour'.

This spurious accusation sprang from a misunderstanding, which came about when I was really pissed one night and was unsuccessfully trying to read the specials' board without my contacts. I found it much easier to focus by putting my finger on my eye and slanting it. The manager misinterpreted the gesture and now I'm barred.

On the way to Steve's house I call in at the Tesco Metro and pick up two bottles of their Finest Cava. I could skimp and get the ordinary stuff, but Jenny strikes me as the kind of woman who, apart from not shagging on a couch, doesn't appreciate men skimping. Besides, I'm starting to get queasy feelings in my stomach whenever I think about her. This alone convinces me she is worth the extra four quid.

At Steve's house, there's only a small lamp on in the living room. I watch as he shuffles out of the door and into the light rain. He walks around the front of the car. "Brilliant," he says, climbing in and clicking his belt. "You're shagging and I'm stuck in with a special fried rice and my right hand for company."

"Don't forget the Kung Po ribs," I can't help but reply. "You're stuck in with them as well." He looks over at me dejectedly and I beam my best David Cameron smile back at him. He doesn't say another word on the way to the restaurant.

A short while later, I'm placing tonight's dainty dish to set before a queen near the microwave and, I have to say, the prawns smell good. It's all going really well.

An hour later I drive to the pub where we met only two weeks ago. It's eight o'clock, the rain has cleared away and it's a pleasant March evening. The pub is much busier than when we first met. The smokers are even bracing the night air by sitting at the tables in the beer garden.

77

Inside it's rammed full. There are no seats, so I order a diet coke and stand by the door. I look around, and see that it's a very mixed crew. A coach party of older guys are sitting in the corner and laughing loudly at the day's events, whatever they were. To my left, a group of teens have commandeered the two slot machines and are throwing money at them like Coleen on a New York shopping spree with Wayne's platinum credit card. On the other side of the pub, various couples have taken the tables and are either talking or staring intently into each other's eyes. One couple is doing neither. They're looking away from each other in silence and with that odd, uncomfortable body language that only a relationship truly in its death throes engenders. I can't help hoping that that particular fate isn't waiting around the corner for Jenny and me.

I glance at my watch. It's now a quarter past eight, so no real surprises there. Two minutes later she enters with her usual panache. She looks radiant and there is no sign of the fatigue in her demeanour that might be expected after a week on the piste. "Hi, you okay?" she asks. She looks pleased to see me.

"Yeah, fine thanks," I tell her. "You?"

"Oh, tired after the week's exertions," she replies, taking off her coat and kissing me lightly on the cheek. I decide not to think about what the 'week's exertions' might have entailed. As if guessing what I might be thinking, she squeezes my hand. "Get us a drink then. Diet coke please," she says, her eyes dancing their way across to mine.

She really does seem glad to see me.

When I get back from the bar I see she's dressed in a tight, white blouse and black trousers. She's still going for understated, but with her usual air of casual elegance. I hand her the drink and ask her how the week went. "It was great," she says. "I had a really good time." A bit of a disappointment, but I continue to probe unabated.

"Lots of skiing and drinking, I imagine."

"Absolutely!" she enthuses.

"And lots of late nights?"

"Oh yeah. They were pretty much compulsory. I had the odd early night, but most of the time we didn't get to bed before three o'clock."

"Holiday romances?"

"A few. There always are, aren't there?" Seeing my face at this drop she starts to giggle.

"I didn't say *I* had any holiday romances, silly. There were people in our group that were getting it on."

"Oh ... right, well err ... it seems like you enjoyed yourself, so that's good."

"Well I did, but d'ya know what? I couldn't wait to get back to see you. If my mum knew I'd talked my brother into staying another night I'd never hear the end of it!" Feeling like I need to focus my energies elsewhere I switch track and we chat about skiing for a couple of minutes. A subject I know naff-all about, but I make an attempt to show interest. Eventually it becomes clear I know naff-all, so I ask, "you hungry?"

"I'm starving,' she tells me, unsurprisingly. "I haven't eaten since this morning on the plane. Why, are you cooking?"

"Let's just say, I have some food on the go if you want it and some wine chilling in the fridge."

"You're the man. Sounds fantastic. The sooner I drink this then the sooner I get some food?"

"That's about it." At this, she makes her drink disappear faster than an unlocked Porsche on a late Friday night in Liverpool city centre. We leave the pub and she follows me on the ten minute drive back to my house. I'm feeling a bit nervous and my stomach is knotting again.

At my place, she parks her car behind me in the small space that constitutes a 'driveway' – at least, in estate agent bumph. She's still smiling as she exits her Peugeot. Briefly, I think again about shagging her on the couch, but dismiss the thought. We pass into the narrow porch and I feel her standing very close to me. As I turn round, she leans forward and kisses me passionately on the lips. With the smell and feel of her so close to me I get a sudden rush of blood to the head.

"Thought I'd just better get that out of the way as you clearly had no intention of doing it to me," she laughs.

"I didn't want to be so presumptuous," I lie, not having thought about anything other than putting my mouth all over hers.

"Presume away," she jokes, and walks past me into the living room. "Can I have a quick shifty at the house then, while you get me a drink?"

"*Mi casa es su casa.*"

"You don't need to try to charm me with your Pulp Fiction lingo. You had me at hallo." With this, she makes that noise like a camera clicking, winks at me, then heads off upstairs like she's on a house-viewing jaunt and I'm an estate agent.

This is good news: I don't want her anywhere near the kitchen. I head off in that direction and open the cava. Two minutes is all it takes for her to view the entire house. She walks back into the living room. "It's nice," she says, taking a glass of cava out of my hand. "The two main bedrooms are a good size and the box room makes a nice, little study. Though, I can't believe the people you bought it off left the bathroom in that state. It's a disgrace."

"Err … yeah. I went mad about that and phoned up the estate agent to complain. I'll get round to it soon."

"Anyway, where's the food? I'm starving. Is there anything I can do to help?"

"Yeah, stay out of the kitchen. You wanna see the state they left that in." With this, I go and set the food out. "Come through and sit at the table," I tell her.

I've removed the Chinese food from the oven, placed it in bowls and put it on the table in front of my best, well only, crockery set. Jenny sits herself down in candlelight with an empty plate in front of her. She eyes the food in a similar fashion to the way Dracula might eye a sign in a hotel foyer saying: Blind Virgin's Convention - 3rd floor. "Go ahead. Tuck in," I order.

"Mind if I have some of these prawns?" she asks, already scooping them on to her plate.

"No, I got them for you because I remembered you said you liked them."

"How sweet." She smiles, but doesn't look up. She's all business when it comes to food. I blush slightly as I think about how Steve assured me on the phone that he was changing my order because, "everyone knows prawns are shagging food".

I reach over and top up the glasses of cava and we begin to chat some more about her week away. I do a bit of probing but she keeps returning to the subject of how much she missed me and so I keep telling her how much I missed her. We're so comfortable that anyone would think we've been seeing each other for years, but the looks in our eyes are a dead giveaway. This is something very new and exciting.

Finally, she finishes the last prawn, slams her empty cava glass on the table, puts her hand out and grabs mine. We look at each other like we're human dessert.

I break away first and look down. I mention that there's a Meg Ryan movie on Box Office. "We could sit and drink a glass of wine and watch it if you want."

"That's really thoughtful of you, but I'd prefer it if you took me upstairs before I pounce on you."

Thirty seconds later, we're on the bed and kissing furiously, but despite the fact that she's trying to take my trousers off, I'm a little preoccupied. Maybe because she senses some uneasiness, she breaks away from me. "What's up?" she asks. "You seem a bit distant."

"I'm thinking it's a really good job I put some clean sheets on the bed earlier today," I joke.

"No, come on, really. What's up?"

"Well, you remember the last time?" I ask her, nervously.

"Go on."

"Well, this time won't be any different. It's not that I don't really fancy you, because I do. I really, really, do. It's just my little problem, the one I had last time, hasn't gone away."

"Ah ..." she mutters, as if only just getting the gist of things. "I've been thinking about your problem and I want to tell you that I have a solution to it."

"Which is?"

"I've decided to see you exclusively," she informs me. I say, informs me, but I have to admit to having no idea what she's talking about – no idea whatsoever. "Exclusively?" She makes it sound like some article in a trendy women's magazine. Most likely one entitled 'Men Who Can't Put A Condom On And Give You A Good Seeing To, No Matter How Sexy You Look'. She grabs my head, looks straight at me, and, as if sensing my growing bewilderment, says, "you don't get me, do you?"

"Err ... no," I say truthfully.

"I've decided I'm not going to see anyone else. Only you!" This is said in the same excited voice electrical retailers use when they tell you they're going to give you a special warranty package on the HDD television you've just bought because you're such a good customer.

She then gives out a large sigh. "Look, I'm not going to be sleeping with anyone else. I haven't had sex with anyone else without a condom and you aren't sleeping with anyone. Therefore, if I'm only sleeping with you, and you're only sleeping with me and I'm on the pill ..."

"Then you can't get pregnant?"

"NO. WE DON'T NEED A CONDOM!" she exclaims.

"Ahhhhhh! Now I get it."

"Now he gets it."

And, as usual, she was right!

Chapter 13

Girl Interrupted

It's been over two weeks since Jenny made the decision to see me 'exclusively'. The prospect of being in her company has now become an event to look forward to, rather than some kind of ordeal to be endured. Although my anxiety levels have generally diminished, this evening they have crept back up the scale a little. This is because I'm driving down the M56 towards Jenny's house and meeting her for the first time at her home.

The real reason for my current nervous disposition is the fact that she lives in Wythenshawe. Whilst I don't think I have a particularly strong accent, anyone who lives outside of Liverpool would probably disagree. True scousers think I sound like a 'woollyback' – a pejorative term for people who aren't from Liverpool. From what I've been led to believe, my particular accent isn't very popular in Wythenshawe. I've never been to 'The Shaw', as it's colloquially known, but I've imagined it many times since meeting Jenny. In my mind, it's a dangerous place where packs of menacing pitbulls roam drab council estates, tracksuit-wearing teenage mothers push snotty-nosed babies in expensive, designer buggies and ice cream van drivers receive remuneration packages that include full medical insurance to the value of several million pounds.

Turning off at the airport junction, I follow the directions Jenny gave me. Lamentably, I don't have satnav but once again, Jenny's instructions turn out to be idiot-proof, which is just as well in my case. A left, then a right, then another left and I'm on her street looking for number 75.

I make my way slowly down the road trying to make out the house numbers in the dark. Meanwhile, it hasn't escaped my notice that it's a really nice estate; much nicer than my own. It's lined with oak trees on both sides and each of the detached houses sits easily back from the road. I realise that I've been in Wythenshawe for about five minutes and haven't yet seen a single pitbull. The track-suited, teenage mums are also conspicuous by their absence. I look over to the right and catch a glimpse of the number 97. Shit! I've passed the house. How did I manage that? I panic and think about the dangers of driving on to the wrong estate as I really don't want to get lost here.

Eventually, I find it. God, it's big! It has two drives and two garages. It's not the dump my fertile imagination had created. It's a large detached house, built with red sandstone brick. The front is covered in Boston ivy and a large porch supported by two white pillars stretches across the full length of the house. There's elegant and expensive looking decking beneath. A six foot high laurel hedge grows along the front of the garden which stretches at least 50 feet. All this merely shatters my preconceived ideas even further; something Jenny's been doing ever since we met. I park on the empty drive, feeling a little uncomfortable – this is her ex's old space. Men are fiercely territorial about their parking spaces. It's probably some primordial fear that dates back to caveman days. Parking on another man's drive is almost akin to shagging his wife which, ironically, is exactly what I intend to do.

I walk slowly to the front door taking in the house's impressive façade again. I'm a little apprehensive in case the kids haven't left yet; they should be staying at their dad's tonight, but one never knows. I feel guilty about my earlier thoughts, but the idea of playing happy families with three teenage boys is not high on my current agenda. The idea of eating a candlelit dinner, drinking a glass of wine and then ripping off Jenny's scanty underwear with my teeth, is. In fact, the last time I had the pleasure of seeing Jenny in her underwear – last Saturday night – I asked her if she owned any underwear that wasn't sexy. She very matter-of-factly declared, "I don't possess any non-sexy underwear." I'm very tempted to go searching through her knickers drawer this evening to confirm the accuracy of this statement, but it's probably not such a good idea. If I get caught it just might not create the right impression.

I ring the bell. Somewhere in the deepest recesses of her house a pseudo-electronic Glenn Miller bell trumpets the opening bars to *In the Mood*. The fake electro-trumpets create quite an appropriate herald to my arrival – I certainly hope Jenny is *In the Mood*. As the bell ceases its swing-time ring, I can also hear loud music blaring out. We haven't yet broached the all-important subject of musical taste, but this is a worrying development as it sounds suspiciously like *Gabrielle*. I hate *Gabrielle*. Jenny's silhouette glides down the hall towards me. She springs the door open and greets me enthusiastically with the now customary, "Hiya!"

"Hi!" I reply, glancing around.

"Did you find it okay?" she asks.

"Yeah, I just didn't know which drive to park on."

"The empty one is usually best." She kisses me on the cheek and marches off even more purposefully in the opposite direction. I take it that this is an invitation to come in, so I do.

She heads towards an open door that leads to the kitchen, I follow slowly down the hall behind her looking around – it's a bit like organised chaos without the organised bit. Strange objects are festooned all over the place. There's the usual stuff you might expect to find in a house inhabited by three teenage boys: a scooter jammed up against the wall, roller blades and a football. But there's also a wok leaning against the radiator and a toilet seat still in its packaging propped up against a cabinet.

I look over to my left and see a huge wooden bookcase. This interests me as I have a theory that you can discover a lot about people from the stuff they read. Okay, not highly original or foolproof, but I like my theory and I'm interested. I take a quick shifty. The first thing I see is a book entitled: *Overcoming Low Self-esteem: a self-help guide using cognitive behavioural techniques.* Next to this is a title that certainly scares me: *Feel the Fear and Do It Anyway.* I guess that these must be products from her time in 'counselling'. I still find it difficult to believe that anyone as fit as Jenny could be in need of all that nonsense. I quickly lose interest and leave the room.

In the kitchen, Jenny is stirring a large pot on the gas cooker with a dark mass bubbling close to the surface. That dark mass smells very appealing. In addition to stirring, she is also attempting something that might, on a very bad day, pass for singing. I find myself watching her. She's completely absorbed in what she's doing, so I take the opportunity to look her up and down. I love doing this. My earlier guess as to what she might be wearing tonight is confirmed. She's dressed in a short-ish, black skirt, white cotton blouse and, best of all, a pair of high heels that wouldn't be out of place in a fetish club. I also make an educated guess that those ever so long legs are harbouring a pair of black stockings. I smile inwardly.

I'm really looking forward to my night. Totally unaware of what I've been doing, she breaks from the stirring and turns to find me staring intently. "Well ...?" she says, fixing her eyes on mine.

"Well what?"

"Give me a kiss." I see that Jenny is still issuing orders, but, hey, I'm not complaining; this is one order I'm more than happy to acquiesce to. I step towards her and plant a rather large one on the side of her cheek. "What d'ya call that? Come here," she says, not hugely impressed. This time she reaches over and pulls me towards her. She kisses me expertly on the lips, leaving me a little dazed. "I've made African stew," she says, breaking away and looking over the pot. "Hope you like it."

I have to tell you that I have never heard of 'African stew'. God only knows what might be in it. My mind conjures up images of her trailing around Wythenshawe Civic Centre attempting to buy elephant steaks and water buffalo tails. On returning home, she's mashed them all up in a great big wooden bowl with lashings and lashings of papaya juice.

"Great." I say, more than a little apprehensively.

At that moment her mobile phone, which is centimetres from her hand on the kitchen worktop, rings. "It's my mum," she groans, and thrusts a large wooden spoon into my hand whilst picking up her mobile. "Would you mind stirring? I won't be long."

"No problem. I am the Stirmeister General."

25 minutes later, my arm feels like it's dropping off and I've learnt that African stew has an atomic weight consistent with that of boiled concrete. Worse still, I'm sure that deep down in the bowels of it I've seen something resembling crocodile teeth. I rub my right arm painfully, grimace and continue to stir.

She breezes back into the kitchen as if she's never been away, kisses me lightly on the lips and pushes her body very close to mine. Suddenly my right arm feels much better, in fact, if the evening goes the way I'm hoping it will, I probably won't be needing it anytime soon. She breaks off the kiss and leans over the pan. "It looks like it might be done now," she says. "What d'ya think?"

"I can't really pretend to be much of an expert in the field of African stew. You know? Not knowing what the hell it is!"

"You'll love it. As long as you like testicles that is," she laughs.

"I'm insulted. Do I look like I eat testicles?"

"I don't know. You might be hiding things from me." With this she winks, stirs it once more and giggles. Then something large and black pops momentarily to the surface. It looks as if she's not joking about those testicles.

She takes the pan off the cooker, pulls two warm plates from out of the oven and begins to dish the dark remains on to them. The slapping out ritual is a little 'Oliver Twisty' and I'm tempted to shout 'more'. "Come on let's eat," she says, picking up both plates and marching off to an adjoining room. "I'm starving."

She does a lot of marching off, this woman.

In the dining room, she places the food on an ancient, wooden table that looks like it would bring David Dickinson to a very large orgasm. To give it its due, the 'African stew' tastes really great. It turns out to be made from meat and vegetables that you can find readily enough in any supermarket, but contains a few exotic spices which qualify it for the moniker. We sit down at the table and enjoy a very pleasant half-hour where she expands on a previously discussed film topic. "*The Matrix* is so a religious film!"

"How is it a religious film?" I ask her, stabbing my fork into a piece of beef.

"Okay, think about it. His name's Neo. Neo! Get it? The *New* Testament."

"That's a bit tenuous," I reply, laughing.

"All right then. What happens at the end? I'll tell you. He dies and then he comes back and saves the world. Just like who?"

"Yeah, but Jesus didn't save it with an Uzi sub-machine gun. And he definitely didn't do it walking around in slow-mo wearing a big, leather coat."

She's not the slightest bit perturbed and is clearly enjoying the debate. "Okay. Tell me then: who's his sidekick?"

"Err ... Trinity," I say, placing my head in my hands.

"Exactly. The Father, the Son and the Holy Ghost. I won't even begin to tell you about Christian choice: the blue pill and the red pill.

I smile at the sheer passion on show.

"Okay, okay. It's a religious film," I agree, throwing my hands up in mock surrender.

"Dead right, it is." With this she laughs loudly and we change the subject. We talk about our respective days at work.

Then her mobile rings again. The second this happens I realise the evening isn't going to go quite as I'd imagined. "Oh, err ... I'll just get that," she says, with a hint of embarrassment. "I really won't be a minute."

Now in my experience, whenever a woman answers a phone and says, 'I won't be a minute', they're telling you the absolute and utter truth. Because there is absolutely no way on God's sweet earth they'll be a minute! This time is no different. Jenny picks her phone up from the table and walks over to the other side of the room (a very bad sign). "Hello? Hi! How ya doing?" she exclaims.

She then proceeds to gesticulate to me in that way that only women do when on the phone. It's like a game of charades in which you have no idea what the film could be. After a few seconds, Jenny grasps the fact that I can't really tell what she is gesticulating about and breaks off her conversation to tell me that she will only be a short while and promptly leaves the room for 40 minutes.

After the first two minutes, she pops her head round the door. "It's Gail," she says, and apparently this qualifies as sufficient explanation as far as Jenny's concerned.

So I'm sitting here on my own, listening to *Gabrielle* sing *Dreams* for the third time this evening and trying hard not to think about my little contretemps with Gail on *UR-date*. During this second prolonged absence, the only thing that interrupts *Gabrielle* and me from our evening alone is the sound of Jenny's laughter emanating from some remote corner of the house.

38 minutes later (not that I'm counting), the wanderer returns. "I'm really sorry about that Rob," she tells me. "Gail needed to talk. She's met this bloke on *UR-date* and she's not sure if he's gay or not. She thinks he might be as they've been out on several dates together and he's not even tried to shag her yet!"

I don't reply to this, or make any interpretable gestures, especially as I'd only narrowly managed to stop the obviously psychotic Gail from casting her insane aspersions in my direction last time. The fact that the bloke hasn't yet tried to shag her has sent him up in my estimation anyway.

To be honest, I'm a bit pissed off that she hasn't realised that being out of the room for so long is just plain rude. I decide I'm going to challenge her on her table manners out of self-respect, but then I change my mind. This is because I look straight into her gorgeous eyes and tell myself that she does seem to be really sorry, even if she hasn't said it enough, and, well, Gail's problem does seem a really big one and ... let's face it, I want sex. "Look, it's fine," I whimper. "I was listening to the CD anyway." I couldn't have lied more proficiently if I was Joan Rivers being asked about her age. "Any more stew left?"

She beams back one of her beamiest smiles. I like it when she beams; she probably has the best beam I have ever seen, even better than the one on the Starship Enterprise. She leaps up, heads straight for the kitchen and returns in an instant with the pan of leftovers (probably the last pieces of the zebra by now). "More cava?" she asks, as she scrapes the food out on to my plate.

"Please." She tops my glass up and in doing so, empties the bottle. Then she sits down opposite me with a wild look in her eyes, puts her wine glass to her mouth, and takes a large and unladylike gulp.

"What d'ya wanna do after you've eaten?" she says, putting her glass down on the table. I allow my mind to wander around the various options. Just as I'm about to verbalise what I think we should do next, the house phone rings.

Okay, so she does look a bit awkward, but there's no real chance that she's not going to answer it. Women cannot ignore a ringing phone. I'd love to do a sociological experiment. I would place a gang of women in a room with Brad Pitt in his boxer shorts. As Brad approaches with his gale-force 'nine', I would trigger their mobile phones. I reckon that the decision – to answer or not to answer – would be too much for most of them and they'd simply pass out.

She flashes me a look – which, whilst not wholly apologetic, goes some way to appeasing me – and tentatively answers the phone. "Hello? Hiya! You're joking? Oh no! Paul!" She holds the phone to her chest and looks at me with a face that would make Bambi look like a vicious bastard. "It's Paul from work. He needs to talk to me. Really, this won't take long. Five minutes at most. I promise."

Amazingly enough I smile back and make an upward glance in the general direction of the phone followed by my very weakest 'it's okay' smile.

The truth is that I really don't care. I'm losing the will to live now and my discomfiture with the night's passing is not just down to the fact her phone keeps ringing.

No, my stomach is slowly beginning to gurgle in a way that can only spell trouble. With the benefit of hindsight, I can now state that African stew and my stomach are never going to be the best of friends.

As she vacates the room for the third time, I search frantically for the downstairs toilet. When I find it next to the kitchen, I'm only mildly surprised to find an electric guitar propped up against the wall. I plonk myself down on the toilet seat and think about how utterly surreal it would be to twang a few chords.

Can I tell you that sitting on your temporarily estranged girlfriend's downstairs toilet, playing a guitar, whilst having an attack of IBS and listening to *Gabrielle* sing *Dreams* for the fifth time, is something you should avoid doing if you ever get the chance?

Chapter 14

Hot Fuzz

After that first date at Jenny's house, our relationship settles into a kind of pattern. At weekends I stay over for the odd night, depending on which night her ex has the boys. I haven't, as yet, met them and can't say I'm in any hurry to do so. Jenny is equally reluctant to let me meet them. This is because she's devised a 'two year plan' to help her to cope with her divorce. Evidently, I ruined the plan because she hadn't intended to get serious with anyone for the first two years.

Meanwhile, I'm surprised at the ruthless efficiency with which I begin to unceremoniously dump my football mates. The 'serious' football's finished now until the new league in September. Having real mates and having a new relationship is, in my opinion, a difficult tightrope to tread. I don't fancy trying that particular circus act and losing both and besides, Jenny is performing all the tricks I need. Still, I try to maintain some contact with Steve during the week and continue to play the kickabouts at the weekend, but can't help wondering: is losing contact with your mates the inevitable price of starting a new relationship?

During the week, if Jenny has the boys or if I have football, I stay at my own house. I spend these nights going to the gym, watching sport and thinking about doing some marking. Yet, even though I enjoy the football and gym, I still find myself thinking about her while I'm doing them. We speak on the phone every evening. I don't know if this is healthy, but it feels like it's the right thing to do. We spend most of the time telling each other how much we love each other, how we really wished we were together and how we hate it when we're not and so on. This doesn't always happen in one phone call. Sometimes there are 'disruptions' in the background – the sound of child-on-child violence being a frequent one – during which she will take herself off to find the perpetrator and promise to call me back later. 'Later' can mean any time up to 11.30 p.m. Sometimes I'm tired, but there is no way I won't wait up for her call.

It's a Wednesday night and we're talking about arrangements for the following evening. Thursdays have, kind of, become our evening, because that's when her ex nearly always has the boys. She confirms that the boys are at their dad's tomorrow and we agree that I'll come over to hers after I've been to the gym. I'll bring a bottle or two of cava. The weather is unseasonably good and we've taken to sitting outside.

As usual we're chattering aimlessly about our days when Jenny suddenly stops me and interjects with a strange, but thoroughly understandable question. "Rob, do you miss me tonight?" she asks.

There's something disconcerting about her tone. "Yeah, 'course I do. I always miss you when we're not together – you know I do."

"No Rob. I don't think you understand," she corrects me. "Do you miss me in that way?"

"In what way?"

"God! In *that* way!" In *that* way? What the hell is she going on about? Clueless as usual, I revert to the time-tested standard reply that I use whenever a woman asks me a question that I don't understand: "Yeah."

The advantage of the time-tested reply is that it can quickly be flipped 360 degrees to, 'no, I mean ...' followed by, 'sorry I wasn't really listening'.

"Do you want to do something fun?" she asks me. There's a hint of mischief in her voice. I wouldn't say I'm naïve but I swear that at this moment, I think she's going to propose that we take a day trip to Alton Towers. This is because, in 38 years, the most fun I have ever had on a phone was ordering unwanted taxis for the old ladies who lived in the bungalows opposite my house when I was 13 years old.

So my reply is slightly apprehensive. "Err ... depends on what you mean by fun," I tell her.

"Well ... you know ... phone sex."

PHONE SEX!

"Phone sex is sordid and disgusting," was the reaction Rebecca had to an article she'd just read in one of her magazines.

But wow! I'm sensing here that although it might be 'sordid and disgusting', it might also be fun!

The closest I've ever come to phone sex is reading about it in a few trendy magazines – and I once heard Julian Clary make some witty comment on the Jonathan Ross show about allegedly doing it with Prince.

An immediate concern is that, although the prospect appeals, I'm not entirely sure how to do it. The only vague idea I have of what it might entail comes from a (thankfully vague) image of TAFKAP and Julian Clary simultaneously inserting their knobs into the phone mouthpiece.

I would also have thought any opportunity for such fancy, newfangled ideas at my age had long gone. As usual though with Jenny, the whole concept of something new, like phone sex, proves to be much easier to realise and nowhere near as sordid as I'd thought. So I'm on the brink of another famous first.

My initial discomfiture is followed by a brief moment of silence, where I (wrongly) think she's waiting for me to respond with some kind of acceptance, refusal, or discussion. But no, the next thing I hear is a loud buzzing on the line. I take the phone away from my ear and knock it against the arm of the sofa in an attempt to clear what I mistakenly believe to be another shit BT line. That's when I hear the moaning, which isn't easy to hear because of the buzzing. In fact the moaning and the buzzing are fusing into a kind of … muzzing.

Finally the penny drops and the legendary 'raging' status occurs in my pants. Meanwhile, her moaning, the buzzing and the 'raging' all begin to take over my thought streams. I have to think quickly about how I can join in, or I'm going to miss out on the fun.

My initial thought is to end my payment dispute with BT (over an administration charge to my last bill) and sort out a new direct debit first thing in the morning. As she continues to 'muzz' I sit here like someone who has just taken LSD whilst listening to Sgt Pepper's for the very first time. In other words, I'm smiling absent-mindedly, doing nothing and imagining the weirdest stuff. It's whilst I'm in the midst of this hypnotic trance that she decides to make her only intelligible contribution to the whole conversation, but it's enough to kick start me into action. "Mmmm! Rob, tell me what you'd do to me if you were here."

Now I have to admit that, although this is my first ever trawl in the murky seas of phone sex, I take to it like a duck to water. I begin tentatively. "If I was there, right now, the first thing I would do is … "

Not a bad start if I say so myself. "And then I would …"

A faint gasp on the phone encourages me to continue. I need to continue because she's not contributing any real dialogue anyway. So I add: "And I would make you …"

I have to tell you that, while I am in the throes of reprising the entire screenplay of a Hollywood porn blockbuster at my end of the phone, at the other end there is what can only be described as a 'crescendo' building. And the crescendo has begun to make its slow, inexorable way towards a climax in much the same way as a really good Rachmaninoff piano concerto does.

The philosophy underpinning her noise could be described as: look, you know and I know that this might take some time, but we all know where I'm going with this, and we all know I'm going to get there in the end.

At the beginning of this session, the noise level emanating from the other end of the phone was so low that even moles might have had difficulty picking it up. Now, however, it has increased to a level so high that Alsatians might struggle.

Yet the concerto has not struck its ultimate note, merely its penultimate one. As men all over the world have discovered since the dawn of time, that penultimate note can go on longer than your mother can about how she preferred your previous girlfriend. I realise that if I'm to finish this, and, perhaps more importantly, if I'm to keep my phone bills down to a manageable level, I'll need to get even more imaginative. So I go for it, "And then when you think I've finished, I'm gonna … "

There is a multiple moaning sound, and it's not Manchester United's back four having a go at the ref. It's followed by a momentary silence. Finally (and very disconcertingly) by laughter as the line clears and the muzzing noise stops. "Mmmm! That was really nice," she tells me. "You're really good, very imaginative."

"Err ... thanks," I reply, somewhat flustered. "I've never had someone compliment my phone sex before; probably because I've never done it before."

"Really? I'd never have guessed."

"Well, once I got going, I got the hang of it – if that's not some crappy pun. Though you seemed to know what you were doing."

"I couldn't possibly comment," she says evasively. "Anyway, I'd better be going. I've got a few things to do before I turn in. Love you."

"Err ... love you too," I reply.

"Night, babe. See you about eight tomorrow?"

"Yeah, around eight. Night."

"I couldn't possibly comment." What in God's name did that mean? It's only at this moment that I notice the bulge that remains in my trousers. It seems I still have a lot to learn about phone sex, because up until this point, one of my other misconceptions about it was that it was supposed to be a two way process.

As I climb the stairs to bed, another one of those uncomfortable thoughts that seems to be part of the furniture in this relationship pops into my head: that was my first time, but there was no way it was her first time.

And there is also the sneaking suspicion that I've been used in some way, but I'm not quite able to figure in what way. Sure, it was a very nice way to be used, and I'm not going to complain about it, but I was still used.

As I hit the sack I think about all the times I've used women over the years and not in as pleasant a way as she's used me. That enables me to sleep a little easier.

And no, I don't wank myself off!

Chapter 15

Riding In Cars With Boys

If the phone sex turned out to be one of Jenny's more pleasant surprises, it's not one that can ever be levelled at the first time I meet her boys. For some reason, Jenny isn't in a hurry for me to get to know them. Looking back I can see how I'd lulled myself into a false sense of security about what it would be like to meet them because, being a teacher, I thought I could 'handle' kids. They say that pride goes before a fall, but what they don't tell you is how far you might fall.

So here I am standing in Jenny's kitchen one Sunday morning and surprising myself by having the temerity to suggest, "we should spend some quality time together, you, me and the boys. Maybe go bowling and get some pizza. That way we could all get to know each other. What do you think?" To my amazement, instead of running up to throw her arms around me and exclaim, "Rob! You're the most amazing man in the world!" she merely shrugs her shoulders.

"I'm not sure," she says, absently sliding her finger around in a bowl of eggs as she tries to remove a piece of eggshell. "It might be a little soon, to, you know? Rush things."

Rush things! Give me a break. By now, I'm beginning to think that Jenny's horror stories of the boys being 'challenging at times' are due to the fact that she can't really see them for what they are – and I know what they are: they're boys. They're no different to any of the boys I come across every day of the week. Boys will be boys, and doesn't she realise that, being a teacher, I'm an absolute expert in child management and psychology.

Hell I've even been on a course and got a certificate!

The course was called: *Under-performing boys: how to get the best out of them.* Some doddering 60-year-old granny ran the whole thing; forget the fact that she probably hadn't seen the inside of a classroom since chalk was considered a major teaching innovation.

Still, Jenny is unimpressed. She says nothing, but smiles at me in a way that means: 'look I know you mean well, but I really do know best on this one. I'm not about to be patronised'.

"We'll have to get to know each other at some point," I insist, "and the sooner, the better, in my book."

"I know. It's not them I'm worried about – it's just - I know what they're like," she tells me, turning round to wash her hands. "We don't have to rush anything. I don't want to expose you to them too soon. Really, that's all it is."

Expose me to them too soon? She makes them sound like they're some teenage version of the Ebola Virus. I know I can handle them, so what is all this negativity? I'm not taking no for an answer. "Listen. If I didn't think I could handle them I wouldn't suggest it. Really, I want to," I persist. She looks over at me again, her face the very picture of uncertainty.

"Well, okay, if you're sure? But I want to go on record to say it wasn't my idea."

"If it goes wrong it's my own fault. But it won't. It'll be fun." Talk about famous last words. That one's right up there with 'no sign of the Indians, General Custer'.

We agree that the following Sunday is as good a day as any to start. I arrive at Jenny's about 12.30 and park on, what I'm increasingly coming to think of as, 'my drive'. Knocking lightly on the front door, I wait for Jenny to appear and let me in. As she opens it I notice that she seems flustered. "Hi Rob. Come in," she says, rolling her eyes. "The boys are in the front room."

I walk apprehensively into the room, followed immediately by Jenny, and see the three boys sitting on the couch watching the TV. They remain engrossed despite my entrance and only one of them even bothers to look up. Jenny pushes past me, goes directly to the television and promptly switches it off. This produces howls of derision. "Boys, this is Rob," Jenny tells them.

Silence. Two of them at least look over at me, whilst the one sitting in the middle of the sofa continues to stare at the television even though it's no longer on.

Jenny does the introductions by going down the line. "This is Chris," she says, pointing to the first one, a small, wiry, blonde-haired boy who is clearly the youngest. He's dressed in skater gear and has Jenny's eyes, except that whilst hers are a sea of tranquillity, his are a whirlpool of unbounded nervous energy.

"All right, mate?" he says, far too confidently for my liking.

"And this is Daniel," Jenny continues, moving down to the boy in the middle. He has much darker hair than the other two and is taller and more athletic looking. But the really striking thing about him is his clothing. He's dressed from head to foot in white. He's wearing white Nike trainers, white Nike three quarter pants and a white T-shirt. He looks me up and down with wide, dark brown eyes. Jenny has previously informed me that Daniel has mild Asperger's syndrome, which affects his social skills. He also suffers from diabetes, which the whole family helps to manage by watching what, and when, he eats.

"Nice to meet you innit?" he says, looking back at the television before he says it.

"Daniel's going through a bit of a white phase at the moment," Jenny tells me, as if that explains everything. "And this is Curtis." The one furthest away turns to face me with a movement that, were it an artistic movement, it would harness the name of 'reluctance'.

"Right, mate," he mutters, almost inaudibly. Although he's a couple of inches shorter than Daniel, I can tell he is the oldest. He possesses every inch of that world-weariness only obtainable by mid-teens. Already his shoulder-slouch and mumbling are perfectly honed. Although he has a little work to do on his manners, which are currently edging towards overly polite on the spectrum.

"Come on everyone," Jenny says, with a sigh. "Let's go and have some fun."

The first indication that it's not going to be any "fun," whatsoever, becomes apparent once everyone is outside. Before we even get into the car, something approaching World War III breaks out over which boy is to sit in the middle of the back seat. Throughout the heated debate, which is less like a heated debate and more like two rival baboon troops fighting over a watering hole, I keep smiling and shaking my head at Jenny when she looks anxiously in my direction. I want to indicate that I've seen it all before, so that she knows it doesn't matter and that I'm in it for the long run. In reality, I'm wondering how I can start up the car, put it in reverse and get the fuck out of here without anyone actually noticing me. As it turns out, I can't and I have to go.

Ten minutes later, we're on our way and the matter has been sorted in the way that these things often get sorted. The youngest one, whose name has already escaped me, has bagged the middle seat but fair dos to him; he's in deep consultation with Jenny about who will be sitting there on the way back. He's making it abundantly clear that it will not be him. The middle one, Daniel, is staring out of the window and like some satnav android, is loudly reciting the names of every street, trunk road, ring road and the odd motorway that we're proceeding along. I have to admit, the guy knows his roads.

The oldest one, Curtis, is also looking out of the window, but he's not reciting anything. In fact, he's making it abundantly clear that he's in the middle of the biggest teenage sulk since Jedward were booted off the X Factor. He's also making it abundantly clear that he's 'not talking to anyone'. This is a fact we're only too well aware of as he repeatedly tells us every two minutes. From time to time he breaks off from the staring out of the window, and the accompanying non-too-silent sulk, to turn his head and shout at Daniel, "Shut up! You're doin' my 'ead in. I don't care what road we're on. Mum, tell him to shut up."

His unfortunate mood is due to the fact that we're not going to the bowling centre that he wants to go to, which is much, much, further away.

No, we're sensibly going to one closer to home instead. Apparently, there might be 'some of the crew who know me' at this centre, which could be 'totally embarrassing'. Looking at the two muppets sitting next to him, I concede that he just might have a point.

Jenny instructs me to take a left at the lights and I'm now being reliably informed, by the human satnav behind me that we've 'just turned on to the A34 via Gatley Road'. I'm becoming increasingly empathetic with the oldest one.

All of this is consternation enough, but it's Jenny that's holding the bulk of my attention. The font of female calmness and serenity that I've fallen in love with has obviously been taken over by some alien from *Invasion of the Body Snatchers*. Right at this moment 'pod-like Jenny' is shrieking at the three boys like a demented banshee. Moreover, and more worryingly, the boys seem completely oblivious to the fact that aliens have killed their mother and are accepting 'pod-like' Jenny's behaviour as a seemingly normal state of affairs.

I decide to intervene in the hope of calming the atmosphere down a little. If I can get Jenny's attention for a minute she might not notice the fact that this is a less than auspicious start. "Jenny, am I going the right way?" I ask. Jenny turns around and looks back at the sign we've just passed. Without pausing for an intake of breath (a sure sign of alien pod invasion) she turns around and starts shrieking again.

"Rob's missed the bloody turn now thanks to you lot. God, you're so selfish. The lot of you shut up now or you're all grounded for a year!"

The car goes silent for a second.

"Take a right here," the human satnav pipes up. "Then take the M60 ring road west and head towards the roundabout at junction 8. Take your second exit and then turn left at the lights onto Acacia road ..." I drive in an uncomfortable silence the rest of the way to the bowls.

The mood has lightened, a little, by the time we reach the bowling centre.

It doesn't last.

On the walk from the car to the arena, Curtis skulks 20 yards behind us with his hoodie up, 'in case anyone sees me with you'. Though he has his hoodie up, I don't think anyone particularly wants to hug him.

When we reach the bowls it appears that nobody in Didsbury can be bothered to do anything else on a cold, Sunday afternoon in April; the queues are enormous. I hate queuing at the best of times. It's a uniquely British disease and one I have no desire to catch. I can only think of two things I would rather do less than queue. One is to sit nailed to a chair whilst my eyes are kept open with rusty staples, and be forced to watch a Jennifer Aniston film. The other is to cover a year 11 science lesson during last period on a Friday afternoon.

Eventually, I will add being in a car with Jenny's three boys to that list, but for the moment, I'm labouring under the misapprehension that what has just happened is a one-off.

Thankfully, Jenny eyes the queue with similar disdain. "What do you think Rob?" she asks.

"Well, to be honest, I'm not keen."

"Me neither. Shall we just go next door to Pizza Hut and get something to eat?" This produces loud howls of objection from the youngest two. The youngest one has the sort of look about him that suggests he was really looking forward to breaking something.

The middle one, Daniel, is waffling on about his scoring average over the last few years and explaining to me how, "I like bowling; I am very excellent at it." There are no howls of derision from Curtis. He's many yards away at the pool tables and it looks like he's found some hoodies to form a pack with. He's happy enough grunting whilst doing that juvenile fist touching thing with them. He looks as if he might be about to sniff their arses and start mating.

The thought of not having to go bowling with these three kids is instantly appealing. For a start, I can't help but wonder how much the cost of a broken bowling lane is. I bet it's a lot of money.

When Jenny and I first went shopping, I questioned her wisdom as she purchased rip-off extended warranties for every electrical appliance you can think of. Then I saw how everything – and I mean everything – in her house seems to break. Jenny is the only person in the country who is making those warranties pay. In some ways, Jenny's kids are testament to the old joke about coming from a broken home: they broke it!

So for the first, and very possibly only, time ever, going to Pizza Hut seems like an attractive proposition. "Yeah! Great. Pizza. Let's go," I shout enthusiastically.

When we get inside, after about half an hour's wait, there are no tables for five. I'm somewhat comforted by this as we split into two groups. Jenny, Daniel and I sit down at one table and the other two sit across the aisle from us.

The waitress arrives with her little white pad and announces that she will be our waitress for today. She asks if would we like any drinks, and I surprise myself by the speed at which I say, "a bottle of San Miguel please." She tells me they don't have any and I reluctantly order a Beck's.

For some unknown reason, I'm craving alcohol desperately. Meanwhile, after being seated for about 30 seconds, the youngest one has started to roam the restaurant with what can only be described as 'gay abandon'. Moreover, Jenny has either not noticed him, or cannot give a toss. I have a feeling it's very much the latter. She's more interested in looking at the menu with Daniel. He, in turn, is in the process of naming the complete range of Pizza toppings currently available and tentatively arguing with Jenny about the size of the diet coke he's allowed to order.

The youngest is now going around collecting helium-filled balloons with a confidence that suggests he's intent on world domination. I'm perplexed: I cannot for the life of me work out what an 11-year-old boy could possibly want with balloons. All the same, I have a knowing, sickly feeling in my stomach that his master plan will soon be revealed.

I'm right. He sits down again and opens one up. Taking a huge gulp of air from the mouth of the balloon, he starts squeaking like Mickey Mouse on crack. A few customers turn round to stare. I'm mortified to see that Jenny is laughing along with him. I'm not sharing her enjoyment. I'm very uncomfortable and concerned about the impression he's making. I realise that such discomfiture about impressions is probably a luxury that can be ill afforded when around Jenny's boys in public, but I'm still feeling it.

Next, he gets out of his chair again and starts to wander around the restaurant talking to people in his demented, helium-fuelled voice – customers and waitresses alike. Even his brothers start to laugh because it is very funny and yet, at the same time, hugely embarrassing. I want to leave. I want to leave before anyone notices he's with me, especially after I catch the eyes of some of the people who are watching him. I realise, by the sad looks on their faces, that some of them probably think he's mentally handicapped. They have those fixed, plastic grins that people resort to wearing when they don't know the correct response in an uncomfortable social situation.

I can't tell you how relieved I am when the food comes because this is his cue to show an almost psychic aptitude for knowing when food has arrived. He promptly sprints back down the restaurant and is settled before the first plate hits the table.

Meanwhile, my eyes are drawn to Daniel. He has whipped out a needle and is in the process of injecting himself in the stomach. I hate needles with a passion, so I'm struck with admiration for this 13-year-old boy who is injecting himself in the same matter-of-fact way that you and I might lazily scratch ourselves.

To begin with, Jenny has ordered three 'combo' starters. This, in theory anyway, means there is plenty of food for everyone. As the boys wade into their starters I wonder if eating disorders might be hereditary. The boys all eat like Jenny. As Jenny and her posse descend on the food like hyenas on the carcass of a crippled water buffalo, I'm content to merely scavenge around the edges, where I find virtually nothing. Not to worry – I'm rapidly losing my appetite anyway.

When the pizzas arrive, what can only be described as 'every-man-for-himself' ensues. Jenny seems to compete adequately enough and manages two large slices of cheese and tomato. I reach across to pick up a single slice of thin and crusty, spicy beef, but before I get it to my mouth Daniel pipes up. "Will you please put that back on the plate Rob? You have made a mistake." I look to Jenny for some help on the spicy beef front, but it's not forthcoming. She dresses up the bad news with one of her sunniest smiles.

"Daniel always has the spicy beef Rob. He doesn't really like to share his food."

Daniel too, smiles at me and I see, for the first time, something of his mother in him. "Spicy beef Rob, innit?" he states. "It's always mine."

Slowly, I put it back onto the plate, as if that statement is all the explanation one could possibly need. Under the table, Jenny grabs my hand and gives it the faintest of squeezes. If this is an attempt at manipulation it has the desired effect. I smile at her. Things do not seem out of hand at this moment; perhaps the worst is over.

It isn't, dessert has yet to be ordered and there is an offer on.

It's an 'all-you-can-eat-and-drink' with the ice cream and full-fat coke. I know, from past experience, that there are more Es in that lot than can be found in your average Amsterdam dance club on a wild Saturday night.

Let me tell you now: the youngest and gallons of full-fat coke do not mix well. As he sits down to drink his third glass, he starts to look increasingly like ET. His eyes couldn't have got any wider if I'd told him Santa Claus really existed and was coming to tea with his elves on Saturday night. The ET look, in combination with his helium balloon voice, are eliciting more than their fair share of strange looks. I wonder if Pizza Hut provides a straightjacket, because it's clear that one will be required if we're to get him home in one piece.

Still, no one, except me, seems overly concerned. In fact, once again, Jenny and Curtis are finding his antics highly amusing. Daniel, sitting across from me, is reciting the different types of E numbers in modern food and the possible medical dangers of each one. He doesn't need to convince me; living proof is before my very eyes.

I begin to look for an exit strategy. "You know, it's getting quite late," I say, looking anxiously at the empty Beck's bottle. "I should be thinking about getting back."

"Rob, it's half past four in the afternoon," says Jenny, raising her eyebrows.

"Yeah, but I do have work in the morning." Jenny looks at me quizzically. Her quizzical look involves a slight turn of the head to an angle of 45 degrees and a half-smile.

It puts me in mind of the look a CIA operative would give you after he's lit the tapers under your fingernails. I begin to squirm in my chair and the desire to order another beer is overwhelming – but I'm driving. Jenny notices my squirming.

"Rob, relax!" she exclaims. "Chris is just enjoying himself. We can go when he's finished." I glance over to his table in time to see him setting off in search of bowl number four. I begin to hope beyond all reasonable hope that even Pizza Hut runs out of ice cream eventually.

Twenty minutes later, Jenny has finally paid the bill and we're on our way towards, what I assume will be, a perilous journey home. I cannot help but notice that we're walking in a very strange formation. Fifty yards in front of the group is the youngest, leap-frogging over the entire row of metal posts that line the path. Jenny and I follow hand in hand, and Daniel is by my side, explaining the subtle nuances of spicy beef pizza etiquette to me once again. As it's the 15th time he's explained this, I can confidently say that any breaches in said etiquette will not be repeated anytime soon. "I think he's taken a shine to you," says Jenny, squeezing my hand again. "He never really talks to anyone."

"Great." I reply, looking behind me nervously. "Aren't I the lucky one?"

Ten yards behind the three of us, with his hood still over his head and clinging even closer to the wall than Spiderman could manage, is Curtis. If there were such a thing as the European skulking championships, he would be the clear favourite to land Great Britain the gold. This is all, again, 'in case anyone recognises me'.

When we finally reach the car the youngest one lands at full speed on to the middle seat. We all pile in and Daniel starts to give me directions out of the car park. I speed away not daring to look back. As I reach a speed approaching 40mph in the car park, Jenny leans over, kisses me on the cheek and whispers in my ear, "well that wasn't so bad was it?"

Chapter 16

Home and Away

After the initial trauma of meeting the boys, Jenny relaxes all restrictions on my visits to the house and I stay over even when the boys are home. We're in the full throes of an amazing passion. One effect this has had on me is that I've become incredibly spontaneous. In fact, if I were any more spontaneous I'd probably combust. With some of the rapidly depleting remains of the £30 grand windfall from the sale of my house, I book Jenny and me on a weekend in Barcelona. It's one of those silly romantic gestures that typify the honeymoon period of our relationship.

I also find myself grabbing flowers from garage forecourts and adding them to the bill when I pay for petrol. It won't be long before I start writing poetry.

Charlotte's offered to look after the three boys while we go to Barcelona for the weekend. She's about to start her exams and for some reason thinks it will be easier to study here than the noisy, student house she lives in. She laughed when I told her the noise levels at Jenny's will be much worse. I got the impression she thought I was joking.

When Charlotte and Jenny meet for the first time I'm nervous. I want the two people I love most in the world to get on.

I needn't have worried. When Charlotte arrives I usher her into the kitchen where Jenny's making coffee. As usual Jenny is charm personified. "Hi Charlotte!" she says, leaning over to kiss her on the cheek. "It's lovely to meet you. Your dad's always talking about you."

"You too," Charlotte replies, smiling. They stand opposite to each other and I can't help noticing that they don't feel the need to shake hands in the way that men would. Instead, they're comfortably taking each other in as if they were both window shopping in the high street and have spotted an outfit they like.

"You look *really* nice in that dress," Jenny tells her. "Is it a Versace?" (Ver-sa-cheh) This comment puts Charlotte even more at ease. Jenny has immediately spotted the fact that my daughter has a penchant for designer clothes and will talk endlessly about them given any opportunity.

"Yeah, but I didn't pay Versace prices for it! It's a knock-off." Sometimes it's a dead giveaway that Charlotte spends a great deal of time with friends in Liverpool.

"Well, it doesn't look it," Jenny laughs, turning to pour milk into Charlotte's coffee. "You look amazing."

At this Charlotte looks over at me and mouths, "she's lovely."

Five minutes later the two of them are upstairs and going through Jenny's wardrobe to see what to pack for the weekend. I get myself a beer from the fridge, go and sit on the patio and listen to Jenny and Charlotte laughing loudly. It's more than sweet music to my ears.

Our trip to Barcelona is amazing. We spend our mornings ambling up and down Las Ramblas hand in hand. In the afternoons we find a small restaurant, order tapas and a bottle of cava, before returning to the hotel for an afternoon sex and siesta.

On our second night we go into the port area of Barceloneta. We dine in a restaurant that serves exquisite seafood. We drink cava and recharge our batteries. Walking around with Jenny is an entirely new experience for me; I'm stunned by the looks she solicits from men of all ages. These looks are generated by a pair of legs that are barely covered by a pink micro-skirt that girls half her age would baulk at wearing.

I question her about it when we stop off for a drink on the way back in a small square off Las Ramblas. "Does it bother you?"

"What?" she asks, innocently.

"All these men, staring at your legs like they'd never even seen a woman before?"

"No, I hardly notice it. Why, does it bother you?"

"No not really. I quite like it," I say grinning.

"Perv," she giggles.

"No, not like that. I mean, it's flattering," I explain.

"How do you mean?" she asks.

"Well, to think that they're all looking at you and I'm the one who's actually …"

"Shagging me?"

"No. I mean, I'm actually with you. You know me: Mr Not Very Confident!"

"Well, I don't feel like that. I feel lucky to be with you. Anyway, in my experience, I find that some blokes might look, but when I'm out with Gail she's the one who gets all the attention."

"Maybe they're intimidated by your looks."

"I wish! The truth is blokes are more interested in Gail's big tits than my legs. I'd swap my legs for her larger breasts any day of the week."

"Well, I don't get it,' I say, twirling my glass of cava. "I think your breasts are fine. Yeah, you'd be even more stunning if you had bigger ones, but God's probably decided that it wouldn't be fair on the rest of the male population." This is said to make her feel better about her lack of boobs.

However, the look this produces on her face makes me think it wasn't one the smartest things I've ever said. "Is that supposed to be some sort of backhanded compliment, because if it was, it's had the opposite effect?" It's the first time that I've ever heard her say anything that sounded, sort of, bitter.

"No. Sorry. I meant ... you've got nothing to worry about Jenny," I say, in my most reassuring tone. "And anyway, it's human nature to want what you've not got."

"Hmm ... I suppose so," she replies, knocking back half a glass of cava. "It's just I can be a little sensitive in that area. Anyway, shall we head off then? I want to see the cathedral." It's clear as can be that she's terminating further discussion.

"Yeah, I'll get the bill," I say, feeling slightly anxious. Sensing my mood she leans over and grabs my leg.

"Mmmm. Good. I love hearing you speak Spanish."

"Well, I'd like nothing better than to whisper a few naughty, Spanish words into your ear later."

"Feel free," she laughs, and for the moment, seems back to normal.

Later that afternoon, with cava pulsing through our veins, I taught her one or two new words.

We return from Barcelona even more in love than when we left and, to my mind, it was money well spent. We were relieved when Charlotte said it all went like a dream and the oldest one, Curtis, seems particularly smitten with her.

Some weeks later, Jenny proves the spontaneous, romantic gestures are not all one way. It's my birthday the following month and she resolves to take me walking in the Lake District. I say 'resolves to take me' because resolution is what she needs to get me anywhere near the place. I've never been on a walking holiday in my life and do not intend to start now. "Come on, it'll be fun. You'll really like it," she tells me.

"I'm not going walking. I just don't get it. What could possibly be fun about walking? Even worse, walking up some stupid hill, while it's pissing down on you and then you have to walk back down it again. I take it they don't have chairlifts for getting down."

"No Rob, they don't," she laughs. "Anyway, it's not a bit like you describe. It's great. You see some amazing views; fresh air; the countryside and all that."

"I hate to tell you, but I've already been to the countryside and I don't like going to places I've already been to. I went a few years ago. So I've got the T-shirt, done that." She looks at me with raised eyebrows.

"Have you ever been to the Lakes?"

"No. Isn't it just a load of old water all strung together for effect?"

"No it isn't just a load of water. It's a gorgeous part of England, especially at this time of year. We can go right up the Langdales!"

It's only because I think this is some kind of euphemism, known only to walkers that I agree to go. The thought of another weekend away and going 'right up the Langdales' with Jenny seems too good an opportunity to turn down.

To my absolute dismay, I love walking. I become addicted to it almost immediately. We go to a large, family-run house on the outskirts of Keswick. On the Saturday morning Jenny takes me on a forest walk, which cuts back and to across the river before we circle back on the foothills of some very large peaks. The sheer sense of solitude and peacefulness engendered contrasts so starkly with my very modern, urban life that I quickly give way to its seductive appeal. At mid-afternoon, and after I have WALKED seven miles, we stop off at a pub to enjoy a well-earned pint of lager. "Well how was that?" she asks, plonking two pints down in front of us.

I can't help loving her even more at this moment. She even goes to the bar! No woman I've dated before has ever, actually, gone to the bar. Yes, women will give you money for their round, but that's usually where they feel their responsibility ends. So, as if Jenny isn't perfect enough, here she is with the drinks and I am answering her question. "As much as it pains me to say, and although I'm knackered, I really enjoyed it," I say, after downing half the contents of my drink in one. "I never thought I'd like walking; I just never got it before."

"Didn't I tell you I was always right? Stick with me, kid!" she winks, and clicks her tongue against the roof of her mouth like some old navvy.

"You're not normal, you," I say.

"And you better not be as knackered as you claim," she tells me, with a glint in her eye.

"Oh, I'd better not be, had I?"

"No, you'd better not be, or I'm not bringing you walking again."

"Well, let's face it, after you've finished with me I'm not usually able to walk much anyway." At this she throws her head back and laughs. I can't help thinking there are walkers out on the top of the peaks who can hear it. I take a very large gulp of my pint and stare right at her.

"What you looking at?" she says, looking more than a little disconcerted.

"Let's go back to the hotel and go right up the Langdales."

When we return from the lakes Jenny has a major surprise in store for me. It's a Sunday morning and we're having coffee in the kitchen. As it's before three in the afternoon the boys are still sleeping. Jenny's clearing up the remains of last night's Chinese takeaway. I'm reading the Observer and trying to come to terms with another disappointing England defeat.

"Rob, I've been thinking," she says, slowly removing her rubber gloves. "Why don't you move in?" It's fair to say that she's captured my full attention at this point.

"Think about it," she continues.

"Do I have to?"

"It makes sense. You keep telling me how much you hate your house and you're here four or five times a week. I miss you when you're not here and you say you miss me. So why not?" I'm struggling to think of an appropriate response, this was the last thing I'd expected.

"Err ... it's a big step," I say, falling back on a tired cliché.

"No it isn't, Rob," she states, totally ignoring my cliché. "Like I said, you're practically here all the time. What's the difference?"

"Well ... there's a big difference," I reply, trying to think of what it might be. Jenny looks at me with her head slightly tilted to one side. She doesn't speak and is patiently waiting for me to spell out the difference. "Look, if I don't like it here I can always clear off back to mine." A salient point I feel.

"But you don't need to sell your house," she says, crushing my argument. "You can rent it out. Then if it doesn't work out we can go back to how it was." This isn't going well, but I have something up my sleeve.

"I don't know Jenny. Think of the boys. I'm not sure it's good for them so soon after the split." I'm playing my ace card here.

"But I think it *will* be good for them." Eh? "They need a male role model Rob," she tells me. "Having a positive one like you will be good for them."

I'm convinced she's right about that.

Early observations have led me to believe Jenny is a 'Mother Earth' figure. That is to say, whenever I look at her parenting, I constantly think: what on *earth* are you doing mother?

By now she's crossed the kitchen and is sitting on my lap. Worse still, she's scratching my head with her long, sexy, red painted fingernails. It feels sumptuous. "Mmmm! I don't know if I should -"

"Come on Rob. Give it a trial at least," she exhorts. "One month. If you're not totally happy about things you can move back; no strings." She sounds, at this point, like a double glazing salesman offering one of those great win-win deals. The only difference is, they don't usually scratch your head while they're doing it.

"Well, if you promise you won't hold it against me if it doesn't work out?"

"It will work out," she whispers in my ear as if that's that. "Why don't we go upstairs and you can hold *it* against me all you like." And that was indeed that.

Three days later I've put the house up for letting and collected the few remaining things that were still there. Jenny has a set of keys cut for me and I've moved in. It's all happened so quickly that I can't even pretend that I was badgered.

Meanwhile, Jenny has spoken to the boys who, quite frankly, don't seem to give a toss. I suppose they're so used to me being around that it's hardly going to make any difference to them.

It's a week later and Jenny has to go to London on business so she won't be home until around nine. I'm back from school a little after four and decide her absence is a good opportunity to do some tentative parenting. There's a hideous thumping sound emanating from upstairs, so I head off to investigate.

When I get to the source I'm not in the least bit surprised to find it's coming from the youngest one's room. So I just ignore it.

I decide to check on Daniel first as I haven't seen him for three days. Jenny's assured me on countless occasions that this behaviour is perfectly normal for Daniel. Knocking loudly on the door I'm only mildly surprised when he doesn't reply. So I enter in spite of this. He has his back to me and is on his computer. "All right Daniel?" I say, stepping cautiously into the room.

Nothing.

"All right Daniel?" I repeat loudly. At this he turns around and fixes me with a hard stare.

"Yes. I am fine," he tells me, turning back round to stare once more at the screen in front of him. Not knowing what to do at this point, I fall back on a tried and tested question I've heard Jenny ask. "You haven't eaten yet, have you?" I enquire, at a bit of a loss.

"Not yet. Can't innit?" Surprised by this statement I make a tentative enquiry.

"Why not?"

"Need my arm squeezing." Jenny's told me he's very funny about who squeezes his arm, which is his preferred injection site when taking his nightly insulin.

"Won't Thingy do it?" I ask.

"No. He is not good at it."

"What about Curtis?"

"He is not good as well." I feel like I don't have much option here.

"Well, what about me? I'll do it … if you want me to." He swivels around on the chair and shines his big dark lamps on me.

"Okay, let us try," he says, after very careful consideration. Then he goes over to his wardrobe and pulls out a small, black bag. He has his back to me. He turns, with needle in hand, and walks over to me. I shudder a little at the sight of the instrument. "Squeeze here," he tells me, whilst holding out his arm. I grip nervously. "No, tighter." I squeeze a bit harder. "Yes, that is correct."

He puts the needle in where I've forced up his skin and pushes down hard. I let go, he puts his arm down by his side and looks at me in a very odd way. Under the dark glare of his gaze I feel like a guilty suspect in an identity parade. "So now are you going to eat?" I blurt.

"Yes. Spicy beef pizza. It has a more than adequate amount of carbohydrate." There's not a great deal one can say to a reply like that. He turns back to his computer and sits down.

Desperate to change the conversation, or lack of it, I ask him "what are you doing?" It's only as I do this that I notice a foul smell emanating from within the room.

"I am competing in a role playing game called *Tekken Wars*, innit?" he tells me, without turning around. "At this moment I am trying to capture Stellion Six because I need lyrillium for my photon cruisers."

I haven't got a clue what he's on about. "Right. Err ... well done," I mutter, and back away from the smell and head rapidly towards the door.

"Please close the door behind you. It is very annoying when it is left open." There's no chance of that as I want to keep that smell contained as much as possible.

Having had some small success with Daniel I head towards the youngest one's bedroom. His door is also shut. However, the horrible thumping noise from inside is causing it to vibrate so much I'm surprised it's not fell off its hinges.

I bang loudly on the door twice and, as I expected, there's no reply. I push it open and peer inside. My first thought is that there appears to be an attempt at the Guinness record for the largest number of teenagers in a box room in progress. Eventually, I spot the youngest one amongst the many hooded faces scattered about. Turning down the noise he looks at me. "Yo. Safe, Rob."

I can't help noticing he's says this in an accent that makes him sound more like an under-privileged gang member from a New York ghetto rather than an over-privileged white boy from Manchester.

Still, I have no idea what this means. However, I've read somewhere that anthropologists, when encountering a tribe for the first time that they can't communicate with, have often found it advantageous to repeat what's being said. "Err ... safe!" I parrot. His reply elicits a rapturous response from all the tribe members.

"Safe. Yeah safe," they all answer, in a similar accent to the youngest one.

"Yeah, safe mate. Wassup?" says one hoodie, who should at least be credited with attempting a more detailed sentence construction than those of his peers.

Feeling rather pleased with myself I make the grave mistake of not quitting while I'm ahead. "What you guys doing?" I ask, noticing the hundreds of crisp packets and glasses festooned all over the room.

"We're settin' down some bars, yo," says Curtis, who I hadn't even noticed up until this point. "Chris's mixin' a beat an' the posse is jus' chillin."

I'm clueless again. This Manchester 'ghetto' speak is a whole new language to me. "Well, okay. Good. I'll leave you to it then," I reply, anxious to get the hell out of there.

"Safe Rob," says Curtis.

"Yeah, safe Rob," says the youngest one.

"Yeah, well safe," I reply, shutting the door behind me to further echoes of "safe" from the rest of the tribe. It's only when I get out of there and sit down in the front room, with a glass of Tesco's Finest, that I really do feel, 'safe'.

When Jenny gets home I'm keen to question her about the apparent open-door policy of the house. I've made her favourite meal: king prawns with pesto. We're sat in the kitchen on stools. I'm drinking cava from a large glass and Jenny's shovelling food down her like it's the only thing she's eaten all week. "Well, I like having lots of young people around the house," she informs me, between mouthfuls. "They give off a lot of positive energy."

"I don't know about giving off lots of energy." I say, "But they certainly consume a lot of energy."

"How do you mean?" she asks, with her fork mid-air.

"Well, there must have been about ten of them in Thingy's room. Let's ignore all the lights that are left on in every conceivable nook and cranny in the house. What about all the food they're eating?"

"Rob, you're exaggerating again," she laughs. "It's a few packets of crisps."

"Right, if you say so. It's your food bill," I say, thinking about how it's about to become my food bill. "And what's with the gangsta speak they're all talking in?"

"It's just a phase Rob. You know what teenagers are like." With this she pushes her plate away. "Mmmm, that was lovely. Thanks Rob. By the way did you check on Daniel, like I asked you to?" she enquires, now picking up her wine.

"Yeah, he's playing some weird, computer game."

"He's eaten though, hasn't he?"

"Yeah. A more than adequate amount of carbohydrate."

"Eh?"

I tell her about the arm squeezing incident. "Wow Rob! I'm impressed. That's a big thing for Daniel. He obviously likes you. He won't even let his brothers squeeze his arm, you're honoured. If I'm not around he'll inject it into his leg, but he doesn't really like to do it there. He says it's uncomfortable."

108

"Well, he freaked me out walking towards me with that needle. And another thing: his bedroom smells like he's been torturing small furry animals in there." She giggles at this and then pulls a stern face.

"Rob, that's cruel."

"It might be, but I can assure you that *'Essence de Daniel's Boudoir'* is unlikely to be a future, best-selling fragrance."

"I'll speak to him again and tell him to take a few more showers. He won't open his window though, which doesn't help."

"Anyway, now that I have a vested interest in it, how much is your food bill?" The words have no sooner left my mouth when I feel that I may have overstepped the mark. So I backtrack a little. "Don't get me wrong," I continue. "It's your house and you can have as many people in it as you like, but I can't help wondering if it's a good thing."

"Rob, I know how much of a shock all of this must be for you. Your life has completely changed since you moved in. You've gone from a household with no kids to one that's full of them. But can we leave it for the moment? I promise you we can change things, but it has to be slowly."

I know she's at least right about that. Things tend to change very slowly in this house.

Chapter 17

My Blue Heaven

Of course, honeymoon periods never last and our relationship hits its first little snag at the end of June. To the casual observer our 'connection', as Jenny likes to call it, appears to be going from strength to strength. But behind the veneer, subtle aromas from the first flowerings of problems are beginning to emerge. There's nothing *too* serious, I admit. They're just little things, like an unprecedented urge on my part to start taking Viagra.

The reason I want to start taking Viagra isn't so much a problem with my knob, as with my head. It's ironic really that the moment I arrive at the most sexually sumptuous period of my life, I feel the need to start taking a sex aid drug. For the first time in my life I actually feel the pressure to have sex rather than the pressure of not being able to get it. The irony isn't lost on me, I can tell you. I have also started to worry about Jenny and if she's really enjoying sex as much as she claims.

For some reason, known only to myself, it's become important to me that I'm the best shag that Jenny's ever had. Not that I have any idea how women measure these things, but I'm utterly convinced that they do. I'm also worried because I think I'm running out of stamina.

That certainly seems to be the case where my football's concerned. In my mind, sex has started to ruin my performance on the court. There's no summer league this year so official hostilities with Drysdale's mob are suspended until the autumn. The only game I consent to play now is the odd Saturday 'friendly' that Steve arranges with them.

We've just finished a match and I was absolute pants. We lose easily and Steve's quick to point the finger in the pub afterwards. "God, you're shit at the moment," he complains, handing me my pint. "You couldn't score in Amsterdam's red-light district."

"I know. But give me a break," I say, after swallowing most of my pint. "I've got a lot on my mind at the moment."

"Yeah, and not much room up there to store it. Well, you'd better sort it out for the autumn. I have no intention of letting the Fat One get his grubby hands on our cup. Did you see his face today when they walked off?"

"No, it's not something I look at if I can avoid it. Anyway, don't worry about me. I'll turn it around. It's just that I'm a bit tired at the moment."

"Probably all that shagging you're doing," he smirks.

"Yeah, yeah," I say unconvincingly.

"Like too much shagging could be bad for you, anyway," he grins, lightly punching my arm.

"I'll get the next round in," I say, trudging off to the bar in the hope he won't see me grimacing.

When I return, with his pint and my diet coke, I make the mistake of not letting things drop. "It's all right you joking about sex, but it can cause as many problems as it solves you know," I bluster.

"Only someone who's actually getting it on a regular basis could come out with crap like that," he replies, whilst tapping his top pocket in search of his cigarette packet. "I'll trade places with you anytime you want." I have to concede he has a point. So I change track.

"I'm not saying it's better not having it. I'm just saying that sometimes a load of sex isn't all it's cracked up to be."

"Yeah, well, I'd like to be in a position to make that judgement for myself." And with this he nods behind him and we head outside while he takes his ciggy break.

All the pressure I've created for myself comes to a head one evening in early July, after another silly attempt in the bedroom to be the best sex Jenny's ever had. We dress and wander out onto the patio. I wait until the moment feels just right. Jenny sits opposite me sipping cava from one of her elegant glasses. The patio heater is on, the candles are lit and the mood is perfect. It's now or never; time to find out.

"Was that the best sex ever, or was that the best sex ever?" I ask wishfully.

She smiles, and ever so slightly – and I mean ever so slightly – she averts my gaze and replies brightly, "it was amazing."

This, you might not be surprised to hear, is not the answer I want. Alarm bells begin to ring in my head and it's not the local Kwik Save being broken into again. I should have listened to them and made a swift exit stage left from this conversation, but part of me stupidly wonders if she's even understood the question. If I'd looked at her with anything other than insipid, male egotism I might have noticed that a stern and assuredly steely look has descended across her face. A look I should have recognised. It's very similar to the one Clint Eastwood gets when he asks some punk, "do you feel lucky?"

You'd think a look like that would be warning enough, but instead of letting it go, I stupidly rephrase the question. "It was amazing wasn't it? I mean, have you ever had better sex than that? It was brilliant!"

She flinches ever so slightly in her chair and I can see there is now not even the faintest trace of a smile on her face. She's firmly holding my gaze though. The only time she ever does this, and does it without a smile, is when she's about to say one of two things. It'll be either "I need to tell you something," or "I need to be honest with you." This was to be the "I need to be honest with you" conversation. Previous experience has taught me that it will possess all the brutality of a depressed, Gestapo officer having a bad day at work.

You see, Jenny believes in what I refer to as 'brutal honesty'. Not your normal 'I'll tell you the truth, but I will water it down to protect your ego a little' honesty. No, it's the sort of honesty that makes you feel like you've been booted in the bollocks and could do with a good lie down. This honesty is usually delivered in the most annoying, irritating, serene voice you can imagine.

Jenny looks at me, takes a deep breath and then that irritating serene voice starts to speak. "Rob, it was amazing and I loved every minute of it. But no, Rob. It wasn't the best sex ever, if that's what you're getting at. I've had better sex. I think it's best to be honest about these things."

As my gigantic, egotistical bubble deflates before my eyes, my first impulse is to lean over into her face and shout as loudly as I possibly can in my most petulant voice: "Oh, you fucking have, have you?" But even at this early juncture of our relationship I've learnt that the serenely calm voice doesn't appreciate you acting on first impulse and it most definitely does *not* take kindly to you shouting at it.

I take a deep breath, exhale and move on to the next impulse that is waiting impatiently in line: childlike denial. "Better than me?" I splutter. "You mean, better than that in the bedroom? I don't get, what … I mean, how? It's not possible."

"Look, I'm being honest with you," she repeats. "What's the point of telling you that you're the best if you're not? It wouldn't mean anything. What we have is amazing and I love you. Can't you just accept what we have? I've never felt the closeness I have with you with anyone else. It's just that I'm able to detach myself emotionally when I want to and that has led to … other experiences."

"Other experiences!" For once, my mind goes totally blank. She looks over at me. I must cut a pathetic figure. In fact, I probably couldn't look more pathetic if I was an 80-year-old Mick Jagger prancing about singing *I Can't Get No Satisfaction.*

Thankfully, she feels the necessity to fill the void before I do. "Are you okay? Is it going to be a problem?" she asks softly.

"No, but I want to know. All of it," I say grimly. With that, the serene voice begins to speak again.

And she tells me all of it; every depressing detail. It was a *UR-date* shag. It happened a number of times and all of them were, apparently, great. There was a physical attraction and there was real, mutual respect. He had a good body, he went to the gym; he was good looking, he had been in the Navy; he'd been around and done things. He did things to her; good things, things she liked, apparently; things that she liked more than the things I did. There had been, 'no emotional connection' whatever the fuck that means. But somehow, that only makes things worse.

There is one little positive that emerges from her story, though, and I try to focus on it in the hope that it will provide me with a future coping strategy. Bing Crosby springs to mind – 'Accentuate the Positive' and all that. The more I think about it the more important it seems. She only mentioned it in passing, but surely, it's vital, isn't it?

It's this: my knob is bigger than his! Oh yeah - blah blah blah - she loves me, has an emotional connection with me and she didn't love him. But still: my knob is bigger than his!

Under ordinary circumstances this might be enough to help me move on, but as he knew how to use his better than I know how to use mine, I can only think about how dynamic he would have been if he'd had mine. God, mine is wasted on me; *he* should have it!

After five minutes of silence that feels like hours, she comes over, sits down beside me and gently lays her hand on mine. "Are you okay?" she asks.

"Yeah, I'm glad you told me. You know? That you were honest." I'm not. I'm not glad at all.

"Is it going to be a problem?" I smile and nod, but don't answer.

The truth is: I can't answer. I don't know if I can handle not being the best. I don't know if it will affect me the next time we have sex. I only know that, for the moment, I will handle it the way people in my family always handle complex emotional matters: I will push the whole thing to some dark corner of my mind, mull it over and then attempt to forget it. So I tell another lie. "No. I'll cope with it. It won't be a problem."

But it will.

The first sign that it will be a problem appears four days later as I find myself back at my own house. I haven't been organised enough to find a tenant for the place yet, and neither have I managed to cancel my BT account. So here I am, booting up my laptop.

I google 'Viagra' and wait with bated breath. It doesn't take long. There are around three million hits. Clearly, purchasing Viagra will not be a problem, but the fact that I refuse to confront the issues of why I want it in the first place just might be.

The reason I'm buying it is, of course, that I'm unhappy with my position of second place in the Premier League of Jenny's previous shags. Sure, that's enough for a place in the Champions League, but I want the trophy. More worrying, though, is the fact that in the long run I might not even maintain second place. I fear I might become one of those teams that has a brilliant start to the season, starts to fade around Christmas as the injury list piles up, then falls quickly down the table and into obscurity as the season nears its end.

So I'm about to make a new signing, something to bolster the team, as it were. Captain Viagra will be purchased to provide the team with a backbone. Not that I'll need the captain for every game. No, he can play on those occasions when I'm tired, suffering from injury, or am merely stressed. Can you see how delusional I am at this point?

Deluded I may be, but despite three million hits, Viagra is proving trickier to purchase than I'd originally thought. The problem is that there isn't just one type of Viagra on offer, but a whole plethora of Viagras. I wonder what the correct collective noun for Viagra is. Perhaps it's a 'cockload'? If it is, there sure is a 'cockload' for sale. There's generic Viagra, non-generic Viagra, Siagra, Silagra, even a Milagra. The only thing they have in common is that they're all blue and claim to make your knob stand on end for longer.

What's also confusing me is the fact that it comes in different strengths: 25 mg, 50 mg, 100 mg, or a whopping great 200 mg. I have no idea which one I would need, or how much of it. Which is ironic, I suppose, seeing as I don't really need it in the first place.

I decide to google 'Viagra strengths' and ten minutes later, I'm armed with some answers to most of my questions. Okay, they're questions a normal healthy male with fully functioning tackle shouldn't even be asking, but what the hell.

I discover that a perfectly working member would require a dose of no more than 25 mg to keep it in the swing of things, as it were. I wonder who is purchasing 200 mg tablets, outside of zoologists trying to sustain the mating habits of 70-year-old bull elephants.

Then there's the question of the price. Obviously highly concentrated tablets are more expensive, but you can purchase these and cut them into pieces, which would make them more cost effective than buying smaller ones. Having done a year of economics at Liverpool University I'm surprised, and highly delighted, to finally find a useful application for my acquired knowledge. I work out a formula for calculating cost per shag. 100 mg cost £4 each, which, for a bloke with my problems, would have a total cost of £1 per shag. Great value really. I decide to buy 16.

I'm not even sure if it's legal to buy it over the net. Consequently, after ordering it, I'll have recurring nightmares in which the drug squad swoops down on my house and carts away bags of blue pills. I'm then led away in handcuffs and photographed by the Daily Mirror as Britain's 'Viagra Mr Big'.

I decide it will be safer to buy them from America. I settle on a site that has positive feedback and is run by an old couple from a ranch in Montana. There's a picture of the owners – Lloyd and Marlene – who look like they ought to be more familiar with the usage of mashed bananas than Viagra. Still, they claim they're regular users and that it has

114

'transformed our sex lives'. I don't really want to think about old people having sex, which ironically is what Charlotte says whenever I mention the subject.

Ten days later a missed delivery card appears on the mat. I go down to the local collections office where a man in a blue shirt gives me a very knowing smile, asks me to sign for a brown package and hands it over.

After a quick glance around to see if there are any suspicious looking vehicles belonging to the drug squad parked up, I sign the piece of paper. Without even giving him a cursory glance, I take the package and head home.

Back in my bedroom, I rip open the package and empty the contents on to the bed. Three items lie before me: a packet of sixteen blue tablets, a plastic pill cutter and a set of instructions/health warnings. I look at all three briefly, pondering where to start, then take the obvious course of action that anyone embarking on a course of new and possibly harmful medication would.

I throw the instructions on the floor, pick up the plastic tablet cutter and begin to hack away at my secret, oval-shaped stash with all the fury of a seasoned addict.

Chapter 18

My Blue Heaven 2

The next evening, I arrive at Jenny's with newfound confidence – the sort of confidence you can only get from knowing that Captain Viagra is in crushed, powdered form inside a sweet wrapper in your back pocket.

The previous evening, I'd sneaked back to mine, briefly acquainted myself with the instructions and read the one thing that I really needed to know: take 45 minutes before required.

I park the car on what I now consider to be my drive and bang very loudly on the door. I've left the keys Jenny gave me in work so this is absolutely necessary in order to gain access to Jenny's house. The three computers and four televisions that are blaring inside can easily compete with the volume levels in a home for the deaf. I've learnt that adolescent hearing is on a par with any 90-year-old granny's. Though I doubt the latter watch MTV cribs.

I say hello to the youngest one, who manages to open the door whilst bouncing up and down on a pogo stick. Under normal circumstances I'd be impressed at his multitasking, but I'm too edgy to appreciate it right now. Trying hard to concentrate, I make an effort to remember the name of the face that's bouncing up and down in front of me. What *is* his name?

It became clear to me on my first day out with them that he's suffering from an acute form of ADHD that has so far gone undiagnosed. The pogo stick might have fazed me at one time, but I'm slowly becoming used to life around a house with the boys. Although, I have to admit to a yearning for the sight of a toilet bowl in which the water is not the colour of stagnant apple juice. "Hiya Rob, mate. Mum's out in the back," says the bouncing muppet, and promptly bounces off in the direction of the main road. I try not to think about the national rise in car insurance premiums that might ensue from this.

I find Jenny on the patio stretched out full length on a sun lounger and totally engrossed in one of those self-help books so beloved by the female gender. It's called *If This Is Love, Why Do I Feel So Insecure?* I shudder. The irony is not lost on me. She's reading a book about insecurity and I'm the one about to take Viagra. God knows what she's got to be insecure about. If I didn't have other things on my mind at this moment, I might have paid a little more attention to that title.

She sees me and puts the book to one side. "Cava's in the fridge babe," she says. "I'm just finishing this chapter." I bend over to kiss her.

"I knew I loved you for a reason."

116

"You love me for lots of reasons."

"Very true," I agree. I turn around, but not before I catch a glimpse of mischief in her eyes. I head off down the path towards the kitchen; it's chaos inside. As usual the house is doubling as some kind of youth club. The unwritten law that there must never be less than 20 people in it at any one time is in operation. Curtis is hanging out with his 'posse' and has three large pizzas on the go. A couple of guys have brought their guitars over and they're all going up to 'chillax' in Curtis's bedroom, probably to create a mini-Glastonbury. On the positive side there's a tacit understanding between me and the boys that they can have the run of the house providing Jenny and I can have the run of the garden.

Having taken a bottle of cava out of the fridge and uncorked it, I'm in the middle of pouring two large glasses when something strikes me. The look of mischief in Jenny's eye has led me to believe that she and I will be intimate later, but I have no idea when this will happen. If I have no idea, how will I know when to take the Viagra?

According to the instructions it has to be taken 'at least 45 minutes before, but no earlier than four hours previous to sex'. Therefore, it's highly likely that the longer before sex you take it, the less effective it will be. This is a dilemma I hadn't previously considered.

What if she pounces on me before I have the chance to take it? Jenny is a pouncer, not that I'm complaining, but right now this might not be a good thing. In my current mentally unbalanced state I'll have no chance of 'rising to the occasion' and therefore risk slipping further down her league table of shags. This is going to be tricky. I decide to play it by ear and keep well out of pouncing distance.

An hour later, we're still sitting in the garden enjoying another great summer evening. The first bottle of cava is showing real promise of turning into a second and a hint of yet more pleasures to come hangs in the air. Oh yeah! And I have Viagra pulsing through my veins.

I took my first ever tablet 20 minutes ago – that is to say, I took my first ever crushed, Viagra powder 20 minutes ago. This was at a point when I was so convinced we were on the verge of going upstairs to have sex that I panicked and told Jenny I needed to go to the toilet. She might have become a tad suspicious as I sprinted up the garden path, spurning her advances to take a desperate piss with a glass of cava in my hand.

Once in the toilet I began to feel like Pete Doherty at an MTV awards party. Feelings of excitement mixed into a heady cocktail containing apprehension, sordidness and outright guilt. Thankfully, I've always been able to deal easily with guilt – my past is shrouded with any number of questionable and morally bankrupt acts, and this would be just one more in a very long list – so I vanquished my misgivings, unwrapped the silver paper and looked down at the crushed remains of a chopped up quarter of Viagra. Another bout of fear crossed my mind – what if something goes wrong further down the line? Thankfully, that idea passed very quickly as I imagined Jenny lying on the bed below my huge, pulsating Viagra enlarged member and screeching "THIS IS THE BEST SEX EVER!"

I picked up the cava glass and lobbed the lot straight in. Salud!

I returned to the garden and I'm sitting here now, smiling at Jenny as if nothing has happened – but she doesn't smile back. Not quite. She looks at me in a very quizzical way. Come to think of it, whenever I ever, and I mean *ever*, do something questionable, or something that I'm not totally comfortable about, she looks at me quizzically, even when she should have no idea whatsoever that I might have done anything. To tell you the truth, it's a bit spooky. "You okay?" she asks.

She has a way of making this sound like a question when you know, really, that it's an accusation. I squirm and want desperately to shout, "NOT REALLY, I HAVE JUST TAKEN A CHEMICAL ENHANCEMENT TO MAKE MY KNOB STAND ON END FOR MUCH LONGER SO I CAN BE THE BEST SEX YOU EVER HAD!"

But instead I mutter, "Yeah fine, why?"

"Nothing – you just look, well, a bit flustered,"

"Me? Flustered? No, why should I be. I couldn't be less flustered. I'm the complete opposite of flustered, whatever that might be," I say, completely flustered.

"Well, okay, if you say so." She gives me one last quizzical look that clearly means we both know that's shite. Then she starts to ask me about my day. Ordinarily I would find this very sweet, but right now I'm not really listening. In fact, I've switched to that primordial mode men possess when the woman they love is talking to them, but they're simply too preoccupied to listen. We fill in the odd gap with vaguely affirmative noises, or the occasional simple structured question to make it appear that a two way process is taking place, but it isn't.

No, there is no two-way process taking place here. She's talking, but I'm too anxious to listen. I'm totally preoccupied. I'm looking for signs that my physiology is changing.

I don't know what I'm expecting really, but I'm pretty sure the Viagra ought to be doing something by now. Perhaps it's a placebo? Anyway, I'm expecting *something*. I'm probably expecting something akin to those old Wolf Man films. You know? Large hairs will appear on my hand, my body temperature will rise to the point where I start ripping off my clothes and, finally, I'll howl at the moon uncontrollably before grabbing her by the hair and dragging her off to my lair.

But nothing's happening. I notice no startling changes. So I decide on a little pre-investigative work. Sliding my hand discreetly down the front of my combats in a way she could never notice, I start to check out my knob.

It's still there – a good sign. I begin to squeeze it to check for any changes in size or temperature, but I'm rudely interrupted. "Rob, what are you doing?"

"Eh? What?"

"Why do you have your hand down the front of your trousers?" she asks sharply. I really can't think straight so I say the first thing that pops into my head.

"Err … I'm just checking." Now that seems like a reasonable answer to an unreasonable question doesn't it? I mean, why does she want to know anyway? Her eldest always has his hands down the front of his tracky bottoms and does she ask him why he's doing it? No, she just tells him to get them out of there.

"Checking for what?" Good question and one that is going to require a really good answer.

"Testicular cancer," I reply, smartly. "You can't be too careful. It's everywhere these days – I read it in the Guardian. They said you should check yourself regularly."

"Rob, I hardly think it's an appropriate time or place to be checking for cancer. I don't think the Guardian is suggesting you check your nether regions at gone ten at night, whilst having a drink with your girlfriend, in her garden!"

"Well, I'm okay anyway," I say, pulling my hand out. "No worrying lumps."

"Glad to hear it. Rob?"

"Yeah?"

"You're really weird at times," she lets me know. "But I kind of like that about you. Let's go up." She picks her book up from the table and takes hold of my hand. Then her mobile rings. As I'm not Brad Pitt there's no way she's not answering it. "Oh! It's Gail," she tells me, looking at the screen.

"Can't you just leave it?" I ask her, in a panic.

"Rob, I'll only be a minute! I need to speak to her; she's going on holiday tomorrow and I've got to look after her cat." I knew *she'd* have a cat.

"Do you really need to do that right now?" I plead desperately. By now she's answered it and is speaking into the mouthpiece.

"Won't be a second Gail. Chill out Rob," she says, putting the phone to her chest. "What's the big rush? Gail's sending the keys round with someone tomorrow and I need to know who and what time. I'll be two minutes." She puts the phone to her ear and walks off chatting to Gail. By now, having been party to a few of Gail's phone calls, I can't help wondering if the four hours Viagra stays active will be long enough. As it turns out Jenny's done in 30 minutes. Not bad for her and Gail.

Anyway, I've just put Viagra to the test. We're currently on our backs, puffing away and catching our breath. "That was great," she musters, after a little while.

"Yeah, great," I say, panting for all I'm worth. But the truth is that for me, it was no different at all. I wasn't any harder, didn't go for any longer and didn't come any bigger. And now we're in the process of telling the truth, neither did she. I can't help thinking it was all a waste of money. She recovers before I do and starts to chat aimlessly. I don't listen and spend my time thinking about how those Americans ripped me off. "I'm tired – it's an early start for me tomorrow," she says. "Do you mind if we get some sleep?"

"Fine by me." She leans over and kisses me.

"Night, babe."

"Night." She turns over and presses herself up against me and then it happens.

Bingo! The last time 'Bingo' happened to me, five minutes after just having had sex, was 20 years ago. She feels it too. "Well, well. Someone's a very horny little boy." She can't see me smiling to myself in the dark. I check for hairs on my hands and think about howling at the moon.

"Less of the little," I reply, and pounce.

After that I'm the proverbial junkie. I'm hooked and getting in way above my head. I'm not just trying to use it for the best sex ever; I've come to rely on Viagra as my own little sexual crutch. Sometimes I use it if I think I'm going to be too tired, or if I think that she isn't. Sometimes I use it if I feel stressed, or if I'm worried that I might fail mentally, and sometimes, shit, I just use it.

Don't get me wrong, often I don't use it at all, but do you know what? Even when I smuggle my supply into the house, I don't think that I'm doing anything wrong. Words and phrases like 'deception' or 'lying by omission' never even enter my tiny little head. All I have is a vague feeling of unease in my stomach that something isn't quite right, although I can't quite put my finger on what that *something* might be. It isn't long before she will grab hold of my hand and shove my finger right up my metaphorical backside.

It all comes to a head on another walking weekend in the Lakes. We take the rare chance to go away together when the boys' dad takes them to Cyprus for a week just before the summer holidays. Things get off to a good enough start. The Friday and Saturday have gone particularly well, we've done the usual stuff: sun, walking, sex and drink. The sex has been particularly good, but once again my growing confidence is about to play a huge part in my downfall.

After visiting the local pub we return in an inebriated state and, as is its wont, sex happens. I love inebriated sex and it's somewhere in the middle of it that I spit it out. It's as close to a confession as I'm likely to make. "Have I got stamina or what?"

"You certainly have babe. You're the man," she replies, catching her breath.

"Well, I have to confess. I am the man, but with a little help." She pulls away from my vice-like grip at this point, which turns out not to be very vice-like, and gives me the quizzical look. Oh no; am I in trouble. The quizzical look.

"What do you mean?" She asks, eyeing me carefully. "With a little help? What kind of help?"

"Look, don't be angry with me. I did it for you. For us."

"What are you talking about, Rob? *What* did you do?"

"Err ... I've been taking Viagra. Not much. Just a bit now and then, you know, for stress."

"You've been taking what? Rob, tell me you're joking. What doctor do you go to who prescribes Viagra for stress?" This isn't going the way I had hoped.

"Look, calm down. Like I say, I did it for us."

"How did you do it for us? I never asked you to do it. So how on earth did you do it 'for us'?" Scratch that. This is going downhill faster than Jack and Jill on skis.

"Well, it's just, you know, you have needs and I wanted to meet those needs." It's safe to say that this is the highpoint of the conversation. I can't really convey the change that takes place in her tone after I say that. The first word is enunciated in a way that would scare Dracula shitless.

"DON'T you make this about us when this is about you. It's about you and your precious male ego. Do you really think I want sex with you that badly? Do you really think I'm some kind of fucking nympho?" The thought had occurred, but best not to mention it right now.

"No, but I didn't think you would mind," I say, somewhat desperately.

"Mind? Of course I mind. This isn't about me is it? I mean it's not about not fancying me? About my tits?" Where did that come from?

"What do you mean?" I stutter.

"Well, you're suddenly taking Viagra behind my back and giving me shit about my needs, when a better explanation would be that you need it because you don't fancy me anymore. I know you prefer girls with bigger tits Rob. I've seen you looking at them. Don't think I haven't."

"That's ridiculous," I tell her, sounding as if it's anything but.

"So why are you taking it then?"

"Like I said, I was just worried about not being able to fulfil your needs. I guess I've fucked-up, but I don't know why you're so angry."

121

"God, you just don't get it do you? Do you want to know why I am so angry? Do you?" I don't really. "It's about honesty," she informs me. "I demand total honesty in a relationship. If you can't give me that then there is no you and me. You've been deceitful and I don't know if I can trust you, and if I can't trust you, it's over."

Ah! It's about honesty. Honesty is, apparently, everything. So it's drilled into me constantly, because, let's face it, that's the only way any of us blokes can be made to 'get' anything. "But you can trust me. Really, I won't do it again. I mean, I did it for - "

"DON'T you say that again."

"I do get it though, honestly. I mean honesty. It's about honesty." She turns her head away and looks up at the ceiling.

"I need some time to think." I have to say, I've a very poor record in the 'I need some time to think' department. It seems like every woman I've ever met has ditched me just after she's had 'some time to think'. It's why I try not to give them any time to think, if I can help it. In this case I can't help it. She's rolled over and I sense I'm going to have plenty of my own 'time to think' in the future.

When I wake the next morning, she's already up and about. Not a good sign. I glance around the hotel room, but can't see any trace of her. I slide the glass doors open and go out on to the balcony.

Bending right over the edge as far as I dare, I can see the lake somewhere out in the distance. Apparently, this constitutes a 'lake view' in Windermere.

About ten minutes later, the door opens and in she walks. I try to scan her face for a clue as to what she's going to say and where things might go from here. No luck. "Let's talk," she says. "We need to." I look up a bit sheepishly.

"Before you start I want to say I'm sorry," I tell her.

"Do you even know what you're sorry for?" she asks, folding her arms.

"Sort of."

"Sort of? If you don't understand why I'm so upset then you really don't know me half as well as you think you do. I would rather never have sex again than think you were under so much pressure to perform like some monkey. I am NOT interested in sex the way you think. Do you get that? I am not with you for sex. I am with you for who you are, your values, your humour, not your cock size."

"Yeah, but it's big." A slight smile crosses her face, but she continues unabated.

"If I want sex I can get it. I can go back on UR-date. I choose not to because you are fulfilling my emotional needs, which I care about. My sexual ones aren't as important."

I can't help thinking she's made her point eloquently and I'm hoping she's going to shut up. She isn't. "You've been dishonest with me and that's what I don't like. You have to promise never to use Viagra again and not to keep things from me. Otherwise I can't be with you."

"I get it, really I do. It won't happen again. I promise."

"It had better not, Rob. Anyway, I've said my piece now. What do you want to do today?" I smile and look down at the sheets. A large morning lump has appeared. A stern look crosses her face.

"Rob. Don't push your luck." And from the way she says it I can tell that's all I'll be pushing for the next couple of days.

Chapter 19

Who Framed Roger Rabbit

As it happens, my excursion into the state of Viagra is only the beginning of my sexually related problems. I'm discovering that, where the complexities of sex are concerned, I'm at the start of a difficult journey. The problems are so obvious that I should easily see them coming, but at times I find it easier to spot the invisible man. My own personal experience in life is that the patently obvious waits around a street corner and consistently manages to punch me in the mouth.

It's a Saturday morning at the end of July when the patently obvious catches me with a punch Stevie Wonder would see coming. My Viagra days are firmly behind me and it's all a big relief. Sex returns to normal – at least, as far as normality and Jenny go together that is. This being a Saturday morning we have, of course, just finished having sex. Generally speaking, afterwards, if I don't go straight to sleep, I reach for the Guardian and read the Saturday sport section. Jenny will either join me in sleeping, or toddle off and make coffee. It's a very agreeable arrangement as far as I'm concerned.

So you can imagine my disappointment this morning when Jenny chooses to violate it. Instead of the anticipated toddle-off, she remains on her back. I eventually look over to see why she's not moving and she's looking up at me in a very peculiar manner. "So, how was that for you?" she asks.

"Same as always: great," I reply, wondering where this is going.

"Good. I'm glad." She says this ever so matter-of-factly, but I'm a little uneasy. It doesn't quite sound as if she's glad about everything. I put the paper down.

"Why? Wasn't it great for you?"

"Yeah, it was. It was just …" She leaves the statement uncompleted and hanging in the air like a dangerous, David Beckham cross.

"What? It was just, what?" I ask. Instead of answering my question, she employs that most feminine of traits: she answers the question with another seemingly unrelated one.

"Rob, do you know I have a Rabbit?" I'm somewhat perplexed by this, especially as I have no memory of seeing any hutches in the back garden. My first thought is, maybe it's kept in Daniel's room and that's what the smell is. I really don't know what she's going on about. Now, you might find this hard to believe, particularly when I tell you that I've watched *Sex and the City* occasionally with my ex. And you might be even more

124

incredulous when I swear that, at this moment, I'm yet to make the patently obvious connection.

Instead, I do what I usually do when I don't know what a woman's on about: I attempt to ignore the question. I pick the paper back up in the unlikely hope that she won't carry on. Some hope! "Rob! You do know what I'm talking about? A Rabbit?" she says, pulling the paper out of my hands.

"Yes, a rabbit, you have a rabbit. So what?" As I say this I'm shifting about uncomfortably the same way you would if you had a banana stuck up your arse.

"How do you feel about that?" she asks, with her head in the dreaded tilted position. I have subsequently learned to hate the verb 'to feel' in the same way that Lindsay Lohan hates mineral water. Jenny introduces it into any of our arguments, or discussions, with all the brilliance of a time-proven Old Bailey barrister: 'Rob, I'm not saying you're wrong, but that is how I feel.' … 'Rob I don't think you're being honest and telling me how you really feel'.

This usually means any cheap point scoring that I've used in previous arguments have completely gone to waste, as she's been so particular in pointing out: 'It's not about right and wrong; it's about how you feel'.

"It doesn't worry you does it?" she asks me. "You don't feel threatened in any way do you?" The only way I imagine being threatened by a rabbit, at my age anyway, is if she's talking about that thing in Donnie Darko. That thing scared the shit out of me. Charlotte brought it round on DVD a couple of years ago and I didn't like it one bit. Last Easter I dreamt it was chasing me round the school playground.

"The only threat to me," I reason back, "would be if you cut it up and served it in your African stew."

"Rob, are you joking? I can't tell sometimes if you're joking or not. Don't you remember our phone call?" With this, she turns over and pulls open the top drawer of her bedside table. Taking out what looks, on first impression, like a hand-held pink robot, she turns back towards me and holds the object up. I can't help but notice that it's giving me a rather rude 'V' sign. As if that isn't bad enough, she flings it over to my side of the bed where it lands on top of me. "Say hello to Roger," she laughs.

"Get it off me!" I say, at the same time kicking it towards her. She laughs even louder. Clearly enjoying herself, she picks it up and flicks a silver switch on the front. To my horror it begins to gyrate like a hunchbacked John Travolta in *Saturday Night Fever*. I stare at it for a moment.

I'm unwittingly drawn to the small, silver balls that are spinning round and round inside it. The whole effect is mesmerising. It looks more like it's a Star Wars weapon than a bedroom toy.

Jenny catches the look of horror on my face, but this only makes her laugh harder. Giggling with an intense, child-like glee, she presses yet another button. The thing has more buttons than a pearly king. On doing this it suddenly stops gyrating and starts to make a buzzing sound that I recognise instantly. The two fingers that were previously giving me the 'V' now start to vibrate. It sounds like a faulty phone line! And with this, the penny finally drops. After what seems like an eternity, she makes it stop. "Well, what do you think?"

"Err … nice babe," I muster.

"I'm not interested in what you think it looks like. I mean, do you want to have some fun with it?"

"I'm not being funny, but I don't see how I could possibly have some fun with that unless, of course, you're thinking of sticking it up my arse?"

Which I know is highly unlikely.

That's because of a conversation we'd had the previous week. We were in bed and I was reading an article in the Guardian by a well-known comedian. The guy was publicly thanking Jonathan Ross for his championing of bum sex. I took this as an opportunity to question Jenny about any future possible engagements we might have in this area. Whilst it has never been a particular predilection of mine, Jenny had slammed the door of future opportunity firmly shut with the classic comment, "nothing's going up there. I've seen what comes out!"

So, whilst it doesn't take a great leap of imagination to see how she might have some fun with it, I can't for the life of me think how I might be able to.

Anyway, I'm a bit miffed by the whole turn of events and, worse still, something perturbing is surfacing from the darker waters of my mind. This leads me to ask the question that men who have little or no understanding of women's sexual needs always ask when confronted by their particular 'Roger'. "Anyhow, I don't understand why you need that when you've got me?"

The look that passes across her face can only be compared to the one my schoolteacher gave me when I asked her why my cousin Shirley didn't have a penis. "I don't *need* it, silly," she explains. "It's just fun and it helps me relax."

"Well, if it's relaxation you want, I'll give you a massage then." She takes umbrage at this and, judging by the look on her face, stock and offence will soon follow.

"You didn't seem to mind too much when we were on the phone," she reminds me.

"That was different."

"How was it different?" I realise childishly saying, "it just was" isn't going to be enough here. So I try to explain myself.

126

"Because I wasn't there then; it didn't matter so much. But now I'm here, and you've got me, you shouldn't need that. I should be enough." From Jenny's carefully prepared response, it seems that she's heard this particular line of defence before.

"You are enough, more than enough. Why do you think you're not enough?"

"Well, maybe because you're thinking of shoving a big, pink, plastic, battery-operated dick inside you."

"I don't think you really understand Rob, or else you wouldn't be so defensive."

"Look, if I'm defensive, maybe that's because I feel I'm being attacked," I reason.

"You're not being attacked, Rob, and your manhood isn't being questioned. It doesn't matter if you don't want to use it. It's fine."

The subtle inflection in her tone as she says this is a clear indication that, even though she says 'it's fine', it most certainly isn't. Besides, her eyes also say different. They seem to glaze over with a look of mild disappointment, but there's also that little glint in there that she gets when she's not giving in. "Look, let me explain." Shit. This is going to be bad. This is the exact phrase in the exact tone my schoolteacher started with when we had the lack of Shirley's penis conversation. "I love having sex with you and I would rather have sex with you than anyone else in the whole world," she informs me. "But, sometimes, I need to, you know? Come."

"What do you mean? You don't come with me?"

"Of course I do. It's just not like I do with Roger. Roger gives me a different sort of come." This is getting confusing. Surely coming is coming, isn't it? How could it be different? I know mine is pretty much always the same.

"Better than with me? Better than how I make you come?"

"Not better, just different." Just different.

The words spin around and around in my head. The way she said 'just different' could mean, 'just different', or it could also mean, 'much better'. There's nothing else for it. I decide I'm going to have to see a demonstration. "Well, as my preferred learning style is kinaesthetic, show me," I say.

Judging by the look that crosses her face as I say this, she couldn't have been any happier if I'd said, "here's a million pounds go and buy yourself some new clothes."

Fifteen minutes later I know that if 'not better, just different' isn't a lie, it's stretching the truth from here to Australia.

From this point on, I take an instant dislike to Roger. He begins to make more frequent appearances during our lovemaking. It's clear he can

127

do things I can't and those things seem, to me at least, to be better than the things I can do. You only have to listen to the noises he solicits when turning his particular party trick to know that.

To make matters worse, in addition to his party trick, he can also do all the things I can. I begin to wonder if there's any real point to me at all. I mean, Roger doesn't appear to suffer from any nerves; he rarely seems to get tired and, by his very nature, he is always, always, up for the job.

From time to time the little bastard goes flat and that, at least, gives me some small sense of satisfaction. But Jenny has a steady stream of Duracells on constant supply. It's only recently that I've understood the subliminal messages in those old Duracell adverts. You know? The ones with that drumming bunny? Any woman watching it instantly recognises it has nothing to do with a drumming bunny, it's a vibrator advert! It might as well have a tagline that says: 'Duracell, it goes until you come'. Meanwhile, we poor male saps continue to believe it's a pointless advert about how long a toy rabbit can bang a drum.

On a positive note, she doesn't have a Roger that runs on AC current, which is a good thing as the polar ice caps might have melted by now.

After another week or so of Roger, Jenny seems to want to get her drum banged no matter how good I've been. It's as if only he can really satisfy her. Like all men, I've had my fantasies about threesomes in the past, but this isn't exactly what I had in mind.

Then there's the jealousy. I begin to imagine that every time she's at home alone, she's whipping him out and buzzing herself into a frenzy. Not only am I jealous of Roger, I hate him. I resolve that he will have to go.

But of course he doesn't, because I don't dare. I have the feeling that if I uttered the fateful line 'it's me or the rabbit', her first thought may be: rabbits don't piss on the toilet seat.

To my credit, I try all the silly stuff. I exchange the batteries for old ones. I attempt to sever his connections, but even the rudimentary electrics of a vibrator prove beyond me. I even start to hide him whenever I leave the house, thinking this will be a way of stopping her from using him when I'm not around. I hope, at least, it will give me a modicum of control over her self-frigging habits. But no, she always finds him. He's always back in the drawer whenever I return. It's like she and Roger have some deep psychic bond that can't be broken.

Not that Roger can't be broken. She broke him twice in the first couple of weeks that followed his introduction into our bedroom antics. Both times she returned the broken Rogers to Ann Summers in the Trafford Centre, claiming that they were faulty. The only fault they had was that they weren't built with the robustness of a BMW 4x4.

One time I had to hang around in the middle of Ann Summers, whilst Jenny produced the broken Roger from her handbag and complained to the shop assistant that he was faulty. Then the two of them examined him. They attempted to make him rotate and vibrate as best he could. I was totally amazed when the shop assistant sped off and brought back a new one. She promptly put some fresh batteries in, switched him on and the two of them purred like fat cats in front of a December log fire as they imagined him in action.

In the end, like any good general who's taking a shafting, I call a truce. We talk openly and frankly about usage. It's like one of those arms reduction treaties that were drawn up by the superpowers in the 1970s. She agrees to limit herself to once a week without me, usually on a Friday, but the actual day is left open. If I'm there she can use him twice a week. I, for my part, agree that there will be limited wanking. Overall, both parties view the agreement as fair.

So my period of détente with Roger begins. It's another little inkling that problems are starting to surface and it's just one more insecurity for us to ponder.

Chapter 20

The Parent Trap

The software company that Jenny works for is international and every six months they hold a conference in some exotic location. Her job doesn't really require her to go and, with three teenage boys to care for, it's difficult to see a time when she would be able to. At least, that's what I thought.

But as usual, I'm way behind the current thinking of the time.

It's early September and we're sitting in the front room eating a takeaway. I'm watching the six o'clock news and Jenny is munching away on her Chinese. Without warning she interrupts her eating - a very bad sign - and looks up nonchalantly from her chilli king prawn. "I've been asked to go to the conference this year," she says cheerfully. "It's a one-off as Paula can't make it, and they need someone there who can help out with the day-to-day stuff. It's in Cyprus." I let this go for a few seconds.

"Pity you can't go then, you know, with you having three kids and all. And having no-one to look after them," I reply. She is, of course, like most women would be, totally unfazed by this comment. She ignores it in the same way you might ignore a Big Issue seller after you've already bought three copies that day.

"Look, there's no pressure Rob. If you don't want to do it you don't have to. Hell, I wouldn't want to stay behind and look after my kids. So I'm not going to blame you if you don't. Anyway, I haven't said I'll go yet. So you can say no if you want. I really won't mind."

And the thing is: she wouldn't. She's so utterly reasonable about stuff like this; it's genius reverse psychology. I'd downright refuse if I thought for one minute that she'd sulk, or be disappointed if I said I didn't want to do it. But the very fact that she doesn't mind means I'll feel a bastard if I say no. "Do you want to go?" I ask.

I hope at this point she'll say something like, 'I'm not bothered' or 'not really'. This would get me off the hook, as I'd rather be stuck in a house on my own with Norman Bates than her three kids. I say three kids; it's more like two.

That's because I've sort of bonded with Daniel. Well, as much as it's possible to actually bond with Daniel. This is based around the fact that I have become Daniel's 'Arm-Squeezer in Chief'. It's a big joke with Jenny that he ignores her now and comes to me for his nightly insulin jab. Anyway, my tactic is to no avail. She spoils my little trap, as she always does, by resorting to the distinctly underhand tactic that women resort to in these situations: telling the truth.

130

"Of course I do! Who wouldn't want to go to Cyprus for a week and get some sun? But I really will understand if you don't want to look after them."

"Aren't you worried I might molest them or something?"

"Rob, if it's a safety issue I'd be more worried about yours than theirs."

"I suppose it won't go down well at work if you say you can't go?" I ask.

"No one will say anything, as it's really short notice, but they'd appreciate it if I could go." This last statement is said in a tone that clearly indicates she will be very pleased with me if I say yes, and might show me some of her own appreciation if I do.

"Well ... I suppose," I reply, thinking suddenly about how her appreciation might be shown.

"Are you sure, Rob?" she asks. "I don't want you feeling pressured into doing this."

"Look, you better shut up before I change my mind. If you're waiting for me to start doing cartwheels around the room and jumping for joy at the prospect, you might have a bit of a wait."

"Thanks Rob," she says, getting up off the couch to put the Chinese leftovers in a carrier bag. "It's really good of you."

But I didn't realise at the time, just how good it was of me.

In the two weeks before she goes, Jenny prepares us all for her trip on a similar all-encompassing level to how the allies must have prepared for D-Day. There are briefing sessions for a start.

Firstly, I'm instructed on all potential problems that may arise. The main worries about 'Operation Clear Off to Cyprus and Leave Rob Stranded' revolve around Daniel. I am factually briefed on other aspects of his diabetes that are more complex than just squeezing his arm, such as hypos.

After which Jenny gives me careful instructions on managing his eating regime and the ins-and-outs of his blood sugar levels.

Finally, I am tactically briefed as to problems that might arise from his mild autism. "He can get stressed, but it's usually when something out of the ordinary happens. So watch carefully for any breaks in his routine," she tells me.

"How will I know when he's stressed?"

"Oh, you'll know; believe me. But as he's got older it tends to happen less and less. So there's probably nothing to worry about."

Famous last words.

With the other two siblings the briefings simply boil down to making sure they are fed, watered and not engaged in violent activity against each other. And that's it really.

The only other thing of note during this period is that Steve phones me with some bad news about the new league starting next month. The first bit of bad news is that the league has expanded and will now run into late April. This isn't good. Jenny and I have tentatively talked about taking a 'family holiday' at Easter, but I decide it might be better if Steve doesn't know anything about this for now.

The second piece of bad news is worse. "Yeah, err ... I ran into Drysdale," he says, ever so matter-of-factly. "Last night in Frodsham."

"Did you?" I say, wondering where he's going with this.

"Yeah, and we got talking."

"Talking? You and Drysdale?"

"Well, when I say talking, I mean arguing."

"Steve, just remember I have to work with the guy."

"Yeah, well. He was mouthing off about this year's league and how they were going to win it and all, and how we we're lucky last time, and how it wasn't going to happen again. So I ..."

"So you what?" I ask, feeling apprehensive because I really don't want to know the answer.

"So ... so I told him to put his money where his mouth was. I challenged him to a bet."

"Steve, you don't have the money to challenge him to any bets. How much?"

"Well ..."

"How much?"

"£500."

"£500! You're joking? Steve, it's an over-35's kickabout. It's not the fucking Premier League!"

"£500 that we'll finish above them. We don't even have to win the league."

"You don't have that kind of money," I remind him.

"No, but you do."

"No chance. Jenny would kill me. That's two flights to Barcelona you're talking about. You'll have to call it off. I'll see him in work. I'll explain. He'll understand."

"You won't Rob. If you do I'll never speak to you again. Anyway, you won't need it because we're going to finish above them; just like the last time."

"God, Steve. £500." The line goes quiet and I sense his unease.

"Trouble is that Drysdale has insisted the money is put in up front. I need to bring it to the first game next month and lodge it with the refs or I'll look like a total dick."

"Shit! Jenny will go mad."

"You must have some of the house money left."

"Not as much as you'd think," I tell him.

"Please Rob," he says, in a tone not to dissimilar to a young child asking for an ice cream on a hot day.

"I'll get it." And as I say it I wonder what I'll tell Jenny.

The next day the youngest one, who fancies himself as a bit of a St Francis of Assisi type, comes home with a baby magpie. Apparently, he found it at the bottom of a tree near his school and decided to put it into his pocket. You know? Like you do.

Worse still, it turns out to be the only nocturnal baby magpie currently in captivity. And where do the boys decide they are going to keep this screeching little banshee? Why, in the fish tank in Daniel's room, of course.

When Jenny's mum is told about this, she is, '…very concerned about how it's going to breathe in there'. It takes a moment before I realise she thinks we've left the water in. Before the week is out, I'll be wishing we had.

To begin with, and before the novelty has worn off, the three of them take turns to feed it bread dipped in warm milk.

Two days later, and unsurprisingly, the novelty has worn off. This is partly due to the fact that Jenny's boys have attention spans similar to an absent-minded goldfish. So the responsibility falls to Daniel. This is because the bird is in his room. I even feed it myself a few times – not out of any desire to be David Attenborough, but just to make it shut up!

So, on the day that Jenny jets off, I find myself in *loco parentis* of three teenage boys and a mangy, baby magpie. Jenny leaves at seven in the morning still insisting that the trip isn't a jolly. "It won't be a holiday Rob; it really will be hard work."

Now I have to admit, the first couple of days go really well. I have daily contact with Jenny by phone. Curtis has various hooded youths round in the evenings and I watch a couple of matches with them. The youngest one goes out a lot and hardly ever comes back, which suits me just fine. I'm more than happy to let him stay out at friends and give him money to encourage him to do so. Daniel, as usual, spends most of his time upstairs on his computer; so no changes to his routine, which is good. He only ventures downstairs now and again to get something to eat for either himself, or the magpie, or to have me squeeze his arm.

On the evening of her third night away, Jenny phones at six. "Has Daniel eaten yet?' she asks.

"Yes."

"Has he taken his blood?"

"Yes."

"Is it high?"

"No."

"Have there been any fights?"

"No."

"Are you okay?"

"Yes."

"Are you stressed?"

"No."

"Are you sure? I know how stressful they can be. I get worried."

"Look Jenny, it's a doddle. Really. Stop worrying. Enjoy yourself. I have it all covered. Trust me."

"Well, I'm going out for a meal tonight and mobile reception might not be too good."

"Fine, ring me when you get in. It's a really warm night here. I'm going to sit outside with my book."

"Okay, I'll call you later."

"Love you."

"Love you, too."

It's a little later and I'm sitting outside enjoying the new Stephen King novel and my second cup of tea. The youngest one has gone out and Curtis is in the front room with a couple of hoodies excitedly talking about their upcoming gig on Wythenshawe FM. All is well with the world, until I begin to get a sense of being watched.

There's a presence in my eye line. I look up. Daniel is standing quietly in front of me. He rarely, if ever, ventures outside the four walls of his room at this time of night, other than to eat. He's shuffling around and looking decidedly uncomfortable. "You okay Daniel?" I ask, putting the book down.

"Err ... well, it's just thingy ... " he explains, hands in his pockets and looking down at his trainers. "That it's sort of, you know? Innit? The bird thingy."

I haven't got a clue what he's talking about and looking at my watch his timing couldn't have been much worse; the evening racing is about to start on Sky. "Look mate, get to the point will you. I'm in a bit of a hurry," I say, perhaps a tad brusquely.

Eventually he mumbles something about the bird and I get his drift. It's not a huge problem. In fact, it's a bit of result. What he needs is some alpha male leadership.

I get up from the chair, give him a playful punch and tell him what to do. I then make my way to the living room, post haste, to watch the first race on the Racing Channel. Past experience has taught me that, given half a chance, he can become very time-consuming. This is where I have the advantage over Jenny. She would have sat down, got into a deep conversation with him about his feelings and wasted a couple of hours. Then there would have been another two and half hours where she talked him through a resolution. Me? Done and dusted in two minutes. I rest my case, your honour.

Two minutes later, whilst Daniel goes off to sort out the problem, I go back indoors, evict Curtis and the two hoodies out into the garden, and switch the TV onto the Racing Channel. The evening is turning out to be another success on my personal road to step-fatherhood. The boys are going about their business and, before I know where I am, it's nine o'clock.

The only downside is that the youngest doesn't stay out and starts pogoing in the hall. I'm feeling on top of my game, so I shout through from the sitting room and ask him to go and tell Daniel to get his snack. This, I deem, will kill two birds with one stone. He takes this to mean 'pogo all the way upstairs and tell your brother' but not to worry.

To my surprise, he comes back down a few minutes later with some disconcerting news. "Rob, he hasn't moved. He's ignoring me. He's acting well weird. You know, like he can."

"Did you tell him it was an order from me?" I ask him.

"No," he replies.

"So go and tell him," I say, glancing up momentarily from the TV. "Tell him I'll take his computer off him if he doesn't get up and get his snack right now." A smile of self-satisfaction crosses my lips. No need to talk to them, or reason with them – simple threats will amply suffice.

I settle down to watch the last race, but to my even greater surprise, the pogo stick is back very shortly. "He's just ignoring me, Rob. He's staring out into space. He's got, like, the weirdest look on his face."

Curtis comes into the room and having overheard the conversation, decides to make a constructive comment. "He's just a muppet. I'll move him, Rob. Don't worry. I'll knock him out."

I realise I'm going to have to get off my backside and sort this out. Otherwise my credibility as step-enforcer will be seriously undermined. Child-on-child violence was one of the things Jenny distinctly said should not be tolerated.

Pushing past Curtis, I climb the stairs and reach Daniel's room. As I enter I see him lying on the bed opposite. He is, indeed, staring out into space and he doesn't look particularly bothered that the step-enforcer is upon him. "Look, Daniel, you need to get up and get your snack. You've been asked three times now, mate. So come on, get a move on. I'm not messing around now," I say firmly.

Nothing. He doesn't flinch a muscle at the old 'I'm not messing around now' line. He continues to stare vacantly out into space. This is going to take a more serious approach. Faced with situations like these I always resort to a tried and tested method. I begin to raise my voice a little. I'm from a large Irish family so raising one's voice is part of my genetic make-up. This is bound to work. "Look Daniel. Get up now!" I say, in the slightly raised voice. "If you're not downstairs in two minutes I'm going to have to take your computer off you for the rest of the week."

Still nothing. Just for a second, he appears to look over at me, but he still doesn't move. By now, Curtis has joined me in the room. Clearly relishing the chance to shout at his brother legitimately, he sets about raising his own voice. "DANIEL YOU MUPPET! GET UP, OR I'LL KNOCK YOU OUT!" he bellows, clearly enjoying the opportunity presented.

After ten minutes of threats from me, and the promise of all kinds of wanton violence from Curtis, there is still no movement. I'm starting to get a little stressed. The slightly raised voice is not having the desired effect – and I'm running out of ideas. Is he having a hypo? Does he need to eat?

I stand there uselessly for another ten minutes, then give in to the sinking realisation that there's only one real course of action left open to me: I have to phone Jenny.

As luck would have it, I reach her immediately and begin to tell her what's happened, but it comes out of my mouth in a whine. "He won't do a thing I ask him," I say. "He's just lying there staring at me and nothing I do makes any difference. You never briefed me about this."

"Calm down Rob. Have you stressed him?" she asks. "He usually only ever acts like this when someone has really stressed him."

"Oh, that would be right! It would have to be me," I say indignantly. "I haven't done a thing." I realise I sound like one of the boys. Jenny's always telling me I'm more like them than I care to admit, but I'm not.

"Look, I'm not saying it's your fault Rob," she says, as if it is my fault. "I'm just saying that it doesn't make any sense. He used to do this when he was little and stressed, but he hasn't done it for a while now."

"Well, he's doing it now all right and if anyone is stressing around here it's me. Is it a hypo?"

"When did he last eat?" she asks.

"About six. I did his arm and he even smiled. He seemed fine."

"It's unlikely to be a hypo; there'd be other symptoms if it was. It's more likely to be stress."

"I'm telling you he's not the one who's stressed – I am."

"Rob, try and keep calm," she says, her voice breaking slightly. "Go and get Curtis. Give him the phone and I'll speak to Daniel."

Curtis and I go back into the room. Curtis places the phone next to Daniel's head and a strictly one-way conversation takes place. After a couple of minutes Daniel has still not moved an inch, but is now staring at the phone. I pick it back up and tell Jenny he hasn't moved. Jenny says, "he's not responding, but I know he can hear me. I still don't think it's a hypo but you'll have to take his blood to make sure." I have no idea how, if he has not responded, she knows that he can hear her.

"He's really worrying me," I tell her truthfully.

"Rob, for a teacher you're not handling this as well as you might."

"That's easy for you to say, you're not the one going through this. Is he okay?"

"Rob, I don't know. That's why I'm asking you the questions."

"Jenny," I plead. "Can't you come home?" On hearing this she gets quite angry.

"Why can't I just enjoy one trip away? Everybody else seems to be able to – why not me?" She continues to rant on the phone. I feel bad, but I'm at a bit of a loss. She then has an idea.

"I'll phone his dad and see if he'll come and get him. He'll know what to do."

"No don't," I beg, suddenly alarmed. "I'll sort it out."

"No Rob. I'm worried about Daniel. You've never seen him like this before and you don't know how to handle it. I'm going to phone Harry. Don't feel bad about it, his dad knows him much better than you. He'll know what to do."

"I know what to do. Really I do."

"Go on then Rob. What's your big plan?" After 20 seconds of silence from my end she says, "I'll phone Harry." With this, she hangs up. I'm left holding the phone and trying to hold on to what little step-parental credibility I have left. I'm going to have to face the ignominy of the ex coming round to deal with a problem that I can't handle.

There's nothing else left to me. I disappear into the bedroom to hide. Soon, Jenny phones back to say that Harry's on his way and when he turns up 40 minutes later, Curtis lets him in.

I skulk by the door as Harry comes up the stairs. I only catch a glimpse of the back of him, but it's enough to see he's a thickset bloke; the sort that you wouldn't want to mess with. Curtis follows him up and looks a bit embarrassed as he glances over to me. He follows Harry into Daniel's room.

From my skulking vantage point I can hear Harry talking softly to Daniel and, amazingly, he gets a muffled response. The next minute Harry is walking out of the room with a groggy-looking Daniel leaning heavily on him. As they navigate the stairs Harry looks over to me and I just shrug my shoulders. To be fair, he just raises his eyes slightly and continues on his less than merry way.

I go and lie down on the bed. I feel like a complete dick. Just when I'm at my lowest ebb the door opens and Curtis strides in. "Don't worry Rob he's just a muppet. When he gets back I'll knock him out." I roll over and try not to think what Jenny's going to say when she gets back.

The next morning I am woken by a tap on the door. "Come in,' I mutter. It's Daniel. He's stood still and looking a bit like he's been dragged through a hedge backwards.

"Sorry Rob, innit? I had a thingy. It is like I can hear but I am not there."

"Don't worry about it," I say, sitting up. "The main thing is that you're okay."

"Yeah okay. Feel all right now."

"Great," I say. I am, though, relieved that he's okay; having spent most of the night worrying about him.

"Rob."

"Yeah?"

"Will you still squeeze my arm?"

"'Course I will."

When Jenny returns two days later, she makes a beeline for Daniel's room first thing. I'm left standing around, feeling inept, while she pieces it all together like Morse on a shit easy case. It takes her about an hour.

When she returns to our room she's smiling at me, but I know that particular smile. It's the smile she wears when she's right. "Rob. You're a muppet."

"Go on then," I sigh, putting my cold coffee down. "Enlighten me. I knew it would be my fault somehow."

"Did I tell you he was stressed, or did I tell you he was stressed?"

"How was he stressed? If he was, it was nothing to do with me!"

"Really? Then you don't remember him telling you the magpie had died?"

I cast my mind back. I vaguely remember the conversation in the garden.

"Err ... yeah. But surely it can't have been anything to do with that."

"Rob, you're unbelievable. Do you know how it died?"

"Well, yeah. They always die outside the nest when they're young," I guess wildly. "It's usually just a matter of time."

"No, Rob. It was screeching in the middle of the night. So Daniel got up and gave it a little tap to, 'help it get to sleep 'cos it was sleepy, innit?' Probably killed it outright. He then got up in the morning and felt highly stressed all day about what he'd done. This was before plucking up the courage to come and ask you to help him to bury it. Burying it was important to him as it was the only way he could cope psychologically with his actions. And when he came to see you about it you told him ..?"

"To put it in a crisp packet and throw it in the bin."

"Yes Rob. You told him to put in a crisp packet and throw it in the bin. Rob, you're unbelievable!"

Guilty as charged.

I have to admit that, I'm afraid. I am unbelievable. But then some truly unbelievable things will happen over the course of the next few months.

Chapter 21

Kinsey

To my amazement Jenny doesn't take it badly when I tell her about the £500 bet I lodged with the referees to cover Steve's idiocy. "It's your money" is the extent to which she's prepared to comment on the matter. This makes me feel like I can at least do something right. I've been honest about what I've done and haven't tried to cover it up as I would have at one time. Perhaps I'm changing and she recognises this.

Or perhaps she has more important things on her mind?

I know that Jenny has worries about how our relationship is 'progressing'. However, I'm beginning to have concerns of my own regarding Jenny. She's begun to develop an irrational desire for knowledge of my previous sexual history. I realise this can go with the territory in new relationships – lots of couples like to explore their new partner's previous encounters – but Jenny's avaricious questioning soon leaves me feeling exhausted.

We began with discussions about my long-term relationships, which have now moved on to a dissection of my short-term sexual partners. The whole project is being conducted in the name of what she calls 'transparency' and I call 'snooping'. Jenny argues that it's moving the relationship forward, but I'm not so sure. There's evidence to suggest that she's not entirely happy if she believes she can't match up to what has gone before. I can't help thinking she's entering her very own 'Viagra zone'.

I don't understand the point of her searching questions. I put up with the questioning because, sometimes, it's a prelude to sex. I talk for five minutes about hot sex I've had in the past and we end up shagging. I like that bit.

It's the post-mortems I don't like. The post-mortems can be likened to *Millionaire*, where Jenny takes on the role of a warped Chris Tarrant and grills me within an inch of my past sexual life. Not that my topic is a particularly taxing one in terms of detail, but the relentless probing makes it all about as much fun as dangling your dick in a piranha infested bidet.

Things come to a head a couple of weeks after Jenny gets back from Cyprus. We've just had sex and during the hottest, steamiest moments she gets me to verbalise my recollection of a previous sexual encounter. She seems to like this as much as I do but, as usual, trouble is looming.

"So what did you like about it so much?" she asks, as we break away from each other and lie on our backs, panting.

"I liked the way you came. It sounded big," I reply.

140

"Not us silly – what did you like about sex with Melanie so much?" My radar kicks into what Jenny calls my 'defensive mode'. I'm only interested in hot-sex talk while we're having sex, but Jenny is interested in the cold-sex talk afterwards.

"Err … I don't know, she just turned me on," I tell her, trying to sound neutral. I sound about as neutral as I can get, without immediately emigrating to Switzerland and hoisting up a white flag over my house. But my neutrality isn't even acknowledged; she marches over it like a bunch of US marines entering an oil rich country that needs democratizing. "How did she turn you on? Was it the way she looked? The things she wore? What she did for you in bed? What?" She is in full-on Tarrant mode here. I need to be careful.

"Well, I fancied her, obviously," I begin, tentatively. "She was good looking, but not too good looking. And she had a good body."

"What was good about her body?" she probes. At this point in the game, I really want to phone a friend, but I'm strictly on my own. I wonder if I can ask her for a 50-50. Instead, I try to turn the tables.

"Look, where's all this going?" I ask, raising the voice a little for effect. "Why do want to know all this stuff?"

"Don't get defensive. I'm trying to process things about you, so I can work things out. I want to know all about you and what makes you tick."

There's a slight change in her tone. I sneak a look at her. The blue steelies are wide open and she has that quizzical look. I can't hold her gaze for long. I figure she must be 'processing'. One thing about Jenny is that she loves to 'process' things and 'work things out'. I'm convinced women do too much thinking about relationships and eventually think themselves out of lots of good ones for no valid reason.

Not that women need much help to think themselves out of relationships where I'm concerned. I take a deep breath to combat the mounting pressure and think for a moment. That phrase – 'what makes you tick' – makes me sound like a fucking watch. "Well, she had great tits," I say, flustered. This was probably the dumbest answer since one of my students wrote, 'I've never heard of him' in response to the question: 'How did the USA deploy Agent Orange in the Vietnam War?' Jenny clearly agrees.

"And that's it?" she asks incredulously. "That's all that it takes to make someone a great shag?"

This tone could not contain more exasperation if she tried. So I back-paddle. I'm like a canoeist being swept frantically downriver in the direction of Niagara Falls.

"Well, not just that, obviously. God! I'm not that shallow," I say, sounding as if I am, really, that shallow. She's now staring at me intently with a look that's telling me to go on, but that this had better be good. So I do, and it isn't.

"She had a great personality as well, and she dressed really sexily. Black dresses and all that. So, you know, it was a total package thing. I liked the total package." I sound like one of those idiots from *The Apprentice* in danger of being booted off by Sir Alan for going on, as I am, about 'the total package'. I'm hoping that I've succeeded in extricating myself from a difficult situation – but I'm wrong. Sir Jenny Sugar gets straight to the point.

"So, just how big were her tits?"

You now have to imagine a contestant on *Millionaire* losing not only the plot, but also the house that was built on it and all the furniture inside. "Shit, I don't know. I never took the time to measure them! Perhaps I should have got a tape measure out at the time and said, 'sorry do you mind, but I'm going to need this information at some future date as my psychotic girlfriend will need to know the size of your tits'."

"God, you're so dramatic. Here I am trying to understand you." Oh no, it's the amazingly serene voice. "Trying to understand what you're about and you go off on one. You were more than happy to talk about it ten minutes ago."

I'm confused, because she sounds calm and relaxed, and I sound like the psycho. I'm sure it should be the other way around. "Sorry," I mumble. "It's just that I don't see where all this is going."

"I just want to know what gets you off," she tells me.

"Can I just say then, at this point, that it's not being questioned to within an inch of my life about all my old shags?" She goes quiet for a minute and I wonder if that's it for this session of *Millionaire*. No such luck.

"Rob, stuff that has happened in the past is important. It's formative and can affect you for the rest of your life."

'Formative'? Sounds very like that psycho-babble you get in counselling. The very thing she puts so much store on. Still, best not to mention that thought right now. "I get all that. It's just that it gets boring Jenny; being constantly questioned about it. I don't see where this is going to get us." She's staring at me now and looking as if she's mulling something over.

"If you asked me questions you'd learn more about me. But you never show any interest about my past. Let me tell you something I've never -"

I'm not listening by now. So I talk over her.

"That's because the only time I showed an interest in your sexual history I was traumatised by that bloke from the Navy and I ended up taking Viagra."

"I know Rob, but if you'd just listen."

142

"Jenny, I'm exhausted listening. Can we leave it for today?"

"I guess so," she replies, and rolls over.

It's about a week later, on a visit the cinema, when it all kicks off again. To my mind, all that's happened is that we've had a really nice time. We watch a great Irish film with Colm Meaney in it. It seems to be a rule of Irish cinema that he must be in everything they make.

Throughout the film, things are good. We have a drink in the bar before going in; we hold hands like a couple of 15 year olds on a first date and we also do other things that a couple of 15 year olds might do on a first date when the film's tempo drops a little.

Jenny still seems happy enough as we leave the cinema. We hold hands as we walk towards the car. But as soon as we reach it, I know something is wrong. I don't, as yet, know what it is. My mind reading powers haven't yet reached full Jenny-mood-deciphering capacity. I do know, though, that there's definitely something wrong.

This is because Jenny makes it very clear when something is wrong, while at the exact same time making it impossible to know just what it is. She makes it clear that something is wrong by deploying something I've come to call 'withdrawal'. 'Withdrawal', as practiced by Jenny, is where any attempt at affection or communication is met with a vague nothingness.

Not a rebuttal, I might add. A rebuttal would be too simple. A rebuttal would be cards-on-the-table time, and we'd all know where we stood. Instead, Jenny takes on the persona of a member of the Borg in *Star Trek*. She simply smiles in a really fake way and answers any questions with simple yes and no answers. When you seek to hold her hand it feels like holding hands with a lizard that's able to instantly freeze its blood temperature and keep unerringly still even if you stroke it for information.

So I'm in the car with her. All physical contact has been withdrawn and I'm left only with verbal interrogation. It's a warped game of *What's My Line?* She only gives yes and no clues. These are constantly repeated back in monosyllabic form and I have to work out what I've done. Unlike the original game, though, the contestant is seemingly allowed to lie and to use other glib phrases, making the whole thing ludicrously difficult.

"Are you okay?" I ask, attempting to learn anything I possibly can.

"I'm fine," comes the stock reply. This is the phrase that starts the game. When she says "I'm fine," it means: "you're a bastard and you know you are". Still, I check anyway.

"You sure?"

"Yeah, I'm fine." See? I'm a bastard. I hold her hand as I start the car. It has all the warmth of a snake's fanny. "Well, it seems like there's a problem," I say, shifting through the gears in more ways than one. "Are you sure there's no problem."

"Yeah." She stares at the floor, her eyes determinedly blank.

"And I haven't done anything?"

"No."

"Sure?"

"Yeah." At this point, she lets go of my hand and gives me a smile so lacking in sincerity I wonder if she couldn't have a brilliant career in banking ahead of her.

On the way back to the house we don't exchange a word. I can feel myself becoming more agitated by the second, but I bottle it in. This isn't the right moment.

Back at the house, Jenny makes her way straight upstairs and I follow reluctantly. I find her lying on the bed reading a magazine with studied nonchalance. I step inside the room and opt for a softly-softly approach.

"Fancy a cup of tea?" I ask her.

"No thanks," she says, not bothering to look up.

"Sure? I'll make you a sandwich, if you want."

"No, it's fine," she says, flicking a page. "I'm not hungry." I'm at a loss as to what to do here. I know that if I press the matter I'll find out what it is I am supposed to have done. Then things will escalate, because I definitely won't be happy about what I'm supposed to have done. I stand uneasily by the door and then bite the bullet.

"Look, what's the matter? What have I done?"

"Who said you've done anything?" she replies, casually flicking another page. I can't help noticing that the coldness I'd associated with her body language has now crept into her voice. I stand there blinking, unsure of where to go from here but surprisingly, Jenny breaks the silence. "You mean, you really don't know what you've done?"

"I wouldn't be asking if I knew," I say, walking towards my side of the bed. "Go on then. What have I done? Enlighten me." The sarcasm in my voice might have been a mistake. For a moment, it seems as if she isn't going to dignify me with a response.

"Don't you remember that pretty Asian girl who passed us on the way to the car?"

"No." And I don't, funnily enough, but I have a real inkling now where this could be going.

"You don't?" she says, looking straight up at me. "That's funny, as you couldn't take your eyes off her when she passed us."

"Look, I haven't even got a clue who you're talking about. We passed loads of people on the way back to the car. The place was packed."

"So, how many pretty Asian girls with big tits did we pass?" she asks, flinging the magazine down and fixing me with her most accusatory look. My mind has already started to process the key phrase 'big tits'. I'm starting to twig that most of this stuff is to do with that phrase.

"Look, if we did pass such a girl, I didn't see her," I say truthfully.

"How could you not have seen her when you bent your head backwards to look at her?" I can't answer that question. You can't answer a question when you don't know the answer. So instead, I plump for a statement – one which is, I think, fairly conciliatory and one that I hope will get me out of this mess.

"Look, if I did look at her, and I'm not saying I did, I did it without thinking about it. So, I have no memory of either doing it or seeing her."

She shuffles nervously on the bed at my reply, but the corners of her mouth lighten ever so slightly. The scowl that was set on her face has mellowed into a quizzical look. "Truthfully? You can't remember doing it? And you have no memory of her whatsoever?"

"I swear. No memory whatsoever."

"She was really pretty and she had really great tits."

"I'm sure I would have remembered if I'd seen her." As soon as I say that I realise it is a mistake.

"Why? Is that the sort of girl you usually remember?" Why do they call questions like that one blunt? That's not blunt, it's really *sharp*. I take a second to compose myself.

"I don't usually remember anyone when I'm out with you, as far as I know." Her body language relaxes and she reaches out to touch my hand. This is the sign that she gives when I'm no longer on the outside, but back in. She strokes my hand lightly and I bite the inside of my lip at the gesture; it's both comforting and unnerving at the same time.

"It's just that … I can't stand that sort of leering male behaviour. It makes me sick; especially when it's done furtively." I sense that this is a key moment. So I think carefully before answering.

"I'm not lying. If I did look, it wasn't a conscious thing and you probably won't see me do it again."

"Well, you did do it. You did it in Barcelona, but I didn't say anything at the time." She sighs and then continues. "I suppose I'll have to take your word for it that you're not aware you're doing it. You have to understand I find that kind of behaviour, looking at other women when you're out with your partner, *so* disrespectful. I don't like it."

"Yeah. You've made your point. But I don't do that sort of thing. I'm not like that. If I'm doing it, I'm sorry."

"Then you have a problem." And she's more than right about that.

I'm getting so worried about this that I even broach the problem, in a roundabout way, with Charlotte. She comes over to spend a weekend with us. Jenny's keen that we should spend some 'quality time' together so I take her out to watch *A Taste of Honey* at the Cornerhouse.

On the way out of the theatre I broach the subject. "Charlotte, have you ever noticed anything odd about my behaviour?"

"Well, yeah," she says, fastening her coat. "Your behaviour's often odd!"

"Seriously," I say, taking her hand and pulling her across a level crossing. "Like when I've been around your friends." She looks a bit puzzled but seems to get my drift.

"What? Like perve-type behaviour?" I look down at the tram tracks.

"Yeah, that sort of thing."

"Don't be ridiculous. Do you think I'd let you anywhere near my mates if that was the case? God, Dad. I know you're not perfect, none of us are, but I've never thought that. What's all this about?"

"Nothing. Nothing really." But she's too smart to let it go and way too smart to delve deeply. Instead she squeezes my hand.

"Dad, you've already been through two relationships and you've played your part in both going wrong. From what I can see you've got a real chance at making this one work. You've changed a lot since you've been with Jenny. She's really good for you. She's changed you for the better. But nothing good comes without a price. That's all I'm saying. You work out the rest."

And with that she pulls me towards Chinatown and, being a student, the first decent meal she will have eaten in weeks.

Though I try to heed Charlotte's advice over the next few weeks, the problem escalates. Every time we go anywhere I keep looking at girls' tits - apparently. By chance, or by preference, I only ever look at girls with big tits. I never look at pretty girls who don't have big tits. Jenny maintains that 'those girls obviously don't turn you on'.

In one really bad episode at the gym, Jenny accuses me of staring at a blonde, ex-porn star type with a gigantic pair of false balloons. I defend myself by arguing that that if I had been staring, it wasn't because of any sexual desire. It was probably the car crash effect.

To tell you the truth, this is where I am with it. I don't deny I'm doing it anymore. I just find reasons to explain my behaviour. Charlotte's advice rings in my head: "nothing good comes without a price".

We have any number of arguments and energy sapping 'discussions', but we still don't know where to go with it. She says I'm doing it – I don't think that I am. I resent it all.

But I love her.

So what can I do?

146

Chapter 22

Barbarella

It's mid-December and it's a very cold month. This isn't just an observation on the weather; Jenny has really taken this insecurity thing to a new level. And by some strange, twisted quirk of fate it seems that the more secure I've become in our relationship, the further Jenny is heading in the opposite direction.

Her insecurities have manifested themselves in breast-related jealousies, which I find very hard to understand. She's even told me that her and Gail have had discussions about whether I'm looking at Gail's tits whenever she comes round. The fact she's having these conversations with Gail shows she's losing it. There's also a nagging feeling at the back of my mind that Gail could well be egging Jenny on. It's not like Jenny needs any encouragement. But even worse than all this is the feeling that I may, in some small way, even be responsible.

When it comes to breast sizes, Jenny is now at the stage that I would label 'fanatical obsession'. I deeply regret revealing any details about my shags with girls who had large breasts, because now Jenny's breasts are 'far too small' and - worse still – I don't 'fancy' them. It also appears that the more often I look her in the eye and tell her that I don't give a toss about the size of her breasts, the less she believes me and the bigger the issue becomes.

If we're not arguing about me looking at other girl's breasts, we're arguing about me not looking at Jenny's. According to Jenny, I've never paid much attention to her breasts during sex, whereas in my sex stories, all I do is go on how big every other girl's were.

To be honest, I really don't know whether I have or I haven't, but apparently, Jenny does know and has remembered everything. The whole thing feels like she's been keeping some kind of logbook on our past sexual activity, which she's now opened up to metaphorically beat me around the head with. She's even asked me to go to counselling a couple of times, but I don't see the point. Besides, I have a feeling that most counsellors are women and how can they help but take sides? I haven't verbalised this to Jenny, I just told her, "I'll think about it."

We sat on the bed last night after sex and 'discussed' the whole thing again. "Would you fancy me more if I had bigger tits?" she says.

"This is ridiculous. We've been through this a dozen times."

"You can't tell me you wouldn't though, can you?" she says accusingly. "When I was dating Brian he used to go mad for my tits. He was all over them whenever he got the opportunity. He used to say I had the best tits

147

he'd ever seen. You've never even bothered with them, right from the first time. You didn't even touch them, just then, during sex."

"I didn't touch them because I can't win, can I? If I touch them you tell me I'm only doing it because you go on about it all the time and that's the only reason I've done it. If I don't it's because I don't fancy you or your tits."

"But you do only touch them when prompted; that's my point," she says, rolling over. "You have to be prompted. So I get worried in case you don't fancy me and that you only fancy girls with big tits."

"How many times a week are we having sex?' I ask her, getting up and going over to the window. "It has to be four or five on average, right? So are you telling me I don't fancy you? I mean, that hardly bears up to the facts." There is exasperation in my voice, which is never a good idea where Jenny is concerned, but I'm feeling the strain. As usual, she's calm, if not totally rational.

"No, I'm not saying you don't fancy me,' she says, turning back. "I'm merely saying you don't fancy my tits. It's different."

"What does it matter what I fancy about you? I fancy you, all of you. Otherwise, I wouldn't be trying to shag you all the time. And didn't I say that you were the best sex I've ever had, and that I fancy you more than anyone else I've ever been with? So why, suddenly, do I have to fancy a particular part of you?"

"You don't; just my tits." With this she turns back over in bed and places her back to me once more, which seems to signify that the conversation is at an end. But it isn't.

"Anyway, I'm going for a consultation next week to see about making them bigger." I have to give her credit. I can be difficult to stop in my tracks, but Jenny has managed it with this comment. I'm stunned. To understand why it's so remarkable you have to understand Jenny's aversion to boob jobs.

Boob jobs and Jenny go together like the Pope and strawberry-flavoured Durex. Jenny has a hatred of boob jobs that borders on the psychopathic. Before I met her my views on boob jobs could have been described as 'silicone neutral'. My rationale was that they looked good on some girls and not so good on others.

Also, at my age, I've never come across a fake pair; although a younger colleague had once regaled me with a story of a certain lap dancer he'd had the good fortune to date. In the end, he felt he had to finish with her as her boob job freaked him out in the bedroom. "I don't know Rob – it was like sleeping with three people at the same time," he told me. "I swear those things have minds of their own. They went against all the natural laws of gravity and shit. When I was humping her it felt like they were looking at me in a funny way."

148

The fact that he was a science teacher meant that I had to take his comments on the laws of gravity seriously. So I chalked one up against boob jobs in the negative column.

After only a few weeks in Jenny's company, I realised it was more than in my best interests to form a strategic alliance with her and declare open war on the whole country of *Faketitia*.

What is weird though is that, lately, I really have come to hate them. I think this is because Jenny has let loose a sort of plastic-titty, aversion-therapy on me. In *A Clockwork Orange*, Malcolm McDowell is made to watch violent programmes with his eyes held open by metal clamps until, finally, he can no longer bear to see violence. Jenny has had the same effect on me. She's like the Lone Silicone-Hating Ranger, constantly tackling fake tits wherever she finds them. We can be in the middle of watching a film when for no apparent reason, she'll say, "Look at those. How can any man find those attractive?" It's not so much a question as an invitation to dare to disagree. So I don't.

"Beats me." The safest reply.

"You don't find them attractive do you?"

"No."

"I mean, they're just revolting. She looks ridiculous doesn't she? I mean, the size of them; just ridiculous."

"Ridiculous." As parroting can be an effective male tool.

"Natural ones look so much better. Don't they? Don't you think?"

"So much better." See!

"Seriously though. They're horrible, aren't they?"

"Horrible." And so on.

So now you can see why her recent statement might perplex me. The idea that Jenny could be considering a boob job is about as likely as Graham Norton getting the lead role in *Ozzy Osbourne – The Groupie Shagging Years*. So, realising I'm on tricky ground here, but also intrigued to see if Jenny is on the point of recanting her anti-silicone orthodoxy, I delve. "So, what's this consultation then?" I say, somewhat tentatively.

"Well, it's not a boob job if that's what you're worried about. I know you hate them." So far, so good. But I must be careful here.

"I don't understand. If it's not a boob job, what is it?" I ask, cautiously.

"It's called the Brava System. It's a revolutionary new way of increasing your breast size without surgical enhancement." I can't help noticing that she says this as if directly reading the bumph straight off the side of the packet. But cynicism aside, I'm all ears.

"Go on then, explain," I say, moving back to the bed to sit down.

"Well, I don't know what it entails fully, yet," she says, sitting up. "But there's no surgery and they pretty much guarantee success. Also, there are loads of positive testimonials on their website. So I thought: no harm in just finding out about it, right?"

"And it's just a consultation? No monies exchanging hands?"

"You know me and money. Being half-Scottish means I'm not easily parted with it. So, if that's what you're worried about, don't be."

"Hey, it's your money you can do what you want with it. If you think getting bigger breasts will make you happier then go for it. Just answer me one question. This desire for bigger breasts – it isn't anything to do with all our conversations is it?" She only hesitates for a split-second, but it's enough time to tell me what I already suspect.

"No, this is about me and how I feel about myself."

I take this to mean: "No, this is about me and how you have made me feel about myself." But just for a second she looks over at me and something unrecognisable crosses her face. It makes her look vulnerable in a way I've not seen before. "Rob?"

"Yeah."

"I know I ..." she says, clamming up.

"What?"

"I ... it's just, well ... nothing."

"What do you mean 'nothing'?"

"No, really, it's nothing."

When Jenny gets back from her consultation the following Tuesday, she's quite animated. She finds me in the bedroom, trying to read the Sports Monthly from last Sunday's *Observer* magazine. Almost immediately, I sum up her mood and put the magazine down. I'm not going to be able to get away with reading it whilst spouting out the odd monosyllabic answer.

Jenny is chirping like a modern day Moses who has been shown the way to the Promised Land of increased, cup-related size. Her excitement doesn't diminish as she explains the exorbitant cost of the system. Let's just say, you can have the surgery for around the same money. I wonder how she can justify spending that kind of money – but still, I guess it is her money, and at the end of the day, how do you put a price on feeling better about yourself?

Anyway, I needn't have worried about the cost – Jenny has no intention of spending that much. Instead she goes on eBay and buys it for a tenth of the price.

Half-Scottish indeed.

The Brava System arrived by courier today and Jenny is talking me through the procedure. We are, apparently, going live tonight. Already I've gleaned enough information to know that all this fuss isn't going to be worth the effort, especially if you look at it from my point of view – which to be honest, is just about the only one that matters to me.

It turns out that the Brava System is nothing more than two huge, rigid, see-through plastic domes, which wouldn't be out of place in a very bad 1950s science-fiction 'B' movie.

The first piece of bad news – in a bulletin that reads like an extremely tragic day at Sky News– is that in order to achieve 'optimum results', it has to be worn ten hours a day for ten weeks. This must be done without a break. Now, it's pretty obvious that, unless Jenny wants to walk around looking like Lara Croft's deformed older sister while she's at work, she can only get that kind of wear time in bed. This leads me to conclude that for the next ten weeks I'm going to have to sleep next to Wythenshawe's answer to *Barbarella*.

Misery loves company. Jenny has also informed me that she doesn't want the boys to know that she's wearing it. This in itself is fair enough – who would want their sons to know that their mother is a lunatic who will be hiding in her bedroom from nine o'clock until seven in the morning trying to grow a bigger pair of tits? But the ramifications of this are not lost on me. It means that any teenage-related kick-offs taking place after nine in the evening will have to be dealt with by yours truly. I love her and it's my role to show support for her at this difficult time, but I'll do it with all the relish that Oats must have felt when he told Captain Scott he was "… going outside and might be some time".

It's four o'clock in the morning and Brava has been live for 12 hours. On this, the first night of what I've already christened 'Living with Brava', I have discerned that the whole thing is going to be even worse than I had previously imagined. I'm used to looking at things from the worst possible angle. It's just that when I looked at the Brava System from the worst possible angle it turned out that it was just about the best possible angle available.

Get this: Jenny has to sleep on her back the whole night. Obvious really – sleeping on one side or the stomach with a huge pair of plastic tits attached would be a tad difficult, but it means that, although it's mid-winter and I'm freezing, I have less chance of a cuddle than George Bush in a Guantanamo Bay prison cell. This wouldn't be so bad if I were someone who preferred their own space, but I'm not, and neither is Jenny. We sleep together on the space of a postage stamp, usually on my side of the bed, and she fits me like a glove that's been knitted by a grandmother who dotes on you and still thinks you're seven. So the thought of spending ten weeks apart isn't a pleasant one.

Worse still, although it's only the first night of 'Living with Brava', I've been woken up 36 times already. Let me explain.

The scientific principle on which the Brava System is based upon is suction. Breast tissue cells are supposed to replicate themselves in response to suction – really. As Jenny has purchased a cheaper version of

151

the system, she literally has to suck her tits up through a plastic tube to expand them to a much larger size. The plastic 'bra-thingy', to give it a technical name, should then hold them in the enlarged position all night. Over a period of time – ten whole weeks to be precise – they will become stretched into a permanently larger size.

Well, that's the theory, anyway. The reality is that air frequently squirts out of the sides of the 'bra-thingy' in large batches, which means that anyone sleeping within a 20 foot radius is woken at irregular intervals by a large pair of farting tits. And that isn't the end of it.

The system has one more shock in store for the unsuspecting male. After every loud fart, Jenny needs to get her breasts back into the enlarged state, and the method by which this is achieved is, of course, suction.

A tube lies flaccidly on her chest, and Jenny has to bring her head forward to suck on it; the other end is attached to the 'bra-thingy'. Watching her re-inflate her tits is a little like watching a prostrate, semi-naked air hostess giving birth, whilst simultaneously showing you how to inflate your life jacket.

Obviously, we sleep in the dark, so it's not watching the bizarre re-inflationary ritual that really troubles me. It's hearing yet another large fart whilst desperately trying to get some shut-eye, then waiting for the sound of her sucking on that godforsaken tube. I kid you not, it sounds like a flock of vampires feeding on a small, helpless puppy. In other words, it's the least erotic sound I've ever heard in my life.

After another large tit-fart and yet another suck, I eventually fall into a sleep that's unbroken by any more ungodly noises, until the alarm goes off at seven. Jenny leaps up almost as soon as it sounds, and I, through the haze of my much-interrupted sleep, faintly recognise the outline of her body and her hands grabbing at the 'bra-thingy'. As she makes an almighty pull at it, the thing makes a swishing sound – like a door opening on a tube train – which heralds the bra's death knell and it falls lifelessly to the floor.

With no small relief, I turn over hoping to catch a few more minutes of sleep, but that isn't to be. Jenny leaps back into bed and grabs my hand. "Feel that!" she says excitedly.

It has to be said, ten hours of satanic suction have created a much larger lady than I previously remember. As my hand squeezes her temporarily enlarged mammary I also become temporarily enlarged in a sexual area. For the first time, I see at least one small benefit to the many sleepless nights to come. I turn round quickly. "Oh my God. Come on down Dolly Parton!"

"Hardly," she laughs.

"I'll do it hardly or softly, just let me know."

"Rob!"

As my luck would have it, the benefits are short lasting. By tea-time, Jenny has shrunk back to her usual size and the process starts again. The negatives are yet to be exhausted.

During the week, Jenny has to be in bed with her fake tits by nine in the evening - without fail - which doesn't leave much opportunity for a social life, not to mention a sex life. Sex switches from an evening pursuit to an exclusively morning activity.

Jenny also cuts herself away from her beloved boys. Our bedroom door is permanently locked for their own protection (God knows the psychological trauma that her plastic tits could inflict on a healthy, teenage boy), but on those occasions when they genuinely need her, Jenny has to pull the sheets up to her chin and talk to them like the demented role-playing wolf in Little Red Riding Hood. Thankfully, none of the boys ever gets to utter the line, "what big tits you have grandma."

Finally, the blisters start to appear. The Brava people predicted that the silicone rim of a big, plastic bra might cause irritation when pressed against the skin for ten hours a day. So they provided special wipes to form a barrier and prevent blistering. Jenny runs out of wipes and finds they can only be purchased from America at an extortionate cost, with a shipping delay of up to three weeks – but she is undeterred.

After three days without wipes – and resembling a victim in a burn's unit – she finds a solution to the problem. Rather than give up and just say to herself, "ah well. I've got small tits and that's that" she takes the elevator up to the penthouse of madness and resorts to smearing a thick layer of Johnson's nappy-rash cream on every square inch of her breasts. This renders her tits completely white. I'm forced to admire two huge plastic domes with what looks like the snow-covered peaks of the Himalayas inside. A ritual that she puts herself through nightly.

In the end, we both endure the plastic tits for the full ten weeks. To her relief, and mine, it does actually work and her tits are slightly bigger – although I'm not sure if it was worth it. I can't have imagined anything worse but then, perhaps, I don't have much of an imagination.

Chapter 23

The Director's Cut

Apart from the fact that we're constantly bickering over my perverted behaviour, and that Jenny's grown a new pair of tits, things couldn't be better. I'm not even mildly surprised, then, when Jenny adds to the ever growing list of things to worry about.

Apparently, she's begun to have what can only be described as gynaecological *issues*. These have also started to interfere with our sex life. The problems culminate in a visit to her GP today and, as a consequence, in some rather distressing news. Not that Jenny seems even slightly concerned about the whole matter – she isn't. But then she has no reason to be distressed because she hasn't received any really bad news.

No, the really bad news is all mine.

As the only time anyone seems able to see an NH doctor between nine and five these days is when they are on the point of dying, or dead, Jenny had a six o'clock appointment. When she returns I'm in bed trying to catch 40 winks after a hard day on a training course. "How did it go?" I say, sitting up. "Everything okay?"

"Nothing to worry about really," she says, taking her coat off. "Just a problem with my age and the pill – apparently, they don't go together."

"Oh, right. Good. Nothing to worry about then?" She comes over to the bed and gives me a light kiss on the cheek. I grab her waist with my arm and pull her down on to the bed.

"I can't," she says smiling. "I have to make the boys' tea."

"I've already done that. Anyway, they're all out, except Daniel. He's in his room asleep – at least, he was when I last looked." With this I begin to squeeze her breast lightly with my left hand, while my right moves to the zip on her short skirt.

"Don't Rob. I need to talk about what we're going to do," she says firmly.

"Do about what?" I say perplexed.

"About the fact that I'm coming off the pill."

"Well, obviously, we'll have to be careful?"

"Careful! I'm not talking about a quick spin in the car down the motorway here Rob. I'm talking about my body. The last thing you or I want, at our age, is a child."

"I know. So we'll take precautions,"

"What precautions? I'm coming off the pill and you can't use a condom. So just what precautions are you talking about?" That's a good

154

question – especially when you consider I don't have a clue what precautions I'm talking about.

"Well, I'll have to make sure I don't come when we do it." It's all I can think of saying.

"Don't be ridiculous Rob. We can't have a normal sex life like that." On saying this she takes my hand and gives it a little squeeze. Oh no. Something bad is coming.

"Look, Rob. We could always get you done." I think about this for about a nanosecond.

"Get me done? You're talking like I'm some randy show horse that's terrifying all the ponies. 'Get me done!' I'm not having anything done and that's that."

"But why not? You know it makes sense. Give me one good reason."

"Here's a good one: I don't want anyone near my knob with a knife. How's that for a good reason?"

"Seriously – is that what you think?" she says, smiling, "because they don't go anywhere near your penis and it's virtually painless."

"Well, it would be for you. I'll give you that much. No. There's got to be another way."

"Well, yeah, there is. I could have an operation, but there are more complications for women than men. So it makes more sense for you to get done." She pauses. I look away from her.

"You don't want any more kids and neither do I. And you like sex as much as I do, Rob. So really, you can at least think it over." She says this in such a way that I have no choice – I will have to 'think it over'. But thinking something over doesn't mean doing it, does it?

It does.

So I'm sitting in my GP's surgery two weeks later, waiting for the little red light to buzz and for the less than helpful receptionist to call my name out.

Over the last two weeks, Jenny has slowly convinced me that there is no other solution. She's right. I love sex. I love her. So what can I do?

My name is called half an hour after my appointment time, but I don't complain. After all, it's not as if I'm in any rush. I get up and follow the signs to Dr Triplett's room. To be truthful, I'm not really worried at this point because I know how long the NHS takes to click into gear in these matters. I figure it will be six months before I get an appointment to actually see anyone and then another six months before anyone gets to hack at my tackle. So, all in all, I figure I have about a year's grace.

When I enter, Triplett is typing away on his computer. Probably on Excel and working out if he can afford a second Ferrari now the new GP contracts have kicked in. "Sit down," he bellows, in that way that doctors do. "How are you?"

"Fine," I say, sitting in the chair he's pointing to and feeling like a fraud.

"What can I do for you?"

"Well, my partner has had to come off the pill and at our age -"

"You don't want any more children." He gets my file up on screen and stares at it like he has just discovered the lost Arc of the Covenant in its bowels. After two or three painful minutes of silence and humming he informs me, "You're 39". Wow! This guy's good. No wonder they pay them so much money. I can't figure out if it's a question or a statement, so I keep quiet. "Makes perfect sense," he continues. "Okay, we use a local service. I'll pass on your details and they'll contact you shortly by post." I don't know if I like the use of the word 'shortly' so I investigate.

"When you say 'shortly', can you give me an estimate?"

"A couple of weeks." Arghhh! Mind you, thinking about the speed that the NHS works, that still leaves me six months plus a couple of weeks.

"Okay thanks," I say, getting up out of the chair. "But ... just one more thing."

"Yes?"

"Does it hurt?"

"No, it's virtually painless." God! Is that woman ever wrong about anything?

When I get back in from work on the following Wednesday I find Jenny in an excited mood. She has in her hand a letter from Kenton's Family Planning. We have an appointment there next Tuesday. Apparently they're experiencing a bit of a slow period in the demand for snips and '... are able to fit us in at short notice'.

"Isn't it lucky?" she states, all too enthusiastically waving it around.

"Yes, isn't it?"

The following Tuesday Jenny and I make our way to the family planning clinic. An odd name, don't you think? Especially when the complete opposite is true. I mean, you're definitely not planning a family when turning up to one of these places.

As we enter the building Jenny grips my arm, ostensibly because it's cold, but I also have the feeling I'm being frogmarched. She's taking no chances.

Inside, a no-nonsense receptionist greets us. After a couple of minutes she gets us coffee, sits us down in a bleak, whitewashed room and gives us a questionnaire and some patient information leaflets. Jenny gets straight down to reading the stuff like she's cramming for her finals in 'Vasectometry'.

Meanwhile, I stare vacantly around the room and ponder how many goals I might score on Sunday. Ignoring me, Jenny gets a pen and starts to fill in the questionnaire with far too much enthusiasm for my liking. From time to time she stops to ask me a question to which I respond in a monosyllabic tone, and mostly without thinking. Eventually she finishes and I get a hand squeeze for my troubles.

After about 15 minutes the receptionist comes in, picks up the questionnaire and asks us to follow her. We end up in an even duller room. This time we're talking to some pseudo-psychiatrist who is attempting to make a diagnosis of my current state of mind in order to ascertain that I 'understand everything'. I say 'pseudo' because if she had even a basic grasp of psychiatry she would realise that:

A) I need to be sent home for six months to think about this some more.

B) She'd be on a lot more fertile ground chatting to Jenny about her tits.

Instead, she's thumbing through her diary trying to find a suitable appointment date while chatting away to Jenny like the two of them don't have a care in the world; which, when you think about it, *they* don't. "Okay, how about this Saturday?" says the pseudo-psyche.

"Eh?" I say, almost falling off my chair. "Err ... I can't. I have a big match on Sunday. It's too late to let everyone down. Steve will go mad at such short notice." I look over at Jenny, pleadingly.

"No. Sorry. It's a bit soon. He's only just getting used to the idea. He needs a little more time." Thank God for that. Jenny has gone to bat for me on this one. She totally gets the sacrifice I'm making and has realised that I need a couple of months to get my head round things.

"Okay then," says the psych, thumbing through a diary. "What about the following Saturday?" I look at Jenny, horrified, but she merely turns back to the psych.

"Yeah. That'll be great." With this, they both look at me – at least, they look at a part of me. They both stare down at my right hand, which has inadvertently found its way down the front of my trousers and is holding on to my knob for dear life.

When I get back the first thing I do is phone Steve to let him know I won't be around for the game a week on Sunday. "But you're having it done on the Saturday," he argues.

"Yes, I know! So there's no way I can play the following day."

"But we need you: the bet." He's right. They do need me. I'm playing better than ever. I'm tackling harder, running faster and shooting harder. In short: I'm doing a Gazza. I'm taking the frustrations of my personal life on court with me and making them work for me. The sheer irony's not lost on me I can tell you.

"You're only playing B+Q," I remind him.

"Yeah, but it could turn a bit nasty."

157

"Steve, there's not a player under 55 in that team and they play in 'Happy to Help' T-shirts. Just how nasty could it get?"

"Yeah, well, we don't want to break up the consistency of team selection. It's important; any good manager would tell you that," he moans.

"Think of it as a rotation policy; one followed by all the big clubs. Anyway, I can't play. It's highly unlikely I'll be able to walk." He makes one last, futile effort.

"Rob, do I need to remind you? We're only level on points with Drysdale's lot and we have the big game in a few weeks. It'll likely settle the bet."

"Well, you should've thought about that before you made it. Anyway, I'm off. I'm sure you can appreciate, I've got more important things on my mind right now than your stupid bet." As I slam the phone down it doesn't occur to me that I'm displaying all the tetchiness of a heterosexual male who's about to have another man fiddle with his bits.

Over the course of the next week, I badger Jenny for all the information I should by now already know, but don't. As usual, she takes it all in her stride and I can, at least, now temporarily worry about something else other than where our relationship is going. "But what if it goes wrong?" I ask her.

"It only goes wrong one time in a thousand."

"What if I'm that one time?"

"You won't be."

"What if I can't come anymore?"

"That won't be a problem. You'll be able to come normally."

"What if it feels different without any come?"

"It doesn't feel any different. Harry had it done and it wasn't any different. And he was as misinformed as you. You still produce seminal fluid. You just don't have any sperm in it. Why do all men think that you don't come normally?"

"What if I need my sperm?"

And so on.

I have to say she's been a bit of a rock for me, putting up with it all. It's like she said though, "it's easy, because I've already had to deal with one big daft baby; having another one's no different."

So it's Saturday and here I am, in a drab, northern NHS hospital with Jenny beside me and my nerves in a knot. The waiting room is full of us: middle-aged guys all looking nervously at each other. Most of us have a partner holding our hands and we're all thinking the same thing, but no one is actually saying anything. Each one of us would, at this moment, probably take a three-day, all-inclusive city break to Baghdad if we were offered it as an alternative.

158

"Look, are you sure you want me to go through with this?" I whisper in Jenny's ear. "It's not too late to change your mind." She giggles.

"I bet you don't even feel it when they do it."

"Yeah right! John at work was limping for weeks."

"They all say that. It's nonsense. You won't even know it's been done."

When they call my name, I take a last anxious look at Jenny, who looks right back into my eyes and tries to give me the most reassuring smile since Adam said to Eve, "you sure God won't be arsed if I take a bite?"

A young, pretty nurse appears at my side. She takes me to a booth and pulls a green curtain across its entrance. The interior gives a new meaning to the word sterile. There's me, a shitty NHS trolley-bed and a chair. God knows how anyone is going to perform life-endangering major surgery on me in here. I seriously consider making a run for it at this point. Jenny couldn't blame me if I did. I reckon I'd be more likely to get a better job done by one of those witch doctors in Nigeria than in here. At least those guys know what they're doing; they do hundreds a year. And the facilities would have to be better than this.

The nurse hands me a green bundle. "Take all your clothes off please Mr Smith and then put this robe on."

Now, I can't even tell you how many fantasies I've had involving an attractive young nurse asking me to take my clothes off. It's just typical of my luck that the reality would have to be in circumstances such as these. I smile weakly in her direction. "Don't worry," she says, clearly picking up on my body language. "Doctor's very good and it's all over in a few seconds. When you're ready, lie down on the bed. Someone will be along shortly."

She breezes out of the booth and I'm left with the 'robe'. I say 'robe', but it looks more like my gran's old washing-up apron. I reckon that when I put it on I'll look like one of the patients from *One Flew Over the Cuckoo's Nest*. I take off my clothes slowly, put on the robe and look down at myself. I think it's fair to say that Vodafone's mobile coverage in Siberia is probably better than the coverage I'm getting from this robe. Despondently, I go over to the bed, lie down and wait.

Two minutes later, I get the shock of my life. The curtain pulls back and another nurse enters the booth. This one is definitely *not* as pleasing to the eye. But it's not her looks I'm concerned with here. No. It's the fact she's carrying a bowl and a very large, shaving razor. "Right," she says, pulling the curtain back across. "I'm going to give you a quick shave my love."

"Eh?" I grunt, the horror of what is about to happen only just beginning to dawn on me.

"I said: I'm just going to give you a quick shave."

It's clear that she thinks she's talking to a mental patient. To be fair, who could blame her? With my nonsensical reply, and my appearance in the robe, I am doing a fair approximation of one. "Is this really necessary?" I ask, playing for time.

"No lovey. I just like doing this sort of thing. Now let's have look."

I don't even have enough time to be irritated by her sarcasm before she's taken my tackle in one hand and a shaving brush in the other. I never could have imagined that having a woman take your knob in her hand could be so un-erotic.

Up until this moment in my life I guess I never really knew what true humiliation was. But now I can give you a really good definition: true humiliation is lying on a hospital trolley with just a green, washing-up apron on and your tackle firmly in the hands of nurse, who looks like a Bulgarian shot putter, while she shaves your pubes off. Oh! And you might want to add having the nurse say, "don't worry son, I've shaved much bigger than this," as she does it.

Two minutes later the harridan departs, taking her bowl, the razor and half of my Sherwood Forest with her. Thirty years I've spent cultivating that and she's dispensed with it with all the proficiency of a Brazilian cattle farmer setting fire to his fiftieth rainforest. I would like to think that it couldn't get any worse than this, but, of course, it can. Very soon a doctor will be coming in to rearrange my tackle; probably with some large scalpel, or something worse.

Two minutes after that, I'm proved wrong about the scalpel, but right about the something worse, as the nurse, cheery as can be I might add, waltzes back in. This in itself would be bad enough, but she's holding a very large needle in her right hand. Judging by the look on her face she also seems to be enjoying herself. "Right my love. Lift up your robe."

"You've got to be kidding me!"

"Doctor needs it to be numb."

"Don't worry – just looking at that, and thinking what you might do with it, it couldn't possibly be anything else." She doesn't even crack the faintest of smiles. Instead she dives straight in.

"Just a little prick."

I'm still not entirely sure what she was referring to.

I'm lying here terrified, but now with the added joy of having icy-cold bollocks. The needle felt like someone had just pumped half the Arctic Ocean into my gonads. I couldn't be more numb if someone had just told me Charlotte was the milkman's daughter.

Still, I only have to wait a few minutes before the doctor finally shows up. To my relief, he's not carrying any gigantic scalpels – not that I can see, anyway – and seems fairly relaxed about the whole thing. "Right, Mr

Smith. Not taking any medicines and have no family history of any of these on the list?"

"No. Can I just ask is this going to hurt? Only I was thinking that maybe -"

"Nothing to worry about at all. Maybe a little soreness for a day or two, that's all."

"What about time off work?" I say, hoping beyond hope, for a few weeks off – I may as well salvage something positive from this disaster.

"Well, stay off on Monday if you feel a little tender. Otherwise, you should be okay by Tuesday." Typical. Still, at least I won't have to face Monday morning briefing.

"Right, let's have a look," he says, as if about to view a new buy-to-let flat he's thinking of purchasing. I feel his fumbling fingers on my leg and then nothing. I get a little worried in case he can't locate anything. Then I start to worry about the operation. What if it goes wrong? A cold shudder passes down my spine at the thought, but even that is nowhere near as cold as my balls.

Seconds later, his head is up and out of my gown and he appears very tickety-boo. "Good. Yes. That's fine."

"So you think you can do it then?" I say, desperately hoping he's located a problem and is about to call the whole thing off.

"Sorry?" he replies blankly, as if, maybe, I've just asked him if consultants declare all their income from private work to the exchequer.

"Do you think there are likely to be any problems during the operation?" I ask.

"I'm sorry, you don't seem to understand. I have just performed the operation. It's done. You can go home."

"But, I didn't feel ..."

Jenny doesn't say a thing on the way home in the car, but there's just the faintest of smiles at the corners of her mouth.

Chapter 24

Airport

Right now our relationship boat couldn't be rocking any more if it was Bill Haley and the Comets' personal river boat. It's the Easter holidays and Jenny and I are going off to southern Spain. We're hoping the break will take our minds off everything.

I'm not sure how we arrived at the decision to take a break, even though Jenny keeps telling me how amazing I am for suggesting it. I don't recall even having the idea in the first place. Somewhere along the line, I think I've been manipulated – again – but the idea does seem like a good one.

As far as I'm concerned, anything that will give us a break from Brava systems and my problem of inadvertently trying to view the Great British Tit is a good thing.

There are other problems it might give us a break from, too, such as my relationship with Jenny's boys. I've been tetchy lately, what with all the recent issues, and some of my irritability has spilt over into my relationships with them. I've been snapping and moaning at them far more than I used to. Not that they've said anything to Jenny – most of the time they're too busy just being teenagers to worry about my changing moods – but I worry.

And I'm not the only one to worry. Steve's worried when I tell him about my planned sojourn in the pub, after a hard fought 3-2 victory over *Civil Service Vets*. That result kept us level with *The IT Crowd* on points and meant that the £500 was still very much up for grabs.

Yes, the holiday doesn't play too well with Steve. "I can't believe it," he moans, blowing hard out of his mouth. "Two weeks holiday. And right in the middle of the bet with Drysdale."

"It's ten days," I inform him, flicking my finger aimlessly at a tatty beermat on the table in front of me. "I'll only miss one game: the return with *B+Q*. Who, need I remind you, you beat seven-nil last time without me."

"But you'll be back for the big one," he implores.

"I'll be back for the big one. That £500's not going to end up as Dryslade's takeaway budget for the next month." His eyes sparkle at my quip and he chugs the last remnants of beer from the bottom of his glass.

"Another?"

"Nah, best not, mate. I'm getting off. Text me with the result on Sunday will you. Not that I'm sweating too much."

162

"Will do. Don't hammer the beer while you're away. You can do that when you get back and Drysdale's paying. I want you in shape for two weeks tonight."

"Aye aye, skip!" I laugh.

We are flying to Spain on the Tuesday. The ten day break is not the first holiday I'd had with the boys. We'd previously been on holiday during Christmas week when we took the youngest two to Penrith Center Parcs – a place so adept at parting you from your hard earned cash that it warrants the moniker 'Blackpool for the Middle Classes'. Being in Center Parcs is almost the same as being in a permanent state of just having woken up after the office Christmas party. That is to say: you know you spent lots of money yesterday, but for the life of you, you can't remember how you spent it.

Before this particular short break I'd been under the laboured misapprehension that holidays were meant to be relaxing and fun. My first memory of the holiday is of Jenny deciding to pack three hours before we were due to set off. "Right," she said, looking at the two boys in the back seat. "Remember, it's going to be at least two hours before we get to Penrith and we're not stopping before we get there."

We had only driven 300 yards to the bottom of the street before she promptly advised me that Daniel hadn't eaten. We then drove another 600 yards to MacDonald's drive-in to buy two cheeseburger meals. So much for not stopping.

For the purposes of sanity, and avoidance of stress levels equivalent to an air traffic controller on a bank holiday weekend, we left Curtis at his nan's, which is exactly where he will be staying at for the next two weeks. This arrangement suits Curtis fine as his nan dotes on him.

So on the fifth of April, and 14 months after we first met, we find ourselves getting ready to leave. We're late, which is incredible because we only live two minutes away from the airport and you'd have thought that being late for an airport you live only two minutes away from might be a bit difficult. Not with Jenny. I've once again discovered that Jenny, unlike Rebecca – who creates a list the moment we book a holiday and runs everything with military precision – doesn't even think about packing until the actual morning of the holiday. And even then she only *thinks* about it.

This can be a tad stressful when you have an 11 a.m. flight. And my stress levels are cranked up even further by the fact that as the boys have no concept of space or time. They're not particularly stressed by proceedings either. This leaves the whole job of being stressed to me. And, credit where it's due, I'm good at it.

The boys are oblivious to everything. The youngest one wanders through the whole event in a daydream. His only concern is that his lie-in has been disrupted. Daniel just crawls from bed to couch and promptly goes back to sleep. "He's just stressed," says Jenny evenly.

"Yeah! So I see," I snap.

"No really. It's just a coping strategy."

"I wish he'd lend it to me."

"You don't need it. You have me," she smiles, leaning over to kiss me. "I'm your coping strategy."

"Well, I'm not coping so you'd better wake him up."

Meanwhile, the youngest one sits at his computer talking on MSN to some of his friends who presumably haven't even gone to bed yet. I decide that he can't get off scot-free. My stress levels climb sky-high whenever I see him sitting there, making his usual contribution to any jobs that need doing. I give him a sarcastic smile. "You okay? Don't get too stressed."

"Yeah, fine. Cheers Rob." His voice is so cheerful that it serves only to indicate that my attempt at sarcasm has gone so far over his head it's currently in danger of hitting an overhead plane. I glance down at his computer, at which point he looks up at me and closes the MSN window. It's not like I have any idea what he's writing. The whole screen looks like some lost ancient Egyptian hieroglyphics to me, so now I'm having an attack of paranoia. Is the sneaky little git writing something about me? I storm out. I really hope somebody writes the book *MSN for Adults* one day.

Jenny, meanwhile, is ever so calmly pottering around the house like she's doing a bit of casual late night shopping in the Tesco Metro. She's exuding the kind of serenity that would make Mother Theresa look like a psycho. She calmly organises everyone and everything in her path, occasionally stopping to utter the odd pearl of assurance in my direction.

'It's fine.' 'All in hand.' 'No need to panic.' 'Rob calm down.'

At some point, someone asks who's picking us up to take us to the airport. I shift my glance to Jenny. "Who is picking us up?"

"Good question," she replies.

"You're joking, right?"

"No, I'm not."

"But ..." Jenny does not think that this will be a problem.

"Don't panic. There will be loads of taxis at this time in the morning."

We phone. There are no taxis. Still, she's totally unfazed.

"Right, Chris. Run along to Brian's and knock him up. Tell him we need a lift to the airport and we'll make it worth his while." Somehow she's galvanised the youngest one into actually doing something.

He sets off towards a neighbour's house and I notice Daniel still sleeping on the couch. I aim a light kick at him. "Rob, don't be pathetic – leave him alone," she says firmly.

164

"Why do we have to be late for every single thing we ever do?" She leans over and gently kisses me on my cheek.

"Yeah, but you love me." Eventually we're in Brian's taxi with about ten minutes to final check-in.

Now, being late for planes, especially when you've forked out three grand to catch one, is just one of many things guaranteed to bring out that side of my character that Rebecca named 'Fawlty'.

As Brian, the taxi driving neighbour, takes us on the perilous two minute ride to the airport, I am at this moment in full 'Fawlty' mode. "Brilliant! Two minutes away and we're going to miss the plane."

"Rob, calm down. We're not going to miss the plane," Jenny says, looking in one of those little budgie mirrors and putting on her lipstick. "We've got ten minutes to check in. That's plenty of time."

"How is that plenty of time? I mean, how is it?"

"It is. Just leave it to me when we get to the airport. I'll sort it out."

"Sort it out? You're going to sort it out? Brilliant! What, the cases and everything? I don't have to do anything?"

"Don't be silly. You just get the cases with the boys and I'll get us checked in."

"How are you going to do that? This is one of the busiest days of the year. The queues will be massive. There will be people everywhere."

"Maybe there won't." This is Jenny's usual *glass half full* philosophy. As you've probably figured my philosophy isn't so much *glass half empty* as: *glass completely empty and the bar shut half an hour ago.*

Still, I continue to witter on. I can't help it – I'm not such a good flyer at the best of times (although I'm better than I was), but being so close to the edge of missing the flight is just piling it on. "Have you got the passports? Don't tell me you've forgotten the passports," I say.

"I have the passports."

"And the tickets?"

"And the tickets." I catch the boy's mesmerised stares. They're looking at me like two three-year-olds who've just been introduced to their mum's new, crack-addicted boyfriend. I flash a nervous looking smile in their direction and they return it in spades.

Eventually the taxi pulls up at the airport. Jenny pays Brian and I charge off inside like a headless chicken. Sure enough, once inside, each check-in desk sports a queue that wouldn't shame that at Lenin's state funeral, but this does not perturb Miss *glass half full*. She walks to the front of a very long queue, whispers something into the check-in girl's ear and, within a moment, we're being ushered to the front of the queue.

We all try to ignore the indignant mutterings of those passengers who realise what's going on. It's a well-known fact that airport check-in girls are composed of frozen, helium gas and have no emotions that function

165

above absolute zero, so quite how we get to the front remains a mystery – at least, until we pass through security to airside. Here I'm a little more relaxed as she tells me how she did it.

"I just told them that Daniel was going to go hypo and if they wanted to avoid a medical emergency we needed to get through to airside to eat." Ah! Daniel and his diabetes; he can have his uses.

Once we're airside we all set about our own personal routines. I go to WHSmith's to look for a book that will take me ages to locate and which I won't get round to reading on the holiday, anyway. These days, I just re-read Stephen King and Irvine Welch, but I still buy a couple of books that I'll never read.

Jenny comes with me and makes for the magazines before joining me to buy books. And it goes without saying that she does this more successfully than I do.

Daniel hangs round us obsessing about eating. You can't blame him for this, but combined with his Asperger's it frays the nerves as quickly as a ride on *The Big One* at Blackpool Pleasure Beach. When he gets like this Jenny calls it being 'on one' and when he's 'on one' it's best for all and sundry to stay well clear. He hovers around our shoulders like a wasp on a Cornetto. "Err … probably need to eat around now," he informs us. "It's probably time to eat."

Fortunately, Jenny's had years of on-the-job training in dealing with this. "Yes Daniel. We will eat shortly. You've had breakfast and you're not due to eat for a little while."

"It's just … you know … best if I eat shortly, innit?"

"Right Daniel. Just let me and Rob get a book first."

"'Cos I need, really, to keep my blood sugar up, innit?"

"Yes Daniel. I understand you need to keep your blood sugar levels up, and we will eat. Now just let me buy a book."

"I have not taken my insulin though innit?"

"You can take it when I buy you a sandwich in a minute."

"I need a sandwich really, you know, for my blood sugar innit? Nice fresh ham sandwich because I feel a bit hypo." He feels a bit hypo whenever it suits him. Children are devious gits and will find uses for even the most serious of life's little setbacks.

I head for the far side of the shop where I see the youngest one through the window and he's heading for the arcades. I can't help thinking he's got it right. Stay well away when Daniel gets 'on one'.

Ten minutes later, the three of us are sitting in one of those airport cafes we've all been in. This particular one is trying to create the ambience of the Old Wild West. In reality, it's merely a BAA monopoly rip-off that would make Center Parcs look like good value. Daniel is no longer 'on one' due to the fact that he's shuffling a 'Triple-Decker, Wild West

Trailblazer Ham and Cheese Toastie', (£5.99!) down his neck, and sipping on a large 'Rio Grande' diet coke. (£3.99!) Still, as Jenny wisely proclaims, "It's worth every penny."

I'm also beginning to chill as I down my second bottle of 'Gunslinger' lager and calmly watch while Jenny destroys a 'Ranch Hand Burger' and a medium diet coke.

Five minutes later, the youngest one joins us to announce he's lost £15 of the £20 his dad gave him on the slot machines. A kerfuffle follows, which sees him stripped of the remaining £5 by Jenny. I glance up at the board.

Oh no! The final call for the plane has been made and guess what?

We're late! We start to run the two miles to gate 58.

Four hours later and we're safely ensconced in a luxury four-star all-inclusive hotel. It's an apart-hotel so we're sharing an apartment with the two boys. About five minutes ago the youngest one disappeared with some newly found friends. He has a tendency to make 'friends' as quickly as a playboy model on a stag weekend. So I'm confident we won't be seeing much of him for the rest of our stay. Daniel is muttering to himself about the limited amount of carbohydrate Spanish food is likely to contain. This is because we're about to go down for tea and he's stressing about the changes to his diet. I just hope they have lots of spicy beef pizza on the menu so that we can all catch a lucky break.

I've showered and changed and I'm in the kitchen, waiting patiently for Jenny to join us, but I have to admit – I'm feeling a bit stressed. Unfortunately, it's nothing to do with the possible absence of spicy beef pizza on the hotel menu. Since we arrived, Jenny's been acting a bit odd. There's something wrong, but it's nothing I can put my finger on; she's just not herself. I'm not getting the cold shoulder treatment – not yet – but she isn't acting like the warm and friendly girl I fell in love with.

I wonder if I've been staring at anyone's tits inadvertently. I feel quite paranoid about it, but that's how the whole thing's affecting me. Her behaviour, or my behaviour, depending on where you stand, has me on a roller coaster these last few months and I'm really beginning to feel the strain.

She comes out of the bedroom, looking fabulous in a short, pink skirt, high heels and matching cut-off top. She plays with her hair in the mirror and applies a touch of lipstick, then turns to Daniel and says, "You got your insulin?"

"Yeah. Got me insulin, innit?"

"Have you done your blood today?" This question always produces an inaudible chuntering whenever he hasn't, and that's what he starts to do now. Jenny ignores him with a sigh and turns brusquely in the direction of the door. "Okay guys let's go and get some tea. I'm starving."

167

Without looking in my direction, she leaves the room.

Daniel points to his arm and I nod, then the two of us trail after her like schoolboys being taken to the head's office. I can't help thinking it's going to be a long holiday.

But, in the end, it's not as long as I think.

Chapter 25

Sayonara

I'm sitting alone on the bed, in the apart-hotel bedroom with my head buried in my hands. This isn't right. I shouldn't be sitting by myself. This is supposed to be a holiday, although right now, I'm questioning that definition. I'm on my own, because 15 minutes ago Jenny left me here, presumably to go for a very large drink - which I wouldn't mind having myself at the moment, but I think it's best if I skip it.

I conjure up an image of her sitting in the bar downstairs, drinking relentlessly to dull the pain. The pain that I've caused her; the pain that she's caused herself.

As you can guess, things have come to a head and I'm sitting here now, reflecting on the fact that I Jenny thinks I'm a pervert. It's been proved beyond all reasonable doubt as far as she's concerned.

For the first few days of the holiday I managed to hide my true nature from the world. Yes, I did glance at a group of bikini-clad young girls around the pool area, but there wasn't enough evidence to bring a case against me on that. I managed to mount a reasonable defence, whilst playing cards on Saturday evening. Jenny, lead counsel for the prosecution, reluctantly dropped the case. But today I've been tried and convicted on the charge of being a total pervert.

The scene of the crime is the small, hotel gym. The gym is usually quiet during the afternoon, mainly due to the July heat of the Costa del Sol. Only mad dogs and Englishmen go out into the midday gym – even if it does boast air conditioning. Most people would think you'd have to be a bit of an idiot to go in the gym at this time of day. Whilst I may, or may not be, a bit of an idiot I have, nevertheless, taken to coming here. This is because it's the one area of the complex where there are no scantily-dressed, young women that I might inadvertently stare at.

Jenny usually comes with me to work out her 'fat belly'. It feels nice to do something together without any pressure. I also get the feeling that she, too, needs some respite from the situation – it must be as exhausting for her as it is for me. This makes sense, as I imagine working on a big legal case to prove your boyfriend is a pervert is as taxing to prosecute as it is to defend. So going to the gym together provides some temporary relief for both of us. I also feel that despite all her protestations about my behaviour, the reason she constantly accuses me of acting like a pervert is connected to the fact that she loves me. Sure, it's not how I would want her to show it, but I suppose it's better than nothing. For my part, I'm still in love with her, but I can feel myself becoming a powder keg on the brink of an emotional explosion.

We hit the gym at around three o'clock this afternoon; the hottest part of the day. We haven't discussed this, but we seem to have some kind of unspoken agreement to get away from the pool and all of the problems it might bring.

Earlier I'd noticed there was a group of young, Italian girls playing volleyball and Jenny observed me noticing. As we walked through the hotel together, my eyes were fixed on the floor whenever possible. This was my clear signal to her that I was showing respect and desperately trying to avoid another row. On the way down to the gym, which is on the far side of the hotel from our room, there were no obvious problems, but there was a close call in the elevator when a good-looking, young girl in a bikini got in on the second floor. "Going down?" she asked.

I glanced briefly at Jenny to see if she appreciated the irony, but she stared blankly out of the elevator window. I thanked God for the elevator's glass bottom and pointed my eyes in its direction.

When we arrived at the gym I looked around nervously. There were a few young women with small children in the indoor pool, but no one except an older, foreign looking guy in the gym. I guessed he was foreign because he had a bright, yellow tracksuit on which no self-respecting Brit would have been seen dead in. He nodded in our direction when we entered and we both said, "hello" back.

I made my way to the rowing machine and Jenny started her warm-up routine. I began to relax. After about five minutes the endorphins kicked in and I smiled over at Jenny from time to time. She gave me a few relaxing smiles in return.

I was just finishing on the rower and had bent down to get my towel, when the girl entered. I only saw her for a brief second from the corner of my eye, but I gleaned she was dark haired, pretty, late-twenties and with a very good figure. I instantly understood that Jenny would have placed her within my target audience and the pressure would be on me not to look. Jenny has decided that she knows the sort of girls I'm prone to looking at and has based her findings on empirical evidence. She's asked enough probing questions in the past to know what my type is.

Anyway, sure enough, when I looked over at Jenny she was staring back with an impassive look and a ventriloquist dummy's smile that signified trouble. I could see the girl in my peripheral vision. She walked over and climbed on to the rower next to me and I gripped my towel and gritted my teeth in irritation. Stupid, I know – she was as innocent in all of this as anyone could be – but I took an instant dislike to her. Okay, she had the misfortune to be born good-looking with a nice figure, but this is where I am right now; this is how all of this has got me.

I figured there was only one move to make. If I moved to the cross-trainer, which was in front of her, the girl would be out of my line of sight. I would only be able to see her if I looked directly into the mirror in front of me, which I steadfastly resolved not to do under any circumstances.

Jenny had moved from the free weights to the running machine and seemed, for the moment, to be unconcerned. She must have seen what I'd done, I thought. She must be giving me the validation I was desperately seeking. I began to cheer up. I hoped I might exit it all with flying colours.

On the cross-trainer I looked down and ploughed relentlessly up and down for the next half hour. As far as I was aware I looked at nothing other than my own feet.

Thirty minutes later, Jenny came over. Her voice was surprisingly cold and dispassionate. "Are we going?" she asked, and that was all the evidence I needed. My efforts had been in vain. I dismounted and picked up my towel, fighting the urge to wrap it round a neck, any neck, and pull tight. Somewhere deep inside my very core, feelings of uncontrollable anger started to worm their way to the surface.

On the way back to the hotel room Jenny walked in front of me. She didn't make any attempt to hold my hand. All the little signs of her displeasure created a familiar scenario, except that something new was taking place. For the first time in our relationship, I really didn't care. I was angry. I was very angry. I had reached a new place and it wasn't a very nice place. I knew we were going to have this out, but that this time it wasn't going to be the reasoned controlled discussion so beloved by my beloved. This time it was going to be a nasty, accusatory discussion and it was going to be conducted on my terms.

When we reached the apartment Jenny went into the bedroom, lay on the bed and started to type a text message on her phone. I tried not to lose control, but I did. I lost it. I burst into the room and slammed the door behind me. "This has to stop," I shouted at her. "I mean, why are you doing this?" At this point, Jenny finally puts the phone down.

"Why? What am I doing? *I'm* not doing anything."

"Go on then – tell me. Tell me what it is I'm supposed to have done."

"Why are you asking a question that you already know the answer to?" I began to pace around the room.

"Can't you see?" I said. "I can't take it anymore. I feel like you're destroying our relationship. It's almost like you want to find some reason to end it. Just tell me if you want to end it, but stop looking for excuses."

"Is that what you think?" she said, standing up and folding her arms. "That I'm destroying our relationship? That I'm looking for excuses? God, that's rich. What about you Rob? What about your part in all this? I

171

love you. Do you know how your behaviour affects me? If you did you would stop, but you just can't help yourself, can you?"

"Can't help what? I did everything I could do in there not to look at that girl. But it just wasn't good enough for you was it?"

"Well, if that was the best you could do, you didn't do a very good job. Your eyes were all over her from the minute she entered. You were worried I'd see you turning your head to look at her on the rower, so you positioned yourself on the cross-trainer so you could stare at her in the mirror! It was embarrassing, Rob. I was embarrassed for you. She was half your age!" Momentarily I felt calm. It was all just so ridiculous that some of my anger subsided and for a moment, I was able to see how hurt she was by it all.

"Do you want to know something that says it all?" I said, my voice now holding a reasonable tone. "I can't even tell you what she looks like. Seriously, I can't. I moved to the cross-trainer so that I couldn't see her – not to get a better view. I did everything I could not to look at her. Everything I could, not to go through … not to go through all this shit." I hoped she would understand that I was telling the truth, that somehow I would reach her and we could start to get through this.

"You moved to the cross-trainer so you could keep your eyes on her. That's why you moved there. Every time I looked over at you, you were looking at her."

"I can swear I wasn't. I can swear on my daughter's life I never. I can swear that I wouldn't even recognise her if I saw her now. So you're wrong. Get over it!"

"And I swear you *were* looking at her. You just don't realise you're doing it. It's pathetic." I looked at her. She was holding something back. I could see that in her face. I was totally lost with the utter hopelessness of it.

By now she had begun to cry softly and something turned over inside me. Her exasperation mirrored mine. Desperate to find some kind of solution to a situation that seemed more and more hopeless, I decided to give some ground. It was a gamble, but one I felt I had to take. "Look. Just say you're right," I said calmly.

"I am right."

"Let's just say you are, for the moment. If I did look at that girl then there is a real problem here."

"You don't have to tell me." She sniffled, and reached for a tissue from the side of the bed.

"The problem is that I have no memory of that girl. I have no pictures in my head, none! I swear that no matter how it seems, my motivation is not to look at these girls sexually. I really don't know that I'm doing anything."

172

I broke off here, convinced that this argument would get me off the hook, based as it was on the absolute truth. But we'd gone too far. We were both too entrenched. "Okay, I'm doing it," I said, my anger building. "I'm a pervert. Let's say I'm a pervert. What are we gonna do about it? Do you know the worst thing in all this? The worst thing is that I tried my very hardest not to do it. Get that? My very hardest not to do it, yet I still did it. I still acted like some pervert who can't keep his eyes off anyone with a pair of tits. So, if I was trying my hardest and I still did it, how can I ever stop? Go on, answer me, how?"

She was sobbing continuously now. She sensed that I'd lost the plot, sensed that she had backed me into a corner, sensed that I was a wounded and dangerous animal. I hated myself. I knew what I was doing, but I couldn't stop. She cleared her eyes with the tissue and sniffled. The sound should have broken my heart, but it didn't.

She looked at me, and in an attempt to say the most placatory thing she could, the thing that she really believed would help us. Instead she said the worst thing possible. "Why don't we go to counselling?"

My anger was more than evident as I walked towards her; nevertheless, I walked calmly. I stepped right into her personal space, leant over and said, "why don't *we* go to counselling? Do me a favour. Why don't *you* go to counselling? I don't need it; you're the psycho."

At that, she got up and left the apartment.

So here I am, and I have to say I'm pretty appalled at that. I do have the ability to be appalled by my own behaviour. When anyone acts as appallingly as I do, with the consistency that I do, an ability to be appalled at oneself seems to come with the territory.

I might even be prepared to do something about my behaviour if I weren't full of self-righteous anger and a fair-to-middling modicum of indignation. I do feel though that I'm seeing things with a clarity that hasn't been available until now. I'm also sitting here stewing. I'm stewing over her walkout; stewing about her suggestion that I see a counsellor; stewing about her accusation that I looked at the girl in the gym when I didn't.

The more I stew the more I begin to see things clearly. Without making a conscious decision I pull open the drawer next to the bed and see my credit card in the corner. In my current state of mind it seems to be giving me some kind of message.

In the distant past, I studied in a language school in Spain and had to leave unexpectedly when a rather large Croatian gentleman took a more than friendly liking to me. So I know that planes for the UK leave Malaga airport virtually every half hour at this time of year.

Sadly, I start to pack my case.

I say sadly because I really, really, don't want to go, but I feel I have no choice; she's driven me to it. My whole being is telling me it's a bad idea, but I can't seem to stop myself.

Ten minutes later and I have everything that I brought inside the suitcase and my passport has been extracted from the safe-deposit box. There's still time for me to wonder what it is that I'm doing. There's still time to stop myself from doing it. But I can't. It's the stewing. My brain is stewed. I know I'm right but I still feel I'm making the worse decision of my life.

I'm just about to walk down to reception and get a taxi when the door opens. Jenny walks in. She looks at me and looks at the suitcase in my hand. She takes a step back into the hallway, a look of utter disbelief on her face. I can see through it to the pain beneath, and as I stand there unmoving, she walks past me, with dignity, and goes into the bedroom. Without turning back, she shuts the door quietly. It's such a brave thing to do, but it's just what I would have done. That feeling of closeness her act engenders is almost enough to make me turn around and go to her, but I don't. Feeling even more like I have no option, I leave the apartment.

On the way to the reception desk I see Daniel walking towards me. He's holding a large pizza box and has a big smile on his face. It's a spicy-beef smile. He looks at me for a second and he too is unable to comprehend what is happening. He focuses on the case. As he does so I notice to my utter dismay how much he looks like his mum. "Where are you going Rob, innit?" I can't look him in the eye. I turn my head to the floor.

"I gotta go Daniel. Sorry mate; one or two problems at home." He goes quiet for a moment and his face looks like he is trying to work out why Pi isn't divisible, which, thinking about it, he might very well be.

"Oh! Okay. There's a plane to Manchester from Malaga International at 21:20, 22:45, 23:50 or 01:05. Looked at the timetable on the Internet and memorised it, innit?"

"Thanks Daniel mate," I sigh. "That's a real help." This produces a massive beam on his face.

"Okay Rob. See you when you get back." He heads off in the direction of the pool, presumably to do some real damage to world supplies of spicy beef pizza. I don't have the heart to tell him I won't be coming back.

As I order a taxi at the reception desk, to very strange looks I might add, I can see the youngest through the window. He's still in the pool messing around with the group of Italian girls I saw earlier. The pleasure on his face must be a wonderful contrast to the abject misery on mine.

There then follows a blur. At any time during this blur it would have been possible for me to turn around and make different choices.

I don't make those choices.

Chapter 26

Volver

For the first few days Steve – a new, sensitive Steve – leaves me alone. The only time he really says anything is to talk about the very safe topic of football. He tells me that they beat B+Q 5-1. It's all on for this Sunday's game and the winner takes it all. He's at work during the day and at night I prefer to sit alone in my room drinking. The evenings take on a pattern. I think, I drink; I think, I drink.

Eventually, it's Wednesday. I'm not due back into work until Monday, which is the day after the match. The irony is that it will be the first time ever in my life that I'll be glad to get back because I just can't function at the moment. I can't function without Jenny. I keep replaying my decision to leave her in Spain over and over in my head. I wonder how I can take it back. I know I can't. Like Groucho Marx's hands on a pretty blonde: my head is wandering into places it shouldn't. I take some small comfort from the knowledge that I really believe I'm not to blame this time.

I realise she will be back tomorrow. I know there's no way she will have come home early; she wouldn't give me the satisfaction. I want desperately to phone, but I can't. Neither will she phone me. Such a phone call would be unthinkable. It would be tantamount to an admission of guilt on her part, and she's far too stubborn to accept her failings.

One of the reasons I fell in love with her in the first place is that she has so much self-respect. I like to think that it mirrors my own. Yet, at a time like this, self-respect acts as a wall and it will probably cost us the relationship.

It's clear that my dark and sombre mood isn't just related to how much I miss her; this really was my last chance. It's all the worse because it was such a great chance. It was a once in a lifetime chance and I feel it's gone. Not that any of this stops me from constantly looking at my phone. I keep hoping that she'll text, or call, and we'll set it all right, but it doesn't happen.

When Thursday comes I keep thinking about the three of them travelling back on their own. I know how difficult it will be for her, but I also know that she will cope without me. We like to think that our partners can't manage without us, but they can. We all can if we have to.

I think about how phlegmatic she can be, how she did all that managing shit before I met her and how she'll revert to doing it again without me. Then I ponder the difficult conversations she must have had with the boys after I left, especially with Daniel. Come to think about it, it's unlikely the youngest even noticed I'd left.

Thursday evening arrives and I know she'll back at home by now. At my lowest ebb, around ten o'clock, I nearly phone but I just can't. Instead I take up Steve's invitation to go down to the pub as a way of taking my mind off things. He goes straight to the bar when we get there and I sit down in the corner. When he gets back with the drinks he tentatively probes in that sweet, bashful, endearing manner of his. "So did you screw up again then?" Oddly, there isn't a trace of triumphalism in his voice. He places the drinks on the table.

"It would appear so," I reply, rather feebly.

"Well, don't think you can stay at mine long, because you can't. I need to decorate that room."

"What with? Tin foil?" He doesn't acknowledge the barb. Putting the pint to his lips he takes a large gulp.

"Why don't you phone her? Forget your pride. Forget your self-respect. Call her. If you don't you're going to regret it."

"I can't. I want to, but I can't. I know you're not going to believe me, but this time it really wasn't my fault. Well, yeah, I did the wrong thing by leaving her there and I wish I could take that back, but I was forced into it. Believe you me, Jenny has issues." He appears decidedly unimpressed by my outburst.

"And? So? What? Everyone's got issues! That's what makes relationships so hard. That's why I'm so shit at them. If I had any more issues I'd be a fucking newspaper. Anyway, you don't want to end up like me?"

"Dead right. Who'd want that?"

"So, for once, listen to me. Drink your pint, clear off and call her." I decide to ignore his advice with the single exception of finishing my pint. At any time during the next couple of days I could have picked up the phone and called, but I don't. And she doesn't call me.

It's Sunday and the day of the big game. Kick-off's at seven. Steve's smoked about 30 cigs already and it's only 5.30 p.m. "Excellent preparation,' I chide. "Thirty ciggies before the game, God, no wonder you're so fit."

"I'm nervous," he says, flicking a butt end out of the back door. "There's £500 riding on this game in case you've forgotten."

"A difficult thing for me to do mate, especially when it's my money."

He closes the door and paces up and down the kitchen. Strangely enough, I have no nerves whatsoever. I'm really looking forward to the game and I don't give a toss about the money. No, the game will take my mind off Jenny. I'm missing her so much that I have the whole bet thing in some kind of perspective. It's very difficult to feel that £500 is a big thing in the cosmological scheme of things when you have a void the size of a black hole inside you.

I get up from my chair to go and pack my kit. I give Steve a whack on the back of the head with my *Observer* as I pass him. "Ouch! What was that for?"

"That was for being nervous. You should be like me: super cool."

"You're talking crap or else you've got too much money," he replies.

"Well, I ain't got too much money, that's for sure. So Drysdale better watch out." And with that a small smile breaks over his face for the first time today.

Twenty minutes later we're stood at the front door, having decided that we'll go early in a bid to stop Steve smoking himself to death. As we're wrestling with our coats my mobile buzzes. It's Jenny.

I stand transfixed, looking at the screen with her name on it. "It's Jenny," I say mindlessly, and then lift my head to look up at Steve.

"Don't answer it," he implores. For a moment I stand there like an idiot at a hypnotist's gig; it takes me a few seconds before I snap out of it and press the button.

"Hello?"

"Oh Rob! Thank God. I thought you might be out at football or something."

"No, I'm not," I tell her, switching the phone to my other ear and turning my back on Steve. "What's up?"

"I'm at the hospital."

"At the hospital?" I parrot back. "Is everything okay?"

"Yeah. Well, yeah it is now. It's just, Daniel. Don't worry; he's okay. It's just … look I hate to ask you Rob, but could you come down? I know you probably have football or something tonight, but I wouldn't ask if it wasn't important. I really need you to come and talk to Daniel. He wants to see you. He's being really difficult." I look over at Steve. He can hear what Jenny's saying and by now has his hands clasped together in prayer.

"Right. Of course I'll come," I say, turning round. "Give me half an hour and I'll be there. What ward are you in?" I turn back to see Steve has his head in his hands now; sunk down and sat on the stairs.

"B12, at the General. Thanks Rob. Are you sure you can come? You don't have one of your matches?"

"No, not tonight I don't. I'll see you soon."

"Okay. Thanks Rob." As I put the phone back in my pocket I can't help thinking that her voice sounded distant, even though she desperately wanted me to come. I turn my attention to the desolate figure slumped on the stairs.

"Look we have six, anyway so I'm not leaving anyone short."

"That's not the point," he says sulkily. "You're our driving force, our talisman. You single-handedly out-psyched Drysdale last time. We need you."

"That's shite and you know it! You can beat them without me." I bend down and rest my hand on his shoulder. "I'm sorry mate, I really am, but I need to go to her for Daniel's sake."

"But you're not even going out with her anymore. She's got no right to ask you. Can't you go later? After the match?"

"There wouldn't be any later. This is my big game like it's yours tonight with the Fat One."

"Eh?" he says blankly.

"It's now or never."

When I get to the hospital there's the usual National Health palaver of parking. Eventually I end up shoving it in a space 15 minutes' walk from the main entrance at the cost of a fiver. As I head down to B12 I console myself that my five pounds will probably help to buy a small wing mirror screw for some consultant's new Porsche.

When I get to the ward Jenny's stood chatting to a nurse by the coffee machine. I wait a little awkwardly by the door until she eventually sees me. "Rob! Thanks for coming," she says, striding purposefully over towards me.

"Well, I kind of figured I owed you one."

"I don't think so," she replies, looking down at her feet. There's an awkward silence so I change the subject.

"What's the matter with Daniel?" I ask. "Is he okay?"

"When we got back he seemed so lethargic," she tells me, taking a deep breath. "I just put it down to the stress of telling him about you and me. You know how he is." She tails off, and then continues. "Well, it must have affected him badly, more than I thought. He was really tired, like he had a virus or something, and then this morning he couldn't get out of bed. So I asked him for his blood-monitoring book. That was when it became clear; he hasn't been taking his evening insulin."

"What! Why would he do that?"

"Well, it seems that now he has 'no-one to squeeze his arm, innit?' He stopped taking his evening insulin the day you left. He never asked me and I just presumed that he'd been doing it by himself. And now he wants you Rob. Not me, his mum, but you. He wants *you* to squeeze his arm. He's being a right pain about it, even with the nurses." At this she leans forward on my shoulder and starts to sob.

"I'm such a bad parent Rob, and a nutter."

"You're not. You're neither of those things; except perhaps a little bit of a nutter." She snorts up some phlegm as a small laugh tries to break out from beneath the mountain of sobs. Then she steps abruptly away from me.

"You left me," she continues sobbing. "At the first sign of any trouble, you left me. How could you, Rob?"

Realising that here and now is probably not the best place for this discussion, given the fact that Jenny is highly stressed at this point, I put my arms around her shoulders and pull her towards me. "Let's talk about this tomorrow," I whisper in her ear, trying not to enjoy the physical contact. "You're under a lot of strain right now, with Daniel and us, and everything. Let me go and see Daniel and then I can run you home later, if you want. She snorts again; something that sounds like an okay.

"You go and see him. I'll get you a coffee." I reluctantly allow her to break away from my embrace. She wanders off and I walk past two harassed looking nurses speeding the opposite way. B12 turns out to be a ward broken up into sections. Daniel is located in the end cubicle which has four beds. Amazingly, for an NHS ward, two of them are empty. He's sat up reading a book, which is a good sign. He doesn't notice me until I'm right on top of him. When he does he almost breaks into a smile. "Hello Rob. Not very well innit?" he says, putting the book down. "Not been taking my evening insulin."

I sit down, but not before noticing the book is *Star Signs of the Famous*. "Yeah, I know mate," I say, trying for the life of me to get comfortable on a crappy NHS chair. "You've had everyone really worried."

"I haven't had anyone to squeeze my arm. So I stopped taking it. My brothers are not good at it."

"I know they're not mate. They're not much good at anything really, except eating and using lots of electricity." His eyes widen and then squint.

"But you are good at it Rob! I want you to do it for me. I do not like the nurses."

"It's not that easy mate," I say, my arse slipping round on the chair. "Me and your mum, we're not … well … we're not together since the holiday." His forehead creases, little furrows appear and he goes silent for a second.

"But I told mum I needed you to squeeze my arm so that you would be able to live with us again," he replies, positively beaming at the brilliance of his solution.

"I'm not sure it works like that."

"It does work," he shouts excitedly. "I have read it in this book." He picks the book up and taps it with his index finger.

I have no idea what he's going on about, which isn't unusual. But I'm more perplexed than normal. As his comment elicits no response from me, he continues. "It's simple Rob. You are a Gemini. Mum is one of the Libras. This means that you love each other." I burst out laughing at this and his brow scrunches up further. I see that he's very serious so I suppress my laughter for his sake. "Rob it does work. It does work. It is in the book. It is a fact. Let me prove it. Do you love my mum?"

He has now fixed me with the big brown owls and there is no way out. I'm going to have to answer. I decide that honesty is the best policy.

"Yes Daniel. I love your mum very much, but ..." It's only then that I hear a noise behind me.

It's Jenny with my coffee.

When we leave, two hours later, Daniel is asleep and Jenny has been assured by the nurse that he can come home in the morning. I drive slowly and in silence through drab housing estates to Jenny's house. When we pull up outside, I don't park on the drive. She exhales deeply and puts her hand on my knee. "Rob, do you mind if you don't come in. I'm exhausted."

To tell you the truth I'm not disappointed. I realise that it's better if I don't. People make decisions they regret, say things they don't mean, when they're tired. "No it's fine," I assure her. "I've got work in the morning anyway."

"Thanks for coming Rob, it really meant a lot to Daniel, and to me."

"It's okay."

"Can I call you tomorrow? I'd really like to talk, to see if we can't sort this mess out."

"This mess." It sounds funny when she says it; like it's something silly; something trivial that can be patched up and put back together with little or no effort. But that's Jenny: ever the optimist.

"I'd like to Jenny, but I'm not sure we can sort it out."

"We can Rob, because you love me and I love you. I'm a Libran remember." I smile at this and she bends forward and lightly places her lips on my cheek. Then she seamlessly exits the passenger door.

"I'll call you tomorrow," she promises, closing it behind her.

Before driving off I take out my phone and call Steve. There are no messages and I'm dying to know who won the game. It goes straight to voicemail. "Steve, you wanker. Pick up ... call me back as soon as you get this."

He doesn't.

When I get in it's midnight and the house is pitch black. I flick on the hall light and poke my head in his room. His bed's perfectly made. I head towards the kitchen. It's dark and there's no sound. I flick on the light figuring he's still out celebrating or, more likely, commiserating. As the light comes on I jump back. There's a figure slumped over the table. "Steve! Steve!" I shout, pushing at his shoulders.

"Eh! Wasssup?"

"Who won? How did the game go?"

"Game? Wha's game?" He's totally out of it. I let him go and he slumps back on the table. As his head hits it, he mumbles something and then the index finger of his left hand slides slowly out to point towards

181

the fridge. There, taped to the door, with two strips of masking tape, is an envelope with a large wad of her Majesty's lovely currency inside.

The next morning he's surprisingly chipper, given the fact that when I counted the money last night, there was only £940 left in the envelope. "You should have been there Rob it was brilliant," he tells me, while cramming a burnt piece of toast into his mouth. "It's two-all with about a minute left and we all think it's going to penalties. I hit this shot that I don't even think is going to reach Drysdale, never mind get past him. As it dribbles towards him he slips on some sweat and the ball ends up in the back of the net."

"How did he take it in the pub afterwards?" I ask, feeling slightly uneasy about the answer.

"He didn't even turn up. But one of *The IT Crowd* told me that he'd had to borrow the money off his mum. He told her it was a loan towards eye laser treatment or something. After the way he let that shot in I wouldn't be surprised if he really needed it. I wouldn't want to be him this morning when you catch him in briefing."

"Yeah … err … dead right," I say, looking blankly away and feeling strangely uncomfortable.

When I get to briefing Drysdale's not there. I have a feeling I know where he'll be. I slip away from the Head's rant about the lack of uniform standards and make my way to the IT office. I enter.

He's on his own, which is just as well, and with his back to me. I cough and he swivels on his chair. For a brief moment there's a nervous tick at the corner of his eye but then he recovers. "Come to gloat Smith?" he asks.

"No. Not really," I tell him. "I've come to return this." I slide the envelope, with the £500 inside, over the counter towards him. He gets up from his chair and waddles towards it. He looks down at the envelope, but doesn't touch it.

"I don't understand?"

"To tell you the truth neither do I. So don't ask me to explain." I walk back to the door and turn the handle. As I'm half way out he finally summons the effort to speak.

"Rob." I turn back.

"Yeah?"

"Err … thanks."

"That's okay … Simon." I decide to get out of there before we start shagging each other.

The rest of the day in school is a doddle after that emotional little episode. I get back to Steve's to wait for her phone call. I know it will come at six. It always comes at six.

It comes at six.

I answer immediately; not because I'm desperate, but because I don't want her to think that I'm going to play games. "Hi," I say.

"Hi Rob." She goes quiet, I sense her discomfort but I don't want to fill the void. "Thanks for coming last night. It was really good of you."

"It's okay. I wanted to. I wanted to see you both again. I didn't want to leave it, you know, where it was."

"Me neither," she tells me. "Look, I don't want to do this by phone. Can you meet me? I know it's short notice but Gail's gonna watch Daniel. He's even agreed to let her squeeze his arm because I've told him I'm meeting you." I think about this for a moment.

"I will Jenny but I have to tell you that, even though I still love you, I'm not sure it's enough. I just can't put up with your behaviour anymore. Not unless there are going to be changes."

"Just come to the pub Rob. I love you and you still love me, so that's got to be worth something hasn't it? Just hear me out. Listen to what I have to say and if it isn't enough you can leave and you won't hear from me again." I take a deep breath.

"Okay Jenny. I'll listen to what you have to say." I owe her that much, at least.

I'm sitting in the pub; my hand nervously taps the table in front of me. I'm dressed all in black. I look at the clock on the wall to see it's eight o'clock. She's due. I'm just hoping, like the very first time, that she's not late.

Two minutes later, a real result for her, she walks through the door. I don't miss it. I've been looking intently at the door for the last ten minutes. She doesn't wave over at me like she knows me. Instead, she walks a little less calmly and confidently towards me than before and settles herself on the stool opposite, at a respectable distance. "Drink?" she says, unbuttoning her jacket.

"I'll have a diet coke. It's shite, but I'm driving." She laughs which sounds a little forced, but heads off to the bar.

When she gets back she maintains a respectable distance. She speaks first. "I know I drove you to it Rob. I really do. But you shouldn't have left. We could have talked it through."

"Jenny, I'm exhausted with me and you talking stuff through. I'm sorry about my behaviour; really and truly, I am. If I could go back to that hotel room and do it all over again I probably wouldn't leave, but you're kidding yourself if you think us talking it through would have made any difference. How many times do we need to go over it all before you realise that I only want you? I just don't seem to have what it takes to make you see it." She stares at me as if trying to get a read on me. I look right back at her. I mean every word I'm saying and I hope that she can see it in my eyes.

183

"You're probably right," she sighs. "I have issues Rob. I never said I didn't, but you chose to think that I didn't. You choose to put me on some kind of pedestal that I couldn't live up to."

"Maybe that's true, but that's not the reason why you behave like you do. It's not about me Jenny. For a long time I thought it was. For a while I was convinced that maybe I was looking at those girls but I know now, I wasn't." Her eyes fall away at this comment and the pain, so evident in her face, just makes me feel miserable. To her credit, she doesn't duck the verbal punch.

"You're right. I've tried so hard to change, but I am what I am Rob. I'm messed up like the rest of us. I just know I don't want to lose you."

"And I don't want to lose you, but we can't go on like this it's too exhausting." She doesn't say anything for a moment.

"Rob, I have to tell you something," she says, sniffling loudly. "I tried to tell you that day in the bedroom, but you just wouldn't listen. I know I should have told you anyway, but I feel so stupid; felt so stupid. All this, all what's happened, it's happened before," she carries on, pulling a tissue from her bag. "I put Harry through the same thing. It's one of the reasons we split up. Sure he was controlling and there were other problems but, like you, he couldn't cope with it all: the accusations; the jealousy. So even before he left, I went to counselling and I made real progress, Rob. I gained loads of confidence and when I started dating and saw how men reacted around me, I was like a kid in a sweetshop. I really thought I'd changed for good. But then I met you."

"Thanks."

"No Rob. What I mean is that I fell in love with you and falling in love was wonderful, but there was a price to pay; there always is."

"And that price was you acting like a nutter."

"Yeah. The reason I'm like I am is because I love you, because you matter."

"I know that Jenny but it's not normal."

"I know, but I never said I was. I'm not normal. I thought that's why you loved me." At this she starts to sob uncontrollably.

As I look at her, tears running down her face and I realise that I've learnt something: I've finally learnt that being in a relationship can never just be all love, sex and Tesco's Finest Cava. Sometimes it's pain, hurt and cheap lager, and as Charlotte said, "you have to take the rough with the smooth".

So I decide to take the rough with the smooth. I say something I never thought I would. "Why don't we go to counselling?" She looks up and uses the tissue to brush away some tears. For the first time since she came into the pub I can see the old Jenny. The Jenny I knew before all this bad stuff happened.

"Really? Really, you'd come with me?"

"I'm willing to give it a go. If you think that maybe it can help us." With this she presses her lips together to stop them from trembling. Her eyes well up and, not for the first time, I see how fragile she is. Eventually she asks, "Rob?"

"Yeah?"

"Will you please come home?"

The next day after school, I'm on Steve's front doorstep with a suitcase in my hand and we're looking at each other. It's very nearly as awkward and emotional as it was between Jenny and me last night. "Listen, mate. Thanks again for everything. I really ..."

I can't finish.

"Ah fuck off! Before you try and snog me. If you want to thank me, do me a big favour and don't come back, because you won't be welcome; all that bitching about your room being cold, and all that shite about the shower." I smile at him and let him have the last word. Just for a second, a faint smile crosses his lips and, as the door closes. "Go on then. Piss off back to Manchester."

I walk to the car and drop the suitcase in the boot. As I'm ambling round to the driver's side, the bathroom window opens and his head pops out. "Look, you're such a loser that if you get really stuck -"

"Thanks mate," I shout back. "But I don't think I will."

I drive the 30 minutes to her house with my mind racing. How is it going to be? Pretty uncomfortable, for a while, I reckon. I just hope we can set things right.

When I arrive at the house my parking spot is empty. Although it's not a big thing, the sight of the vacant drive makes me feel better. I try my key in the front door and it works – she hasn't changed the locks. As I enter the hall I'm nearly knocked off my feet by a bouncing muppet exiting on a pogo stick. "Sorry Rob! Mum's in the back somewhere. Gotta go." As he bounds off towards the road I turn around to watch him go.

"Err ... yeah. Thanks ... err ... Chris! See you later."

I put the suitcase down in the hall next to a banjo. I smile. I can smell hot food so I head to the kitchen thinking that maybe she's in there. I enter and Daniel is inside pulling a large pizza from the oven. He places it down on a large plate, turns to me and grins like a Cheshire Cat. "Spicy beef, innit Rob?" After hacking it into tiny pieces, he asks me, "Will you squeeze my arm Rob?"

As I grasp it my eyes start to well a little. Daniel expertly injects himself then wanders off completely unaware of my emotional state, happy as the proverbial Larry, to his room. I look through to the garden where I see two tents set up on the lawn. Curtis and two other dodgy looking characters are sitting on the bench passing round an even dodgier

185

looking cigarette. Curtis looks up, waves warmly in my direction and then resumes his conversation. The tears start to break and slide silently down my face and a soft voice speaks to me from behind. It's full of warmth and understanding, and makes me feel like I'm alive. "Welcome home Rob," Jenny whispers. "Are you okay?" I rest my head on her shoulders and answer in a muffled voice.

"I love you so much and I nearly lost you. I nearly lost you, and worse, I nearly lost something I never even knew I had …

… a family."

Chapter 27

28 Weeks Later

A famous German historian once propagated the theory that Adolph Hitler caused the Second World War as a way of avoiding his sexual inadequacies. I would like to subscribe to this theory and, indeed, take it further. I reckon any number of wars have been started by men who were so depressed about their lack of understanding in the bedroom that conquering the world seemed an easier option. Adolph was probably lying in bed one evening with Eva Braun in late August 1938 desperately trying to get it on with her when she stopped him and said, "nein, nein Adolph. What about der foreplay?"

The invasion of Poland followed imminently.

I don't really 'get' foreplay and so subsequently neither does Jenny, much. Well, not as much as she'd like anyway. I'm not so much 'New Man' these days, as 'Slightly Newer Man'. Before going to therapy sessions with Jenny I viewed foreplay in the way that I viewed breakfast: I skipped it whenever I could. We've had any number of conversations about my deficiencies in this area, and, yes, Jenny has frequently made me aware just how large those deficiencies are.

It's a warm, September afternoon. Ironically, I've already skipped breakfast. Now I don't know what it is about warm afternoons in bed with Jenny but they have a certain effect on me. To be truthful, they don't really have to be that warm – any afternoon in bed will usually do. "Rob?"

"Mmmm!"

"Is that it?"

"Is what it?"

"That. Is that what I think it's supposed to be?"

"What do you think it's supposed to be?"

"I think, you think, that what you've just done counts as some kind of foreplay?"

"What? What counts as foreplay?"

"Well, flicking your cock into my arse a couple of times, slobbering down my back, and making some heavy breathing noises."

"It doesn't count then?"

"No Rob," she sighs. "It doesn't."

"I didn't think it did. I just thought, you know? We could …"

"Well, we can't. You know, sometimes a woman needs a little more arousing and subtlety than a hard cock pushed into her arse a couple of times to get her in the mood. What happened to tenderness, touching and a little love?"

"So you're not in the mood. Why didn't you just say then? Would have saved me a lot of hard cock flicking and I could have had lunch."

"Durrrrr! I didn't say I wasn't in the mood or that I couldn't be in the mood. It's just, sometimes I'd like a little help to get me in the mood."

"So what you're saying is that you don't fancy me anymore?"

"I'm not going to dignify that with a response. You're a master at twisting what I say!"

"But that's what you're saying. You're saying that I don't do it for you anymore. Well, let me tell you, I don't need all that touching and caressing stuff to get me in the mood because you still do it for me."

"That's because you're a man and you don't have the same needs. We talked about this in the sessions remember? Foreplay's really important to me, Rob. I know it's not for you, but I want a little more than a hard cock pushed into my arse at times that's all."

"That used to do it for you."

"It didn't ever do it for me Rob, believe me. It's just that I couldn't be bothered arguing with you. Like all women I mistakenly believed that eventually you would understand my needs. But you don't so now I'm training you."

"But what if I start, you know, doing the whole touchy feely thing, getting you in the right mood and then I lose it? You won't be happy then will you?"

"It won't matter. Like I told you the other week, I won't care. I would rather have the touching anyway. It's better than sex … sometimes."

"What! Better than sex? That's funny because I never hear you on your back screaming 'give it to me now, give me the foreplay'."

"Well, that's ironic, because that's exactly what I do feel like shouting sometimes." She turns over and arches her body slightly away from me. She's a genius at body language; her subtle gesture makes its mark like a hammer on my head. The message is clear: she's not overly pleased with me. I think long and hard about what she says.

"Okay, I take the point. I'll try a bit harder. It's just that I'm not much good at it."

She turns back to face me and takes hold of my hand. "Rob! You're amazing at it when you want to be. It's just that you can't be arsed most of the time. Like all men you'd rather follow the SAS operations school of shagging."

"Eh?"

"In and out as quickly as possible."

"That's a bit harsh. Anyway, my motto tends to be 'quality rather than quantity'."

Putting my arms around her I move my still hard cock slightly to the left so it's no longer in contact with her delicate left arse cheek. This is a clear sign to her that I am no longer in sexual gear and am in the process of switching off the engine. We lie like this for a few moments in silence, until she breaks it.

"Well?"

"Well what?"

"I would like that foreplay now please!"

"I can't. The moment's passed."

"What do you mean 'the moment's passed'? That would indicate the moment was ever present in the first place. I'm telling you categorically that the moment most certainly hasn't passed."

"It's just … it's just that if I did it now it wouldn't seem real. It would seem like I was only doing it because you said I had to. So I can't. It wouldn't be honest."

"Well, I don't see it like that and, if it's okay with you, I'd like my foreplay right now thank you very much."

"But wouldn't you feel like I was trying to manipulate you? Wouldn't you feel cheapened?"

"Rob, when it comes to you and foreplay, I'll take it any way I can get it. Now shut your mouth and get it open," she laughs.

The next minute I slide alongside her and I'm gently touching her. My mouth is well and truly open as she commanded, and she begins to sigh and shudder beneath my soft kisses. As my hands gently explore her body I sense her mood softly changing as she becomes more responsive to my advances. I don't rush things. I know that she will make me take things very slowly. I don't have any physical problems and remain in the mood. I await her and the moment she chooses.

Sometime later, in one of those Star Trek space-time conundrums – five minutes for her, and about four and half hours for me – that moment comes. We enter the full throes of passion. It's soft and gentle and it's fast and furious. At times we make love. At times we have sex.

When we finish, we're breathless and she's laughing. We lie in each other's arms and it's as it should be. She's nestled beneath my chin and as usual determined to have the last word. "Now don't tell me you didn't enjoy that."

"I did, but I'd have preferred to cut to the chase a bit sooner."

"Yeah right."

"Okay. It was all right but it'll never replace sex." I begin to gently kiss her and caress her neck with my fingertips. She lets out a little gasp of pleasure.

"God, your post-play is better than your foreplay."

I smile. "Well that shows you just how much I love you. The fact that my post-play is better than my foreplay is a sign," I go on, despite her incredulous look. "Don't you realise that during foreplay a man is after

189

something, therefore foreplay is not always honest? During post-play a man isn't after anything. So any man can fake foreplay but post-play is only ever honest, that's why I specialise in it. It's pure. It's honest. Just like me."

"Rob."

"Yeah?"

"Could you do something for me?"

"What?"

"Stop talking bollocks and get me a glass of cava."

"Okay."

Follow Steve's ramblings or ask him a question on Twitter @cavaguy

56031983R00108

Made in the USA
Charleston, SC
12 May 2016